Harry Castlemon

A Rrebellion in Dixie

Harry Castlemon

A Rrebellion in Dixie

ISBN/EAN: 9783337205485

Printed in Europe, USA, Canada, Australia, Japan

Cover: Foto ©Andreas Hilbeck / pixelio.de

More available books at **www.hansebooks.com**

A

Rebellion in Dixie

BY

HARRY CASTLEMON

AUTHOR OF "THE GUNBOAT SERIES," "THE HUNTER SERIES,"
"WAR SERIES," ETC.

PHILADELPHIA

HENRY T. COATES & CO.

1897

CONTENTS.

(iii)

A REBELLION IN DIXIE.

CHAPTER I.

IN REGARD TO THE REBELLION.

"NOW, Leon, you will take in everybody. Don't leave a single man out, for we want them all there at this convention."

"Secessionists, as well as Union men?"

"Yes, of course. I had a talk with Nathan Knight, last night, and he says everybody must be informed of the fact. We are going to secede from the State of Mississippi and get up a government of our own, and he declares that everybody must be told of it."

"I tell you, dad, we've got a mighty poor show. I suppose there are at least two thousand fighting men here—"

"Say fifteen hundred; and they are all good shots, too."

"And Jeff Davis has called out a hundred

(5)

thousand men. Where would we be if he would send that number of men after us?"

"He ain't a-going to send no hundred thousand men after us. He has other work for them to do, and when the few he does send come here in search of us, he won't find hide nor hair of a living man in the county."

It was Mr. Sprague who spoke last, and his words were addressed to his son Leon. They, both of them, stood leaning on their horses, and were equipped for long rides in opposite directions. Just inside the gate was a woman leaning upon it; but, although she was a Southerner, she did not shed tears when she saw Leon and his father about to start on their perilous ride. For she knew that every step of the way would be harassed by danger, and if she saw either one of them after she bade them good-bye it would all be owing to fortunate manœuvres on their part rather than to any mismanagement on the part of the rebels. They were both known as strong Union men, and no doubt there were some of their neighbors who were determined that they should not fulfil their errand. It would be an easy matter to shoot them down and throw their bodies into the swamp, and no one would be the wiser for it.

Leon Sprague was sixteen years old, and had been a raftsman all his life. He had but little education but much common sense, for schools were something that did not hold a high place in Jones county. In fact there had been but one school in the county since he could remember, and some of the boys took charge of that, and conducted themselves in a manner that drove the teacher away. Leon was a fine specimen of a boy, as he stood there listening to his father's instructions—tall be-beyond his years, and straight as one of the numerous pines that he had so often felled and rafted to Pascagoula bay. His counte-nance was frank and open—no one ever thought of doubting Leon's word—but just now there was a scowl upon it as he listened to what his father had to say to him.

These people, the Spragues, were a little better off than most of those who followed their occupation, owning a nice little farm, four negroes, and a patch of timber-land from which they cut their logs and rafted them down to tide-water to furnish the masts for ocean-going vessels. His father and mother were simple-minded folks who thought they had everything that was worth living for, and they did not want to see the Government broken up on any pretext. The negro men worked the farm and their wives were busy in the house, which they kept as neat as a new pin. Just now the men had been butchering hogs in the woods, and were at work making hams and bacon of them. These negroes did not have an overseer—they did not know what it was. They went about their work bright and early, and when Saturday afternoon came they posted off to the nearest village to enjoy their half-holiday. They loved their master and mistress, and if anybody had offered them their freedom they would not have taken it.

In order that you may understand this story, boy reader, it is necessary that you should know something of the character of the inhabitants, and be able to bear in mind the nature of the country in which this Re-

bellion in Dixie took place, for it was as much
of a rebellion as that in Georgia, Tennessee,
North Carolina and Missouri, where men were
shot and hanged for not believing as their
neighbors did, and their houses were set on
fire.   They made up their minds at the start
—as early as 1862—that they would not furnish any men for the Southern army; and,
furthermore, they took good care to see that
there was no drafting done in their county.

If you will take your atlas and turn to the
map of Mississippi you will find Jones county
in the southeastern part of the State, and
about seventy-five miles north of Mobile, a
port that was one of the last to be captured
by the United States army.   It comprised
nearly twenty townships, the white population
being 1482, a small chance, one would think,
for people to live as they did for almost two
years.   The land was not fertile, "the entire
region being made up of pine barrens and
swamps, traversed by winding creeks, bordered
by almost impenetrable thickets."   It was
bounded on four sides by Jasper, Wayne,
Perry and Covington counties, which were all

loyal to the Confederacy, and it would seem
that the people had undertaken an immense
job to carry on a rebellion here in the face
of such surroundings.   The inhabitants were,
almost to a man, opposed to the war.   They
were lumbermen, who earned a precarious living by cutting the pine trees and rafting them
to tide-water, which at that time was found on
Pascagoula bay.   They had everything that
lumbermen could ask for, and they did not
think that any effort to cut themselves loose
from the North would result in any glory to
them.   They could not get any more for their
timber than they were getting now, and why
should they consent to go into the army and
fight for principles that they knew nothing
about ?

Of course, this county was divided against
itself, as every other county was that laid
claim to some Union and some Confederate
inhabitants.   There were men among them
who had their all invested there, and they did
not think these earnest people were pursuing
the right course.   These were the secessionists, but they were very careful about what

they said, although they afterward found op-
portunities to put their ideas into practice.
When General Lowery was sent with a strong
force to crush out this rebellion he was met
by a stubborn resistance, and some of these
Confederates, who were seen and recognized
by their Union neighbors, were afterward
shot to pay them for the part they had carried
out in conducting the enemy to their place of
retreat. Taken altogether, it was such a thing
as nobody had ever heard of before, but the
way these lumbermen went about it proclaimed
what manner of men they were. It seemed
as if the Confederacy could run enough men
in there to wipe out the Jones County Repub-
lic before they could have time to organize
their army; but for all that the inhabitants
were determined to go through with it. They
held many a long talk with one another when
they met on the road or in convention at Ellisville, and there wasn't a man who was in
favor of joining the Confederacy, the secessionists wisely keeping out of sight.

Things went on in this way for a year or
more, during which the lumbermen talked

amazingly, but did nothing. Finally Fort
Sumter was fired upon, and afterward came
the disastrous battle of Bull Run, and then
the Confederates began to gain a little courage. They knew the South was going to
whip, and these battles confirmed them in the
belief; but the raftsmen did not believe it.
In 1862, when the Confederate Congress
passed the act of conscription, which com-
pelled those liable to do military duty to serve
in the army, the lumbermen grew in earnest,
and a few of them got together in Ellisville
and talked the matter over. The market for
their logs had long ago been broken up, and
some of them were beginning to feel the need
of something to eat; and when one of their
number proposed, more as a joke than anything else, that they should cast their fortunes
with the Confederates, and so be able to go
down to tide-water and get some provisions,
the motion was hooted down in short order.
There were not enough people there to hold a
convention, and so the matter was postponed,
some of the wealthy ones who owned horses
being selected to ride about the county and

inform every one that the matter had gone far
enough—that they were going to hold a meeting and see what the lumbermen thought of
taking the county out of the State of Mississippi. Leon and his father were two of those
chosen, and they were just getting ready to
start on their journey.

"I don't know as I ought to send that boy
out at all, Mary," said Mr. Sprague, when he
arrived at home that night after the convention had been decided upon. "I have never
seen Leon in trouble and I don't know how
he will act; but the boys down to Ellisville
seemed determined to let him go, and I never
said a word about it."

"I think you have seen Leon in trouble a
half a dozen times," said his wife, who was
prompt to side with her son. "The time that
Tom Howe came so near being smashed up
with those logs down there in the bend—I
guess he was in trouble then, wasn't he?"

"But that was with logs; it wasn't with
men," said Mr. Sprague. "Yes, Leon was
pretty plucky that day, and when all the boys
cheered him I didn't say a word, although I

had an awkward feeling of pride around my heart, I tell you."

Leon and three or four other fellows of light build were frequently called upon to start a jam of logs which had filled up the stream so full that the timber could not move. A hasty glance at the jam would show them the log that was to blame for it, and armed with an ax and bare-footed the boys would leap upon the raft and go out to it. A few hasty blows would start the jam, and the timber rushing by with the speed of a lightning express train, the boys would make their way back to the shore, jumping from one log to another. Sometimes they did not get back without a ducking. On the occasion referred to Tom went out alone, and after he had been there some minutes without starting the jam, Leon was sent out to assist him. Two axes were better than one, and in a few minutes the timber was started. It came with a rush, too, but Tom was just a moment too late. The log upon which he had been chopping shot up into the air fully twenty feet, and when it came down it struck the log on which Tom was standing and soused him head over heels in the water; but before he went he felt somebody's around him. It was Leon Sprague's arm, for the latter struck the water almost as soon as he did. Leon came up a moment afterward with Tom hanging limp and lifeless in his arms, and heard the cheers of the " boys" ringing in his ears, but had to go down again to escape the onward rush of the logs which were coming toward him with almost railroad speed. By going down in this way and swimming lustily whenever the logs were far enough away to admit of it, Leon succeeded in landing about half a mile below, and hauling his senseless burden out on the bank. Tom could swim—there were few boys on the stream that could beat him at that—but when that log came down on him it well nigh knocked it all out. Leon's father never said a word. He walked up and gave the boy's hand a hearty shake, and that was the last of it. Leon had the opportunity of knowing, as soon as Tom came to himself, that he had made a life-long friend by his last half-hour's operations.

"Jeff Davis ain't a going to send no hundred thousand men after us," repeated Mr. Sprague, preparing to mount his horse. "He'll send a few in here to break up this rebellion, and when they get here we'll be in the woods out of sight. Kiss your mother, Leon, and let's go. We have got a good ways to ride before night."

"Now, Leon, be careful of yourself," said his mother.

"You need have no fear of me," said Leon, leaving his horse and going up to the gate. "I've got my revolver in my pocket all handy."

"But remember that when you are riding along the road somebody can easily pick you off," said Mrs. Sprague. "You know you are a Union boy."

"Do you want me to make believe that I am—Confederate?"

"By no means. Stick to the Union. Good-bye."

The farewells being said, father and son got upon their horses and rode away in opposite directions. Leon rode a high-stepping hors'

—he was fond of a good animal and he owned one of the very best in the county—but he allowed him to wander at his own gait, knowing that the horse would be tired enough when he returned home. As he rode along, thinking how foolish the people were to consider seriously the proposal to withdraw from the Union, he ran against a boy about his own age who, like himself, was journeying on horseback. He was a boy he did not like to see. He was awfully "stuck up," and, furthermore, he was a rebel and did not hesitate to have his opinions known.

"Hello, Leon," exclaimed Carl Swayne, for that was the boy's name. "Where are you going this morning?"

"I am going around to see every man in this side of the county," said Leon. "We are going to get up a convention on the 13th, and we want everybody there. The convention is going to be held at Ellisville."

"By George! Has it come to that?" cried Carl, flourishing his riding-whip in the air. "What do you think you are going to do after you get to that convention?"

" We are going to dissolve the Union existing between this county and the State of Mississippi."

" Yes, I'll bet you will. How long will it be before the Confederates will send men in here to whip you out? You must think you can stand against them."

" I don't think we can stand against anybody," said Leon. " If the Confederates come in here we shall go into the woods."

" Well, it won't take me long to show them where you are," said Carl, savagely. " I was talking with uncle about it last night, and he says you haven't got but a few fighting men here, and that it is utterly preposterous for you to think of getting up a rebellion. I know one thing about it: you will all be hanged."

"And I know another thing about it," said Leon. " When it comes we'll be in good company. Will you be down to our convention ?"

" Not as anybody knows of," replied Carl, with a laugh. " I'll get somebody up here to put a stop to it."

"Well, I wouldn't be too hasty about it. You may get hanged yourself."

"Yes? I'd like to see the man living that can put a rope around my neck," exclaimed Carl, hotly. "I've got more friends in this county than one would suppose. I'll bet you wouldn't be one of the first to do it."

Leon picked up his reins and went on without answering this question. He saw that Carl was in a fair way to pick a quarrel with him, and he had no desire to keep up his end of it. Carl was hot-headed, and when he got mad, was apt to do and say some things that any boy of his age ought to have been ashamed of. He kept on down the road for a mile further, and finally turned into a broad carriage-way that led up to a neat little cottage that was surrounded by shade trees on all sides. This was the house of Mr. Smith—a crusty old bachelor who had always taken a deep interest in Leon. He was Union to the backbone, and if he could have had his way he would have made short work with all such fellows as Carl Swayne. He was sitting out on the porch indulging in a smoke.

"Hallo, Leon," he cried, as soon as he found out who the new-comer was. "Alight and hitch."

"I can't do it, Mr. Smith," replied Leon. "I am bound to see every man in this part of the county, and that, you know, is a good long ride. We are going to hold a convention on the 13th, and we want you to come down to it."

"Whew!" whistled Mr. Smith. "You bet I'll be there. What are you going to do at that convention?"

Leon explained briefly, adding:

"I just now saw a fellow whom I asked to come down, and he positively declined. He says he will get somebody to put a stop to it."

"That's Carl Swayne," said Mr. Smith, in a tone of disgust. "Say! I will give half my fortune if we can hang that fellow and his uncle to the nearest tree. They have been preaching up secessionists' doctrines here till you can't rest."

"I think we can get the better of them after a while," said Leon. "When did you get back?" he added, for Mr. Smith had been

down to tide-water to see what was going on
there. "Did you see or hear anything in
Mobile?"

"I got back last night. There is nothing
in Mobile except fortifications. I tell you it
will require a big army to take that place.
By the way, Leon, I want to see you some
time all by yourself. Don't let any one know
you are coming here, but just come."

"I'll remember it, Mr. Smith. You won't
forget the convention? Good-by."

"What in the world does the old fellow
want to see me for?" soliloquized Leon. "And
why couldn't he have told me to-day as well
as any other time? Well, it can't be much,
any way."

Leon kept on his ride, and before night he
was many miles from home. He took in every
house he came to, Union as well as secessionist, and while the former greeted him cordially, the rebels had something to say to him
that fairly took his breath away. If he
hadn't been the most even-tempered fellow in
the world he would have got fighting mad.
They all agreed as to one thing: They were

going to see Leon hanged for carrying around the notice of that convention. His neighbors wou'dn't do it, but there would be plenty of Confederates in there after a while that would string the Union people up as fast as they could get to them. Leon had no idea that there were so many secessionists in the county as he found there when he came to ride through it, and he made up his mind to one thing, and that was, it was going to be pretty hard work to carry that county out of the State.

"But just wait until we get together and decide upon a constitution," said Leon, as he rode along with his hands in his pockets and his eyes fastened upon the horn of his saddle. "Jeff Davis has long ago ordered all Union men out of the Confederacy, and what is there to hinder us from ordering all these rebels out? That's an idea, and I will speak to father about it."

Leon did not care to spend all night with such people as these, and so he kept on until he found a family whose sentiments agreed with his own, and there he laid by until morning. The head of this household had but recently come into the county, and Leon did not know him. When the latter rode up to the bars the man was chopping wood in front of a dilapidated shanty, but when he saw Leon approaching he dropped his axe, took long strides toward his door and turned around and faced him. The boy certainly thought he was acting in a very strange way, and for a moment didn't know whether he was a Union man or a rebel.

"Good evening, sir," said Leon, who thought he might as well settle the matter once for all. "Can I stay all night with you?"

"Who are you and where did you come from?" asked the man in reply.

"My name is Leon Sprague and I live in the other part of the county," replied Leon. "I am a Union boy all over, and I came out to tell everybody—"

"Course we can keep you all night if that is the kind of a boy you are," replied the man coming up to the bars. "Get off and turn your horse loose. I haven't seen a Union boy before in a long while. I came from Tennessee."

"What are you doing down here?" asked Leon, as he led his horse over the bars.

"I came down here to get out of reach of the rebels, dog-gone 'em," said the man in a passionate tone of voice. "You had just ought to see them up there. They have got their jails full, they are hanging men for burning bridges, and when I left home there was two or three thousand men going over the mountains into Kentucky. But I couldn't go with them. The rebels cut me off, and as I was bound to go somewhere, I came on down here."

Leon had by this time taken the saddle and bridle from his horse and turned him loose to get his own supper. Then he backed up against the fence and watched the man chopping his wood.

CHAPTER II.

THE CONVENTION.

"WHAT made you start for the house when you saw me coming up?" said Leon, as the man sank his axe deep into the log on which he was chopping and paused to moisten his hands.

"Because I thought you was a rebel. I reckoned there was more coming behind you, and I wanted to be pretty close to my rifle. I didn't know that I had got into a community of Union folks down here."

Leon was astonished to hear the man converse. He talked like an intelligent person, and the boy was glad to have him express an opinion, for it was so much better than his own that he resolved to profit by it.

"I don't know that you got in among Union people," said Leon, "for I have seen more rebels to-day than I thought there was

in the county; but all the same there are some
Union folks here. You might have gone further and fared worse."

"So I believe. When you came up you
said you were out to tell everybody something.
What were you going to say?"

It didn't take Leon more than two minutes
to explain himself. The man listened with
genuine amazement, and when the boy got
through he seated himself on the log and
rested his elbows on his knees.

"How are you going to take this county
out?" said he. "You haven't got men enough
to do any fighting."

"No, sir; but we are going to do the best
we can with what we have got."

"That's plucky at any rate. I suppose
that if the rebels come in here to capture you,
you will take to the swamp."

"Yes, sir. That's just what we intend to
do."

"Well, sir, you can put my name down for
that convention," said the man, getting upon
his feet and going to work upon his wood-pile.
"I've got so down on the rebels that I am

willing to do anything I can to bother them.
I've got two brothers in jail up there now."

"You said something about bridge burning," said Leon, and he didn't know whether
he made a mistake or not. "Perhaps you had
a hand in it."

" Perhaps I did," answered the man with a
laugh. "And I tell you I had to dig out as
soon as I got home. So you see I dare not
go back there."

"What's the punishment?"

"Death," answered the man. "And they
don't give you any time to say good-bye to
your friends. They don't even court-martial
you, but string you up at once."

The man said this in much the same tone
that he would have asked for a drink of water.
Leon was surprised that one who had passed
through so many dangers as that man had
could speak of it so indifferently. But then
he looked like a man who would have been
picked out of a crowd to engage in business of
that kind. He was large and bony, the ease
with which he handled his axe was surpris-
ing, but his face was one to attract anybody's

attention.   It was a determined face—a face
that wouldn't back down for any obstacles.
If the Union men in Tennessee were all like
him, it was a wonder how the rebels got the
start of them.

"I can't give you as good a place here as I
could at home," said the man, as his wife
came to the door and told him that supper was
ready.   "At home I have a commodious house,
and you could have a room in it all to yourself.   Here I have nothing but this little tum-
ble-down shanty to go into.   It leaks, but I
will soon get the better of that.   Molly, this
young man is Union all over, and he has come
down here to tell of a convention that is to
be held at Ellisville to take this county out of
the State.   Whoever heard of such a thing?
I am going to that meeting, sure pop."

His wife was greatly surprised to listen to
this, but she accepted the introduction to
Leon, and forthwith proceeded to make him
feel at home.   There were two children, but
they had been taught to behave, and did not
try to shove themselves forward at all.   Taken
altogher, it was a comfortable meal, and before

it was over Leon learned some things regarding this man that he wouldn't have believed possible. He had come all the way through the rebel State of Mississippi by telling the people he met on the way that he was going to see some friends, and had, by chance, struck Jones county, the very place of all others he wanted to be.

"I must confess it was pretty pokerish, sometimes," said the man. "The rebels had sent on a description of me as the man who helped burn their bridges, and now and then I had to get under the bundles of clothing and cover myself up there, leaving my wife to guide the horses. But I had my rifle all right, and it would have gone hard with the men who discovered me."

The evening was passed in this way listening to the man's stories, and when Leon went to bed in a dark corner of the room he told himself that he had got into a desperate scrape, and that he had got something to do in order to get out of it. He had never dreamed that men could be down on their neighbors in that way, and here this man had all he could do to keep from being shot.

"By George! I tell you we are in for it," said Leon, pulling the blankets up over him, "and I don't know how we are going to come out. There are rebels all around us, and if they are as bad down here as they are up in Tennessee there won't one of us come through alive. But I am armed, and I'll see that some of them get as good as they send."

It was daylight when Leon awoke, and after washing his hands and face in a basin outside the door he stood in front of the fireplace, before which the woman was engaged in cooking the breakfast, and looked up at the man's rifle, which hung on some wooden pegs over the mantel. It was an ordinary muzzle-loading thing, and didn't look as though it had been the death of anybody.

"That rifle has been too much for half a dozen men," said the woman.

"Why, how did that happen?" asked Leon.

"It happened when they came to burn us out," answered the woman. "They came one

night and tried to call Josiah to the door, but
he would not go. He took his rifle down, but
he wouldn't shoot until they did, and as he is
a good shot, he hit every time. The next day
we had to move, for they came with a larger
body of men."

"There is one thing that makes me think
you are in a bad place," said Leon. "You
are right here close to the river which sepa-
rates the two counties, and if anybody makes
a raid over here they will strike you, sure. I
think if that convention is held you had better come down to our place. We have room
enough there to stow you away."

"Oh, thank you. Perhaps you had better
speak to Josiah about it."

Josiah was out attending to his horses and
cow, and Leon went out to him. He looked
at him with more respect than he did the
night before, for, in addition to burning the
bridges, he had "got the better" of half a
dozen men. He bade Leon a hearty good-
morning, but the boy noticed that all the
while he kept talking to him he kept his eyes
fastened on the woods. Probably it was from

the force of habit. He agreed with Leon
that they were in a bad place to meet raids,
and promised that after the convention came
off he would see what he could do. He
didn't want to trespass on anybody until he
had to.

Breakfast over, Leon brought his horse to
the door, put on his saddle and bridle and bid
good-bye to the family from Tennessee, and
rode off. He was two days more on his route,
and on the third day he turned his horse
toward home. He reached it without any mis-
hap, and his mother was glad to see him,
judging by the hug she gave him. His father
had arrived the night before, but the stories
he had to tell didn't compare with Leon's.
Of course his mother was shocked when she
learned that Josiah (Leon did not know what
else to call him) had shot so many men before
he left Tennessee, but she readily agreed to
shelter his wife and children.

"I never thought to ask him his name,"
said Leon, "but I will ask him down to the
convention. He was dead in favor of it, and
said he would be there. I tell you that man

has passed through a heap. He couldn't talk
to me without running his eyes over the woods
to see if there was anybody coming."

On the next day but one was the time of
the convention, and at an early hour Mr.
Sprague and Leon mounted their horses and
set out for Ellisville. On the way they picked
up a good many more, both afoot and on horseback, and by the time they reached their des-
tination they numbered fifty or more. They
made their way at once to the church, and
found themselves surrounded by a formidable
body of men, all of whom were armed with
rifles. There must have been a thousand men
there, and there was not a secessionist to be
seen in the party. Shortly afterward Nathan
Knight arrived. He bid good-morning to the
people right and left, and went into the
church, whither he was followed by all the
building would hold. Those who couldn't
get in raised the windows on the outside and
settled themselves down to hear what was
going to happen.

Nathan Knight was a large man, with gray
whiskers and an eye that seemed to look right

through you. But for all that his face was kindly, and if you got broken up in business and wanted help, Nathan Knight was the man to go to. He took his seat in the pulpit, just where he knew the folks would send him, took off his hat and drew his handkerchief across his forehead. His meeting was not conducted according to order, but those who were there understood it.

"Gentlemen will please come to order," said he. "Are there any of us who are opposed to taking this county out of the State of Mississippi? If there is, let him now speak or hereafter hold his peace."

Each man gazed into the face of his neighbor; but each one knew that the one he looked at was as much in favor of secession as he was himself. Finally, some one in the back part of the church called out:

"Nathan, there ain't nary a rebel here."

"I am glad to hear it," said Mr. Knight. "But there are some around in the county, and you want to be careful how you deal with them. I will now appoint a committee of six to draw up a series of resolutions of secession.

They will go over to the hotel and come back when they get done."

Mr. Knight had evidently been thinking of this matter before for he appointed the committee without hesitation, and among them was the name of Mr. Sprague. They were all men who would not say a thing they did not mean, and as they were about to go out the president beckoned Mr. Sprague to his desk and placed a piece of paper in his hands.

"There's some resolutions I drew up after thinking the matter over," said he. "Perhaps it will serve as a model to you. You can amend them or leave them out entirely, as suits you best."

When the committee had retired Mr. Knight got up, and for the next half-hour proceeded to arraign the Confederate States and praise the Union, his remarks calling forth loud and long-continued applause. He took the ground that it was a "geographical impossibility" to conquer Jones county, because, the inhabitants being lumbermen, it would be easy for them to slip into the woods, and when there nobody but a raftsman could find them. He kept his speech going until the committee were seen coming back. Mr. Sprague made his way to the desk, and amid the most impressive silence read the resolutions of secession as follows:

WHEREAS, The State of Mississippi has seen fit to withdraw from the Federal Union for reasons which appear justifiable;

And whereas, We, the citizens of Jones county, claim the same right, thinking our grievances are sufficient by reason of an unjust law passed by Congress of the Confederate States of America, forcing us to go to distant parts, etc., etc.;

Therefore be it resolved, That we sever the union heretofore existing between Jones county and the State of Mississippi, and proclaim our independence of said State and the Confederate States of America; and we solemnly call upon Almighty God to witness and bless such act.

When Mr. Sprague ceased reading, the applause which shook the building was long and loud. Not satisfied with that, some of the raftsmen fired off their guns, and for the next five or ten minutes it was impossible to do anything inside the church. By that time the excitement had somewhat died out, and then the president asked if there was any debate on the matter, but no one had anything to say. Knowing that those six men had the good of the county at heart, there was not one who had anything to say against them. Mr. Knight expressed himself pleased, and was about to announce that the resolutions were passed, when somebody on the outside of the building called out:

"Nathan, here's a couple of rebels out here."

"What are they doing out there?" asked the president, in surprise.

"I don't know. They have just come up here. It looks to me like they were going to recruit."

"Well, fetch them in here. Now, boys, not a word out of you. I will do the talking, and if you have any questions to ask, you can ask them; but don't all talk at once."

Mr. Knight settled back in his chair and the most profound silence ensued. Finally the crowd about the door gave way as the rebels and their escort approached, and the Confederates, seeing so many men standing there with their hats all off, courteously took off their own. They kept on until they got up to the desk, and then Mr. Knight drew up chairs for them to be seated.

"Now, gentlemen, what brought you up here?" asked the president.

"We came up here to recruit," replied the ranking officer. "I am glad to see so many of you here, for it will save us the trouble of hunting you up."

"Will you be kind enough to read that?" said Mr. Knight, unfolding the paper on which the resolutions were written and passing it over to the officer.

The official took the paper, and as he read his eyes opened with surprise. When he had got through with it he passed it over to his subordinate, and then turned and looked at the men near him. He was satisfied that there was not a man there who did not believe every word of those resolutions. The officer had nothing to fear now—he was the first recruiting official that ever came there—but after he got away he would not come back at any price.

"These are not all your men?" said he.

"No, sir. We have not more than three hundred men, but these extra parties have come in with their families at odd times. And every man you see is a Union man."

"My friend, you are making a great mistake," began the officer.

"We are ready to stand by it, sir."

"Do you suppose the Confederates will stand by and allow you to take this county out of the State, to be an odd sheep in the flock?" continued the officer. "The first thing you know you will be overrun with men, and you won't have a house to go into."

"What will we be doing all that time?"

"Oh, I suppose you will fight, but it won't do you any good. The Confederates can send twenty thousand men in here."

"We don't care if they send forty thousand," replied the president. "Whatever you send we'll fight."

The men who were crowded in the church and gathered about the windows couldn't stand it any longer. They broke out into loud applause, which continued for some minutes.

When they got through, the officer evidently thought they were in earnest.

"We have a thousand men here, and when we get into the swamp we are willing to meet five thousand," continued Mr. Knight. "You can't conquer us."

"What will you do for grub?"

"We'll steal it," shouted one of the men; and the answer was so droll and corresponded so entirely with the thoughts of the men who were standing around, that the whole assembly burst into laughter. Even the enrolling officers joined in.

"I suppose you can do that, of course," said he, "but supposing the escort is too strong to be successfully attacked?"

"We don't borrow any trouble on that score," said Mr. Knight. "We haven't got all the men we are going to have. You see how they are coming in now. But you are interrupting us, and we shall have to bid you good-bye. You see very plainly that you can't raise any men here for the Confederate army. Another thing we'll tell you, you are the first to come in, and you will be the last to go out."

"Do you mean to say that you will kill any enrolling officers who come here?"

"That's just what I mean to say. We don't want them here."

"Well," said the official, rising to his feet, "we'll go, but we won't be the last officers to come in here. I will tell you that very plainly. You mustn't think that the Confederates are going to allow you to have your own way in this matter. It beats anything I ever heard of."

"We are aware of that, and that's what makes us think we are going to go through with it. I will bid you good-bye, gentlemen."

The men divided right and left to allow the rebels a chance to get out, and when they had passed out beyond the door the president proceeded to call the meeting to order.

"I am pleased with the way you obeyed my commands," said Mr. Knight. "If you will obey as promptly as that, we are going to be hard to whip. The next thing is to elect a president."

"I nominate Nathan Knight as president of the Jones County Confederacy," shouted a man near the door.

"We ought to have a ballot for that," said Mr. Knight.

"We don't need no ballot. It takes too much time. Can I get a second to that?"

He could and he did. It seemed as if every man in the house seconded the motion. Mr. Sprague put the vote before the house, and it was carried unanimously. Mr. Knight did not stop to make a speech, but said the next vote would be for vice-president, and Mr. Sprague was nominated.

"Hold on, there," shouted a voice. "We don't want Mr. Sprague for vice-president. We want him for secretary of war. If there is any man who can put us fellows where we can do the most good in a fight Mr. Sprague is the chap."

And so it was all through the convention. There wasn't a ballot taken for anything, and no man thought of declining an office. By four o'clock the work was all done, and then Mr. Knight thought of something else.

"There is one thing more that I want the convention to decide on," said he. "It is a ticklish piece of business, but we have got to do it. Jeff Davis has been making things very uncomfortable for our fellows out there in the Confederacy by telling them that they have got to light out or go into the army; now, what's to hinder us from doing the same thing? There are many rebels about here—"

"And I say let's get rid of them," said a voice. "I know one fellow who is going around all the time talking secession, and if the meeting says the word I'll go to him and tell him he had better dig out. The county will be a heap happier if he ain't in it."

"Let's all go in a body," said another voice.

"That's what I say," said a chorus of half a dozen men.

"I think myself that would be the better way," said the president. "If a lot of us get together and call upon a man, he will think we are in dead earnest. Give them time to take what they want, and then escort them out of the county. Don't leave a rebel behind you. There being no further business, the convention stands adjourned, to meet again upon call."

And where was Leon Sprague all this time? He was sitting in the front seat, where he could hear all that was going on. He felt proud when his father was elected secretary of war. He supposed, of course, that it was his business to post men in battle, but he learned better after a while. He was particularly anxious about escorting the rebels out of the county, and as soon as the convention adjourned he hurried out to find Tom Howe. As he was hurrying through the door, whom should he run against but Josiah—the " man who had seen a heap," and who " got the best of half a dozen men." He stood with his rifle hugged up close to him as if it were an old friend and he did not want to part from it.

CHAPTER III.

"A WORD IN YOUR EAR."

"WHY, Josiah, I am glad to see you," said Leon, advancing and shaking hands with the man. "The rebels haven't raided you yet? Look here, what is your name? I forgot to ask you when I was up to your house."

"Giddings—Josiah Giddings," answered the man. "No, the rebels have not raided me yet, but I am mighty dubious about them."

"Well, I want to make you acquainted with my father," said Leon. "He will give your wife protection at his house. We have a negro cabin there that is much more comfortable than the one you live in now, for it doesn't leak. And there is plenty of pasturage there for your horse and cow."

Leon drew up alongside of Giddings and in a few minutes his father came out. The introduction was given, and after a few com

monplace remarks Mr. Sprague inquired how
he liked the resolutions.

"They ain't strong enough," said Giddings.
"If you had two brothers in jail waiting for
their death-warrant, I reckon you would put
in more language than you did."

"Where is that?" inquired Mr. Knight,
who came out just at that moment.

"Up in Tennessee mountains. My brothers
were engaged in bridge burning, and now
they have got to suffer death for it."

Leon waited just long enough to see that Giddings was in a fair way to make the acquaintance of the principal men of the county, and
then hastened out to find Tom Howe. After
looking all about, he discovered him sitting
under the shade of an oak eating a lunch.

"Hallo, Leon; have some," was the way
in which he greeted the new-comer. "It's
mighty good, I tell you—chicken and apple
pie."

"A person to look at your lunch wouldn't
think that we Union fellows would be so hard
up for grub," said Leon, seating himself on
the ground by Tom's side. "You heard

what that man said, in reply to the enrolling officer, that if we got short of provisions we would steal them? But I want to talk to you about driving those rebels away from here."

"I know one who will get out of the county with once telling," said Tom.

"Who is it?"

"Carl Swayne."

"That's just the fellow I was thinking of," said Leon, spitefully. "He told me the other day that if we ran into the swamp it would not take him long to show them where we were."

"And he told me that he wished I had been smashed up in that jam while I was about it, for then there would be one Union man less in the world," said Tom. "I'll never forget him for that."

"Well, you come around to the house early to-morrow morning, and we will go up and send him off. I see father is getting ready to go home, so I must go. So-long."

Leon mounted his horse and started on a lope after his father, but when he came up with him he found him surrounded by a lot

of men and boys who were talking loudly of
the secession resolutions, finding no end of
fault with the Confederate Government, and
praising the Union.

"They won't get me, no matter which way
they turn," said one of the men, who lived
away off in the swamp. "I live two miles
from everybody, and right there is where the
fight is going to take place. The river in
front of my house is so narrow that you can
throw a stone across it anywhere, and for a
mile above and below the house it spreads out
into a swamp that they couldn't get across to
save their necks."

"So you really think there is going to be a
fight, do you?" inquired Mr. Sprague.

"Oh, sure. It's just as that enrolling officer said. The Confederates ain't a-going to
leave us to be the black sheep in the flock.
We are going to see some fun before we get
through with this."

That was the opinion of all the men, and
they concluded, too, that the best place to hold
the fight would be right there in front of this
man's house. "But I'll tell you what's a fact,"

said Giddings, "you will have to look out for
your wife and children. The rebels will make
short work of them if they get hold of them."

"The swamp is big," said the man. "If
they get out in there I will risk the rebels
getting hold of them."

Then men and boys dropped off one after
the other when they came to the cross-roads
that led to their homes, and by the time Mr.
Sprague reached his home there were but few
men besides Giddings left. The latter got off
his horse at the gate and went in to take a
view of the cabin in which Mr. Sprague told
him he could live until the trouble was all
over, and he straightway came to the conclusion that it was a much better house than the
one he now occupied.

"You see there was nobody there to tell
me that I could go into that house or I could
stay out of it," said Giddings. "It wasn't
occupied, and so I went into it, and sometimes
when it rains you might just as well be outside. If it suits you, I will come here to-
morrow."

Mr. Sprague told him that the sooner he

4

came the better; but Giddings declined an invitation to supper, because he knew his wife was waiting for him, so he got on his horse and rode off.

"It kinder runs in my mind that that man Giddings will be a good fellow to tie to," said Mr. Sprague, as he drew his chair up to the table. "There's no end to the way he hates the rebels, and it's my opinion that when he shoots at them he will shoot to kill."

"But do you really think there is going to be a fight?" inquired his wife. She asked this in a very indifferent manner, as if she did not care whether it came or not. She had got used to thinking of such things.

Mr. Sprague, by way of reply, told her all about the convention, and described to her the visit of the enrolling officers who had come up there to enlist men for the Confederate army.

"Did they get any?" inquired Mrs. Sprague.

"Not much. There were a thousand men there under arms, and that is rather more than two men want to handle. They know all about our plans, for Knight showed them the resolutions. Of course, they are going back to their headquarters, and are going to make a fuss about it."

"I tell you it won't be long now before we shall see some Confederate soldiers up here, and I wonder if I dare shoot at any of them?" said Leon. "If they will let me alone I believe I'll let them alone."

"How about those rebels that we are going to drive away from here to-morrow?" asked his father. "I think I have heard you say something pretty rough against Carl Swayne."

"Well, that's a different matter. Carl won't let me alone, and I am determined that hereafter I am going to live in peace. He told Tom Howe that he wished he had been jammed up in that log heap, and I don't like to have people talk that way."

Early the next morning Mr. Sprague's family were up and stirring. Leon was surprised when he looked at his father. There was a determined expression on his face, and the boy became aware that he was about to engage in an enterprise that promised at some future time to bring him no end of trouble.

Leon took his cue from it, and from that time
he was not so joyous as he had been. He
took his revolver out, shot it at a mark, and
then proceeded to load it very carefully. There
was only a man and a boy and two women in
the family he intended to send out of the
county, and Leon could not understand that
determined look on his father's face. When
he sat down at the breakfast-table he asked
him about it.

"Father, you seem to think you are going
to have a handful in sending that Swayne
family away from among their friends," said
he. "What do you look for?"

"I don't look for anything now," said Mr.
Sprague. "There will be a time when they
will come back. Old man Swayne is a fighter,
and it will stand us well in hand to get rid of
him entirely."

The conversation was dropped there, and
they ate breakfast in silence. Before it was
fairly ended the five men on whom Mr.
Sprague was depending to assist him stepped
up on the porch and came into the house.
They were all invited to sit down and take

another breakfast, but all declined, having broken their fast several hours before.

"You see, Mrs. Sprague, we got an order from the Secretary of War, and we've got to be on hand," said one of the men. "It would not do to go back on anything he tells us."

"I don't know what they put me in for that office for," said Mr. Sprague. "I don't see that I have got anything to do."

"Well, wait until it comes to fighting, and then you will find plenty to do. Now if you are all ready we'll go on," said the man, forgetting that he was giving orders to his superior officer. "We can't get rid of that Swayne family any too quick. They're all the time boasting and bragging of what they intend to do, and now we will give them a chance."

Leon found opportunity to kiss his mother good-bye, and when he went out on the porch, where Tom Howe was sitting and waiting for him, they fell in behind the men, who shouldered their rifles and marched at a brisk pace toward Mr. Swayne's house. There was no attempt at military movement, for there was not one in the party who knew anything about it, but they went ahead just as if they were going hog-hunting in the woods. In due time they came to a cross-roads which led down to Swayne's house, and here they stopped, for there was something that drew their attention and angered them not a little. Before they left Ellisville, on the day of the convention, Mr. Knight had given several copies of the resolutions to men living in different parts of the county, with the request that they should nail them up on trees (there was no printing-press in the county), in order to give those who were not there timely notice of what they had done. The man who served this notice performed his duty, for the tacks were in the tree plain enough, but it hadn't been able to do much good. The notice had been torn down and the pieces scattered about on the ground.

"Well, I do think in my soul!" began one of the men, "he wasn't going to let anybody see it, was he?"

"Look here," exclaimed Leon, who had grown wonderfully sharp sighted of late; "I know who did it. It was that miserable Carl

Swayne. Do you not see his footprints here in the dust?"

"That's so. Now what shall we do with him? Sprague, you are Secretary of War, and you ought to be able to say what shall be done with him. Knight never thought yesterday, when he gave out those resolutions, that somebody would go to work and pull them down."

Meanwhile Leon had been busy gathering up the torn fragments of the resolution that were scattered around. When he got them together he compared them and saw they were all there.

"I'll fix him," said he. "And I'll make him so sorry that he ever tore this down that he'll go by a resolution the next time he sees it."

"What are you going to do?"

"I'll make him write it over again and come here and put it up," said Leon, savagely.

"That's the idea," said Tom Howe. "He pulled it down, and of course he must put it up. I'll be close at your heels when you are doing it."

Mr. Sprague said nothing, but Leon noticed

that the look on his face got deeper than ever. He led the way at increased speed toward Swayne's house, and in a few minutes turned through the carriageway and saw Mr. Swayne and his nephew, Carl, sitting on the front porch. They evidently grew alarmed at seeing them, for they arose from their chairs and held on to the backs of them.

"Good morning," said Swayne, and his voice trembled and his hand shook as he hauled up some chairs for them to seat themselves. "I did not expect to see so many of you here this fine morning."

"We have no time to sit down," said Mr. Sprague, who was supposed to do all the talking. "You are a rebel, are you not?"

"Well—yes; that is it depends on what you call a rebel," said Mr. Swayne, trying to laugh at his own wit. "I am opposed to your trying to take this county out of the State; because why—"

"So I supposed. We have come here to tell you that you can pack up and leave this county as soon as you please. We don't want to hear any argument about it."

"Why—why, where shall I go to?" exclaimed Swayne, while the boy turned whiter than ever. "If I leave here, I leave everything I have got behind me."

"We will give you an hour to pack up things. If you are in the house at the end of that time, we shall set fire to it."

"Well, now, see here," said Swayne, who grew more frightened than ever; "I can't pack up in an hour—"

"I have told you just what I intend to do," said Mr. Sprague, consulting his watch. "It is now ten o'clock. If you are in here at eleven we shall set the house going. If you are out of it in that time, why, we'll save it. You want to make up your mind in a hurry."

"Of all the brazen-faced fellows I ever saw you are the beat," said Swayne, his fear giving place to anger. "I wish I had half a dozen Confederate soldiers here to protect me."

"By gum! We'll set the house a-going before you get out of it," said one of Mr. Sprague's men. "You ain't a-going to talk to us like that."

"One moment, Bud. We'll sit down here
on the porch until he gets through being mad,
and then maybe he'll pack up. You had better go, Swayne, for as sure as we are sitting
on this porch, so sure will we set fire to it."

In the meantime Leon and Tom had stood
close together, and as Carl flounced into the
house after his uncle, the two bounded up the
steps and went up to the frightened boy.

"A word in your ear," said Leon.

"Well, I don't want anything to do with
you," said Carl, almost ready to cry when he
found himself driven away from his home.
"A man who will do as you have done has no
business with a white person."

"One moment," said Leon, while Tom
cocked his gun and brought it to bear on Carl's
head. "That brings you to your senses, don't
it? Here's a resolution of secession that my
father got up yesterday, and which was left
on a tree down here, and I found it torn up
and strewn on the ground. Did you have a
hand in it?"

"Say, Tom, I want you to turn that gun
the other way," said Carl, who dared not move

for fear that the rifle would still be pointed at him.

"Did you have a hand in it?" repeated Leon.

"Yes, I did," said Carl, who, remembering that his uncle had got off easy by showing some grit, now resolved to show a little himself. "I will tear up every one you put there."

"Well, I want you to go into the house and bring out some writing materials, and sit down at this table here on the porch and draw up a full copy of this resolution," said Leon; and Carl had never heard him speak so before. As he spoke he drew a revolver from his pocket.

"I can't write as well as that," stammered Carl, who saw that he had got to do something very soon. "I wish you would put that revolver away. You don't know how it worries me to have those things in sight."

"You can write well enough. Go and get the pen and ink. And mind you, you want to be out here in short order, or we will be in there after you."

Carl hurried into the house, while Tom uncocked his gun and leaned upon it, and Leon put his revolver into his pocket. They didn't think they would have any more use for them. Carl went at once to the room in which his aunt was busy packing up some of her clothes, and the face he brought with him was enough to attract anybody's attention.

"Well, Carl, this is pretty rough, ain't it?" said his uncle, who was engaged in getting some of his own things together.

"I should say it was," whimpered Carl. "Are you not going to be revenged on these fellows?"

"We'll be revenged on them so quick that they won't know it," said his aunt, in a husky voice. She didn't cry, but her hands trembled and her face was very white.

"Where are your writing materials, aunt? That little Leon Sprague is going to make me write out those resolutions I tore down. I wish, with uncle, that we had some half a dozen Confederate soldiers here. Wouldn't we make a scattering among them?"

"Carl, you can't have those writing mate-

rials," said his aunt, who was struck motion-
less with surprise. "Tell him that we haven't
got any in the house. The young jackanapes!
Where's your rifle, that you don't use it? I
wish I were a man for about twenty minutes.
There wouldn't be so many of them as there
are now."

"But, aunt, they have got fire-arms, and
they pulled them on me," said Carl. "If I
don't get them out there very soon they will
come after me."

"You will find them in the top bureau
drawer," said his aunt, who began to think it
was necessary to show a little speed. "Wait
until I get my things all together and get out
there, I will give them a piece of my mind."

"Now, Lydia, you want to be mighty careful what you say out there," said her husband.
"They have got weapons, and they had just
as soon use them as not. It is a pretty piece
of business, this allowing strangers to drive
us away from our home, but I tell you we'll
have revenge for it sooner or later. Pack up
all your things in a hurry, for we have an
hour left us in which to save our home."

Carl, seeing that his uncle had no way to propose for him to get out of making a copy of that secession resolution, hunted up the writing materials as soon as he could, and went out on the porch with them. He found Leon and Tom there, and they were getting impatient.

"Look here," said the former, "if you want to help your uncle get his things together you will move a little spryer than that. Now, sit down at this table and make out a full copy of this paper, just as it was when you pulled it down."

"I'll bet you won't always have things all your own way," said Carl, as he seated himself and removed the stopper from the ink-bottle. "You don't suppose we'll come back, do you?"

"I suppose you will, and that you will have men with you," said Leon. "But you must bring all of two thousand men to put this rebellion down. Don't let's have any more talk. Go on and write out that paper."

"And remember, it's got to be the same as it was there," said Tom, when he saw Carl arrange the pieces without reference to what came after them. "If you don't, you will have to write it over again."

While Carl was busy with his copying his uncle and aunt came out on the porch. They didn't say a word, but brought with them a large bundle of clothing that they wanted to save. Aunt Lydia showed that she would have annihilated Mr. Sprague if she could, for the glance she cast upon him was full of hate. Mr. Swayne then took a horn down from a nail under the porch and blew two long blasts upon it. That was a signal to let the field-hands know that they were wanted. Presently the field-hands came up, a half a dozen of them, and although they may have been very smart negroes, the clothing which they wore did not proclaim the fact. There was hardly a piece of cloth on them that wasn't patched until it was almost ready to drop off their persons. They looked on in surprise when they saw so many Union men there (they used to say that the darkies were rather blunt in such matters, and that they didn't know who the Union men were), and saw the piles of clothing that had been brought out, but the first words their master spoke to them cleared everything up.

"We've got to go away from home now, or these men are going to burn it," said Mr. Swayne. "Hitch those mules to the lumber-wagons and bring them up here. Be in a hurry, now, for we have no time to waste."

The darkies rolled their eyes in great aston-ishment, and then went about their work with alacrity. In a few minutes the wagons were driven up to the door, and the darkies began to pile in the clothes. While Mr. Sprague was watching them he became aware that somebody was trying to attract his attention. A pebble thrown by a friendly hand hit him on the shoulder. He faced about, and saw one of the darkies behind the house. When he saw Mr. Sprague looking at him he beckoned to him to come where he was.

CHAPTER IV.

CARL BRINGS NEWS.

"SAY, Marse Sprague, is you Union men going to burn dese houses ober deir heads?" began the darky, so excited that he could scarcely stand still.

"We have given them an hour to take their things out," said Mr. Sprague. "If they don't take them out in that time we'll set the house a-going. If they get all their things out and loaded in the wagons we'll save the house, so that they can have something to live in when these troubles are all over."

"Whar do you reckon dey'll go if dey get the things all tooken out?" asked the negro.

"I don't know where they will go; over into the next county, probably. But what makes you so anxious?"

"Well, say, Marse Sprague, I don't care to

5

go ober into the next county wid 'em. Dey's rebels ober dere."

"So I have heard."

"Well, I don't want to go among dose rebels 'cause I won't get no freedom. Dey say we'll get it in a little while if we stays here among dose Union men."

"Who told you that?"

"Your own Mose told me dat, sah."

"Is Mose going to take his freedom when he can get it?"

"Sah? No, sah. He say he's got a Marse who don't stripe his jacket none, and he ain't a-going to look at his freedom. I tell you, I don't care to go ober into dat oder county wid dem people here."

"What are you going to do about it?"

"We-uns didn't know what to do about it. If we slip away from dem while dey are going ober dar can dey catch us?"

"I don't know whether they can or not. There's been an Emancipation Proclamation ssued by Abraham Lincoln, saying that if they don't quit their rebellion in six months he will declare their niggers all free."

"Dat's just what I want to get at, sah," said the negro, pounding his knees and shaking his head as if he were overjoyed to hear it. "Dat's just what I want, sah. De rebels ain't a-going to go and get up such a 'bellion, and den go and give it up 'cause somebody tells 'em to. I ain't a-going into dat oder county, and the first thing Marse Swayne knows my folks and me will be missing."

"Well, you have got to depend on yourself," said Mr. Sprague. "I cannot help you if you do run away from them."

"I knows dat mighty well. But you just watch out and see if you hain't got more black folks up to your plantation dan you ought to have. You is a Union man and I know it, and you ain't a-going to give me up just 'cause Marse Swayne says so."

The negro started one way because he heard somebody calling him, and Mr. Sprague joined the men on the porch feeling as if he had a big responsibility resting upon him. He didn't agree to take all the darkies in the county who might make up their minds to run away from their masters, and how was he going to support them all and find work for them to do?

"I tell you, this thing is coming to a head," said Mr. Sprague to the man who sat next to him. "You remember what Stephens said about having a Government whose corner-stone should be slavery?"

The man remembered it perfectly. They used to get Confederate papers when the war first broke out, but now that they were in rebellion, and the postmaster was a rebel, they didn't get a sight of one. The man who had charge of the office removed to Mobile as soon as he saw how things were going, and since then there had not been any post-office.

"Well, sir, old Cuff has just been talking to me, and he thinks of running away. He says that if he goes over into the other county he won't get his freedom."

"Good, said the man. "I am glad of it. We'll see how their 'corner-stone' is going to hold out when they get their Confederacy. But they ain't a-going to whip."

"But this old Cuff thinks I am going to

support him," said Mr. Sprague. " I haven't got any work for him to do."

" Send him into the woods to cut logs for you," said the man.

" I might do that, but I don't see where I am going to find market for them. But I will get along somehow. Well, half an hour is gone, and they haven't got many things out yet. Leon and Tom seem to be making it all right with Carl, don't they ?"

The two boys referred to stood patiently by until the resolutions were complete; then Tom took his copy and Leon fastened his eyes upon the torn manuscript and waited for him to read it. It was all correct; there wasn't a mistake in it.

" You write a pretty good hand for a boy who hasn't been to school more than you have," said Leon.

" Keep your compliments for them that need them," said Carl, snappishly. " I don't care to hear them."

" You haven't got through with this business yet," said Leon, in a voice which he meant should carry conviction with it. " You found this resolution on a tree, and you tore it down so that people couldn't see it. I intend that you shall go back and post this thing up there."

"But you told me I should have to help my uncle carry out his things," said Carl, anxious to shirk all the responsibility he could.

"Oh, we'll wait until you carry out your things," said Leon, with a smile. "You are going right by the tree, and it won't hurt you at all to stop and nail this thing up."

Carl gathered up the pen and ink and disappeared in the house, and Leon and Tom went down the steps to join the men who were sitting there.

"I got it, but I had hard work in getting it, too," said Leon. "How much longer time has he got?"

"Not quite fifteen minutes," said Mr. Sprague.

"And I see he is hustling things more lively than he did. You won't start the fire when the quarter of an hour is up, seeing that he is doing the best he can to get them out?"

"Oh, no. I wanted to see him get to work, that is all."

At the end of half an hour the furniture and clothes they intended to take with them had been loaded on the wagons, and then the women began to slam the blinds and fasten them securely. When Mr. Swayne came out on the porch he locked that door and put the key into his pocket.

"We have got some things in there yet, but we don't want these traitors to have them," said his wife, in a tone which was intended very plainly for the ears of Mr. Sprague and his friends. "Let them go somewhere else and steal somebody else poor."

Mr. Swayne did not pay any attention to it. He buttoned up the key in his pocket, and looked all around as if he were searching for someone. At last he called out:

"Cuff! Where is that lazy nigger Cuff? Come here this minute, or I will stripe your jacket till you can't rest."

Mr. Sprague was surprised. He thought it very likely that he could tell Mr. Swayne what had become of the negro Cuff. He had been sent with all his companions to the quarters to bring some clothes and other things they wanted to save, and he hadn't showed up since. It would be very easy for them to slip through the cornfield, and so into the woods, and that was right where Cuff was when his master was calling him.

"Carl, suppose you run down to the quarters and hurry them up," said his uncle. " We want to get away from here as soon as we can. There's too many Union people here."

The man who had threatened to burn the house before they got out of it was sitting on the steps a little way from Mr. Sprague. He wiggled and twisted and wanted to say something in return, but there was his superior officer who didn't say anything, and he thought he would hold in for a better opportunity. Carl was away about fifteen minutes, and when he came back his face bore evidence that he was utterly confounded.

" There ain't a nigger about the quarters," said he. " Their clothes, both bedding and wearing apparel, are gone, and that proves that they have run away."

"That's the first time I ever had a nigger serve me that way," said Mr. Swayne, pacing up and down the porch. "Run away, have they? If I ever get my hands on them I'll make it awfully uneasy for them to lie down, now I tell you. Did you follow them into the woods to see where they went?"

"No, I didn't. I saw their tracks leading through the cornfield, and then I came home to report the matter to you. Those niggers think they are going to get their freedom now."

"Yes, and you might have expected it," said his aunt, turning her flashing eyes upon Mr. Sprague. "What are these Union men here for if it isn't to coax the niggers away from an honest Confederate?"

"Mrs. Swayne, we had no hand in inducing your negroes to run away from you," said Mr. Sprague, who now began to get angry. "They said they were not going into the other county with you, and I told them that they must depend entirely upon themselves."

"By gum! You want to see your house go before you get away from it," said the man who had threatened to burn them out.

"Any more such talk as that and I'll set her a-going; by gum I will."

"Carl, you will have to do some driving for us, for we can't stop to hunt the niggers," said Mr. Swayne.

"Oh, now, I didn't agree to do driving," whined Carl. "Let's stop and go into the woods after them."

"You have already got your things loaded on the wagons, and I must ask you to drive on," said Mr. Sprague. "It is my duty to stay by you until you get beyond Ellisville."

"Carl, jump on that wagon and drive after me," said Mr. Swayne. "I don't want to hear any more argument about it."

"Tom, you haven't got any horse, and I advise you to get into that wagon with Carl," said Leon. "When you come to the tree on which the resolution was posted, make him get out and post this one in its place. He'll object, but we can't help it."

While Carl was tying his riding-horse behind the wagon Tom climbed in and seated himself on the table which had been placed

there for one of the negroes who had gone off
with Cuff. Carl saw what he was doing, but
didn't make any fuss about it. He had arrived at his uncle's conclusion that the best
thing they could do was to take no notice of
the Union men. By doing that they would
irritate them, and they would not have so
much to brag of when they talked about driving Confederate families out of the county. But
they didn't know Mr. Sprague and his friends.
The task was one they did not like, but they
did it because they had been ordered to. Carl
kept his mouth resolutely closed until they
came to the tree from which he had torn down
the resolutions. He whipped up his mules
when he came there, but Tom laid hold of the
reins and stopped them.

"Now, Carl, this is the place," said he.
"Here's the notice, and you want to get out
and tack it up. The nails are all there."

Carl didn't know whether to refuse or not,
but just then Leon came up on his side of the
wagon. Leon had a revolver in his pocket.
and Carl did not like to see that; so he
grabbed the notice and sprang out of the

wagon. In a few minutes it was tacked up just the same as it was before.

"There," said Leon, "that will do. Now anybody who comes along here and who wasn't at the convention can see what we did there."

"Now I guess you had better get out," said Carl, addressing himself to Tom Howe.

"No, I reckon not," replied Tom. "I've got to go with you as long as you stay in the county, and I reckon I can get along here as well as I can afoot. Drive on."

Carl at once closed his lips and had nothing more to say. As they were going by his own house, Leon noticed that there was nobody present, for his mother was too refined a woman to take such a paltry vengeance on those who did not believe as she did, but there was one little circumstance that attracted his attention. He was certain that he saw old Cuff's cottonade coat disappear around the house. He did not have more than a glimpse of it, but he was sure it was there. When they arrived at the cross-roads they met ten more men on foot who were escorting four more wagon-loads of secessionists to Perry county, which was the nearest place they could get and be among friends. They never said a word, but fell in behind Mr. Sprague, and followed along after him. They were all armed with rifles, and some of them had revolvers stuck in their belts. The sight of these men made Carl open his eyes. He had not dreamed that there were so many Union men in the county.

"I believe you've got more Yankees here than Confederates," said he.

"These men are not Yankees," said Tom. "They are men born here in the South. But these ain't a patching to what we've got. If you had been down to that convention you would have seen a thousand men under arms. There were so many of them that we couldn't get them all in the church. Some of them had to stay outside and raise the windows."

"Well, what did you do there besides pass the resolutions of secession?" asked Carl; for now that his uncle was out of hearing he seemed anxious to learn what had been going on at that meeting.

"We elected officers," said Tom.

"Didn't you do anything else?"

"Well, yes. There was a couple of enrolling officers came there to enlist men for the Confederate army, and we sent them back where they came from."

"Then the rebels don't allow that this county is out of the State, do they?" said Carl, who was overjoyed to hear it. "You have got your own way this time, but I tell you we are coming back. And I won't forget the boys that drew fire-arms on me."

"Well, that's right. I suppose they won't draw any more on you?"

"No, sir, they won't," said Carl, hotly. "I don't mind talking this way to you, but I do hate the sight of that revolver that Leon Sprague has in his pocket. Where is he now?"

"He is back talking to those men that came up awhile ago," said Tom. "He can't hear you, but you must remember that we can fight tolerable sharp."

Leon had gradually slackened his pace until the single man on horseback, who seemed to be the leader of the party, came up and rode beside him.

"Well, sir, you got 'em, didn't you?" said the man. "You know, when your father said he would go up after that man yesterday I felt rather anxious about him. I thought he would fight, sure."

"Well, he didn't. He did not show any signs of it. He was mighty saucy, though, and so was that nephew of his."

"One of our men was sassy, too. Do you see that man driving the next wagon? He's got a big lump under his eye. Bob Lee hit him."

"Now, what did he do that for? Bob had the right on his side, and there was no reason why he should get mad and strike the man. My father had just as good reason to hit Swayne, but he didn't do it."

"He had no business to be sassy. If Bob hadn't a hit him I would. He said that he hoped to goodness that the rebels would come in and take the last scalp from our heads. When Bob asked him to take it back he said he wouldn't do it, and so Bob upended him.

That was the last sassy word given to us. It showed them that we were in earnest. Hello! There's three more fellows come up and are talking to your father, and by gracious! one of them is a rebel. Let's go there and see what they have got to say."

Leon and his friend urged their horses forward, and in a few minutes drew up beside Mr. Sprague, who was listening to some words the rebel had to say to him. As he spoke he looked at the women and Mr. Swayne, and then sank his voice almost to a whisper.

"Colonel, are these some rebels that you are taking out of the county?" said he.

"We have got so far with them, and we expect to get the rest of the way," answered Mr. Sprague.

"I want you to come off on one side so that I can talk to you without fear of being overheard," said the rebel. "Now," he added, as the men moved some distance down the road, "the rebels are going to move a big wagon-train along that road to-morrow. You see they have got to go around this county, for they don't want to run the risk of being captured if they pass through here."

"We stopped and saw President Knight about it, and he advised us to come on and see you," said one of the men who had acted as guard to the rebel.

"Take his gun away from him," said Mr. Sprague, and the rebel promptly gave it up, together with his ammunition-box and bayonet. "Have you any other weapons about you?"

"Nary one, sah," said the rebel. "My family is down here a little ways from Ellisville, and you may know that I am all right when I bring them with me."

"How did you say you escaped?"

"I wasn't conscripted, as a great many were, but there was such a pressure brought to bear upon me that I thought I might as well go into the army instead of waiting until I was conscripted in reality. I have been in the service only six months, but I have been in three or four little engagements. I live in Perry county, and when I found out what you were doing here, how you had never sent

6

any men into the army, and how there were a thousand men here who didn't intend to go at all, I wrote to my wife, advising her to come here and I would join her after awhile; but she wrote back that she wouldn't stir a step unless I came. On the night I escaped I was on guard, and the corporal hadn't any more than got away from me when I was missing. I travelled all night, and at daylight reached my home. I packed up what few things I wanted to save and came here, and one of my mules dropped dead as soon as I got to Ellisville. I wanted the President to go on at once and capture that train, but he thought I had better come on and see you about it."

"Well, you tell a pretty straight story, and I shall have to put some faith in it until I can prove the contrary," said Mr. Sprague.

"You are at liberty to disprove my story in any way you can," said the rebel, earnestly. "I am dead shot on this thing, and if this county is going to stay out of the Confederacy I am going to stay out, too."

"I shall have to send you to my house," said Mr. Sprague.

"Send me anywhere, sah, but stop and explain to my family why I don't come home. She will appreciate the reason, for she is a soldier's wife."

"Father, come here a minute. I don't see what's the use of sending that rebel to our house," said Leon, when his father had drawn off on one side. "He must have a camp down there in Ellisville, and, now he has given up his weapons, I don't see how he is going to get away. There are fully five hundred men camped around Ellisville now."

"Well, that is so," said Mr. Sprague, after reflecting a moment. "I think I had better take him on to Ellisville and leave him there, with plenty of men to watch him."

"That would be my way, certainly."

"Forward, march!" shouted Mr. Sprague, as he placed himself at the head of his little train, and the cavalcade once more moved onward. The rebel kept close at his side, and Leon rode a little ways behind him. There was one thing that drew the boy's attention, and that was the rebel's horse. Although she was tired, her gait showed that she fretted and fumed at the bit as if she was anxious to go faster. She was a beautiful animal, with limbs so small that they did not look strong enough to support her weight.

"May I ask you where you got that horse?" said Leon, after he had watched her for some length of time.

"I stole her from the wagon-master," said the rebel. "I should not have been able to get home if it hadn't been for her. I did the rebels all the damage I could before leaving them."

"There must be some escort with that wagon-train, isn't there?" inquired Mr. Sprague.

"There are twenty-five men, including two officers," replied the rebel. "But half of them you needn't be afraid of, for they are all Union."

"How many wagons are there in the train?"

"Forty;" whereat Leon opened his eyes in surprise.

"Will the teamsters fight?"

"Fight!" exclaimed the rebel, in disgust. "No, they won't. Half of them are armed, but they don't know what it is to fight. When they see you coming up with your guns all ready the majority of them will throw up their hands."

If ever there was a happy man in that train it was the rebel. He joked and laughed because he said he was among friends once more and could say what he pleased, and all the way to Ellisville entertained his auditors with thrilling stories of his earliest battles. He told how frightened he was when he got into the first one, and how he looked around for a hollow log into which he could crawl and get out of sight; but there were his companions all standing up without being shot, and his pride made him stay right where he was. At three o'clock they reached Ellisville, where the President had located his office. As Leon had said, there were at least five hundred men camped around there, some with their families, some had no homes at all, but all wanted to be where they could feel that they were of some assistance to Mr. Knight. They knew that when a raid was made upon the county it would come from Perry, the county next on the south, and they calculated to be at hand to stop it. Here Mr. Sprague halted his train and went in to hold an interview with the President, taking the rebel's gun with him. He was gone but a few minutes, and when he came out his countenance indicated that he had resolved upon something. He mounted his horse and rode in among the lean-tos and other shelters which the men had erected for themselves, and shouted "Attention!" at the top of his voice, and immediately every man who heard him came running up to see what was the matter. When he thought he had got a sufficient number about him, Mr. Sprague proceeded to unfold his plans. It wasn't the way that a majority of leaders do, for they never let their men know what sort of dangers they are going to meet until they get fairly into them.

"We are going out to-morrow to attack that wagon-train," said Mr. Sprague, "and I want all of you who can go to be on hand here bright and early."

"Good!" exclaimed one. "Then we'll have something to eat."

Mr. Sprague then went on to tell them how many wagons there were in the train, how many teamsters, and how large an escort of soldiers; for he put implicit faith in the rebel's word. He was certain that five hundred men, if he could secure that many, advancing with their guns at full cock, would take all the fight out of them. Mr. Sprague was careful not to talk so loud as to attract the attention of Mr. Swayne, for he knew that he would warn the Confederates. Having given his men something to think about, he rode back to place himself at the head of his train, which moved away toward the county line.

CHAPTER V.

CAPTURING A WAGON-TRAIN.

"NOW," said Mr. Sprague, when Leon rode up beside him, "you want to go and tell your mother the reason that I don't come home to-night. I shall have to stay here with the men, to be ready to start out with them at an early hour."

"Then after that I suppose I can stay at home," said Leon.

"Yes; I think that would be the best place for you. Those twenty-five men, and all of them old soldiers, are not going to give up that wagon-train without some resistance."

"Well, now, I'll tell you what's a fact, father," said Leon, decidedly. "I just ain't a-going to stay at home."

"Why not?" said Mr. Sprague, in surprise.

"If you are going to meet those men, I am going, too. You needn't think you are going into danger without my being close beside you. I wouldn't dare look mother in the face again if I should be guilty of remaining at home."

Mr. Sprague looked down at the horn of his saddle and thought about it. Leon had really more pluck than his father thought he had, and after awhile he thought it would be better to let the boy have his own way in the matter.

"I don't see what is the use of sending any word at all home to mother," said Leon, after pondering what his father had said. "She knows that we are in the service of the county, and she won't care whether we come home or not. The best way would be to stay right down here and go home when we get the job done."

This settled the matter, and Mr. Sprague never referred to it again. About eight o'clock they arrived at the little bridge which spanned the creek that flowed between Jones and Perry counties, and there Mr. Sprague halted his men and motioned to Mr. Swayne to go on. The man complied, and when he had got far

enough across to let all the wagons that came
after him get a footing on Confederate soil he
stopped and jumped out.

"Thank goodness I've got a white man's
ground under my feet!" he exclaimed; and no
one had ever seen him so mad before. He
seemed to be holding in for just this occasion,
and he was so angry that he could scarcely
speak plainly. "I suppose that now I can
talk to you as I have a mind to."

" Draw yourselves in line across this bridge
and hold your guns in readiness to shoot," said
Mr. Sprague in a low tone to his men. "He
may open fire on us before we can get under
cover. Oh, yes, you can say what you please,
now," he said, in his ordinary voice. "But I
wouldn't say too much till I get behind that
bend."

"Well, I want to say this much to you,"
shouted Mr. Swayne; "you have had your
own way this time, but we are coming back in
less than a week to clean you all out."

" And remember this," exclaimed Carl from
his place in the wagon. "I will bear in mind
the boys who drew shooting-irons on me, you

see if I don't. I'll tear down that notice, and every other one that I can find."

"And you, Bob Lee, I'll remember you," said the man with a lump under his eye. "I'll teach you that the next man who says anything about the Confederates—well, you had better let him alone, that's all," he added, when he saw Bob raise his gun to his shoulder.

"If you are all ready, go on," said Mr. Sprague.

Mr. Swayne was a long time in getting into his wagon. He would place his foot upon the hub, and then one of the men would say something insulting in regard to the men they had just left, and Mr. Swayne would take his foot down and stand there until he heard what the man had to say. He was in earnest when he said they were coming back to clean the Union men all out, and that there wouldn't be hide nor hair of them left when they did come, and finally he got into his wagon and drove on. When he looked behind to see what had become of Mr. Sprague and his party, he saw them just disappearing around the nearest bend in the road.

"I wish I dared shoot at them," said he.

"Well, I'll shoot at them, and welcome," said the man whom Bob Lee had struck, as he reached for his gun.

"Don't do it, Jim," expostulated Mr. Swayne.

"Dog-gone it, don't you see the bump under my eye?" said the man. "I can see the chap who did it, and I can pick him off just as easy as you would kill a squirrel."

"If you shoot at them they will come back here and arrest the whole of us, and take us back to their camp and make us stand a court-martial," said Mr. Swayne. "I am not a-going to stand punishment for your deeds and mine into the bargain."

This view of the matter rather arrested the man's hand, and he sat with his gun resting across his knees, muttering curses not loud but deep, until he saw the Union men disappear around a bend in the road. Mr. Sprague knew that he stood a chance of being fired upon, and that was what he intended to do; he would arrest the whole of them and take them to camp. But Mr. Swayne was a little too sharp for him. It was two o'clock when they arrived at the camp, and the men, to show that they knew what sort of respect ought to be paid to the Secretary of War, went off to hunt up some forage for his horse and Leon's before they went to bed.

"Well, Leon," said Mr. Sprague, after the horses had been picketed with plenty to eat and the men had all gone away, "we haven't got any blankets."

"No matter for that," said Leon. "It won't be the first time I have slept out with nothing to cover me. Get some leaves, and they will do just as well."

They walked along the road as they talked, and Mr. Sprague could not help thinking what a big army he was going to have to attack that wagon-train. Every step of the way he saw lean-tos, and he knew that there were stalwart men sleeping under them. Finally he drew up before a lean-to where there was a sentry sitting in front of the door. He did not carry his arms at a "support," nor did he bring his piece to "arms port" and call out, "Who comes there?" when he saw Mr.

Sprague and Leon approaching. But he greeted him in regular backwoods style.

"Hallo, Sprague," said he. "Did you get your parties through all right?"

The Secretary of War replied that he did, adding—

"This must be the home of that rebel, isn't it?"

"Yes. But he has been perfectly peaceable all night. He didn't sleep at all the night before."

"No; but I am awake now," called out a voice from the inside; and there was a little fussing in the cabin and the rebel came to the door.

"Say, Colonel, are you going to stay here all night?"

"That is the intention. I want to get an early start, and it is too far for me to go home."

"Well, now, I know that you haven't got any quilts," said the rebel, disappearing under the roof of the lean-to. "Here's some that will add to your comfort to-night. Take them and welcome."

Mr. Sprague thanked the rebel for his gift and spread the quilts down where they intended to camp for the night, while Leon told himself that it was a good thing to have a father who was Secretary of War, after all. They slept soundly for a little while, but at half-past three Mr. Sprague was awake and busily engaged in arousing the men. In less time than it takes to tell it they were all up and cooking their breakfast, and in an hour more the grove was empty. Five hundred men were going out to attack that wagon-train, and, if possible, secure something to eat. We don't mean to say that they were hard up for provisions, for there was bacon and corn-meal enough in the county to last them for months; but we mean that they had lived so long on these things that they had grown tired of them. They had been used to something better than that before the war, and when their boats came back from tide-water, after their owners had succeeded in selling their logs, the housewife found pickles, canned meat and condensed milk enough to last her family for six months. That was one thing that the men had in view; and another thing, some of them were in need of clothes; and they believed that this wagon-train had something of that kind stowed away for the boys in Mobile. And, better than all—and here was the thing that led the men to look with favor upon robbing the train—it would show the Confederates they were in earnest; —just what the Union people wanted to do.

It was a long march from the grove in Ellisville to the stream that separated the two counties, but the men went about it in earnest and determined to get there in time to stop that wagon-train. Of course, there was plenty of joking and laughing while they were on their own ground, but the moment they struck the bridge a deep silence fell upon the company. We ought by rights to say that the men had been divided into five companies, a hundred men in each, and that each one had three officers to direct them; but the Union men of Jones county had not got that far in military tactics. There was only one man at the head, Mr. Sprague, and he had the full management of them.

Mr. Sprague rode at the head of the line in company with all the men who had horses, and there must have been about fifty of them, and when he crossed the bridge he sent a dozen of them on ahead to travel at full speed, to see if the wagon-train had passed.

"I needn't remind you that you want to go into every house you come to, and if there is a man in there take him in," said he. "Don't say a word to the women, but ketch the men. It won't do to leave any rebels behind us, for they can easily warn the train, and so we must take them with us until we get the job done. Silas, I will appoint you captain of this squad."

Silas raised his hand to his hat with something that was intended for a military salute, called all his men about him, and went down the road at a keen jump, while the rest of the company travelled on as before. An hour afterward they came up with their scouts, and Silas at once rode up to report.

"The wagon-train hain't passed yet, and we've got five men, and two of them are rebels. We had to chase through a cornfield after one, and fired two shots at him."

7

"Did you hit him?"

"No, we didn't hit him, but he was mighty ready to throw up his hands when he heard the bullets whistling."

"Did you get their guns?"

"Yes, we got them all safe."

"Now the best thing we can do," said Mr. Sprague, turning about to face his men, "is to go down the road and conceal ourselves in the bushes. When you see me move my arm this way," here he raised his arm above his head and waved it toward the right and left of the road, "you will all divide and go into the timber on different sides; and when you hear me whistle this way," he put his hand to his mouth and gave a whistle that could have been heard a mile, "then you may know that it is time for you to get down to business. But bear one thing in mind: Don't shoot unless you have to."

The company, or, more properly speaking, the battalion, moved on again, and in half an hour not one of them was in sight. They had divided right and left, as Mr. Sprague had directed, and taken up their positions on op-

posite sides of the road, and there was not the
least noise or confusion about it. Two of the
men had gone down the road to see if the train
was coming, and they were impatiently waiting their return. The prisoners had all been
turned over to Mr. Sprague, and he was having something of a time with one of them,
who was determined that he would not hold
his tongue. He had a very shrill voice, and
when he spoke in his ordinary tone it could
be heard a long distance.

"Now, Sprague, I don't see the sense in
your doing this," said the shrill-voiced man,
and he seemed to have pitched his tones so
loud that they could have heard him at the
end of the line. "You take me away from
my home, who never did the Union any
harm—"

"You are a nice fellow, you are," said one
of the men who happened to be close around
when the shrill-voiced person was talking. "I
take notice of the fact that Ebenezer Hale
wanted to come up here so as to be among
Union men, and you heard his story, and
when he was asleep that night you went off

and got a lot of rebels to surround and carry him off. Where is he now? In jail, likely. And you, dog-gone you, you never did the Union men any harm! You had oughter go to jail until this trouble is all over."

"Well, now, Simeon, I did just what I thought was best for the community. I didn't have nothing against Ebenezer Hale, but I knew that if he went into this fight—"

"That's enough," said Mr. Sprague. "We have listened to you all we want to."

"Now, Sprague, I shan't quit talking until I have a mind to," said the shrill-voiced man. "You have undertaken more than you can accomplish, and I say—"

"Sim, cut a little piece of wood about four inches long, and tie a string to each end of it," said Mr. Sprague. "If Kelley don't shut up we'll gag him."

"Oh, now, Mr. Sprague, don't gag me," said the man, sinking his voice almost to a whisper this time. "I won't say one word more. I won't, upon my honor."

The gag was duly cut and prepared, and nothing was wanting except another word from Mr.

Kelley to induce Sim to put it where it belonged; but the man took just one look at it and concluded that the best thing he could do was to keep still. He never showed any disposition to open his head until the scouts were seen coming back with the information that the train was approaching. They came in a hurry, too, as if they were anxious to get something off their minds.

"Where's Sprague?" were the words they shouted as they galloped along the road; whereupon Mr. Sprague showed himself. "The train is coming," they said, as soon as they came within hearing of their leader. "Every blessed one of them is coming, and are acting as if they didn't fear anything."

"Did they see you?" inquired Mr. Sprague.

"No, they didn't. We hid our horses in the bushes, and then went and lay down beside the road until we saw the train coming. Yes, sir, we're going to get them all."

Mr. Sprague and his scouts went into the bushes again out of sight, and then he noticed that Mr. Kelley wasn't so anxious to keep in the background so much as he had been. He was even disposed to go out of the bushes, but he hadn't made many steps in that direction when Simeon seized him by the collar and stretched him flat on his back.

"Oh, now, Simeon—"

"Not another word out of you," said his guard, savagely. "You will get the gag in your mouth as sure as you're alive."

"Take your stand close behind him," said Mr. Sprague, who was getting angry now, "and with the very first words he utters shoot him down. We are not going to have our plans spoilt for the sake of him."

Leon, who stood close at his father's side and heard all this conversation, grew as pale as death when he found that the wagon-train was coming. He clutched his revolver nervously, and determined that whatever danger his father got into he would be there to help him. The leader glanced at his son's pale face and said, in a low tone :

"Leon, I think you had better stay here as a guard to these prisoners."

"Are you going out there to face that escort?" asked Leon.

"Of course I am. I shall be right in the thickest of it."

"Then I'm going, too."

"But you will be safe here. They can't hit you, even if they shoot at you."

But Leon only shook his head, and at that moment somebody whispered that the foremost wagons were in sight. That turned Mr. Sprague's attention into a new channel, and Leon was left to himself. He glanced at Simeon and his captive, and was gratified to see that Mr. Kelley had been forced to sit down, and Simeon was standing there with his cocked gun ranged within two inches of his head. He wanted to speak, and made a motion to Simeon to turn the gun the other way, but as often as he did this the piece was raised to his guard's shoulder, and the words froze on his lips.

The foremost wagon came along as rapidly as the mules could draw it, and after what seemed an age to Leon the wagons were all in view. When the leading wagon was almost opposite to him Mr. Sprague raised his hand to his mouth and gave a shrill whistle. Never in his life had he given a better one. He wasn't excited at all. There was a moment's silence there in the brush, and out popped the cavalry and infantry, and in less time that it takes to tell it the wagon-train was surrounded. Not a shot was fired. To say that the rebels were astounded would not half express their feelings. Every teamster had three or four guns looking at him, and the cavalry, who occupied the advance of the train, were surrounded with horsemen that were two to their one.

"Well, by George! You have done this up in good shape," said the rebel captain, after he had taken time to get his wits together. "What are you—Union?"

"Yes, sir; Union to the backbone," replied Mr. Sprague. "May I trouble you for your sword and revolver?"

"That was as neat a surprise as I ever saw," said the captain, as he unbuckled his belt and handed it to Mr. Sprague. "You didn't give us time to fire a shot. What are you going to do with us? Put us in jail?"

"No, sir. We shall allow you to go where you please," said Mr. Sprague, accepting the belt and fastening it about his own waist. "We are not making war on your folks now, but on your provisions. We shall have to take your horses, too. Dismount."

"I guess father's all right, and now I'll get some weapons of my own," said Leon, as he turned his horse and rode along the line of the escort. "There must be some rebels in there that haven't given up all their fire-arms."

As he rode along he found a soldier on the inside of the third four who held his weapons in his hand and was looking around for somebody to give them to. When he saw Leon approaching he held his sword, revolver and carbine toward him over his companion's horse.

"Come out here," said Leon. I shall have to take your horse as well as your weapons."

"Well, I can't help it, can I?" said the rebel, who was more inclined to laugh than he was to feel despondent over it. He came out and proceeded to give up his horse and weapons to Leon, and at the same time he took particular pains to place himself on the boy's side next to the woods. In this way he could talk to him without his rebel friends hearing it.

"Say," he added, "you won't take me to jail, will you?"

"Certainly not," said Leon.

"Don't talk so loud. I don't want my companions to know that I have found a friend among Union men. Let me go out in the woods a little while, and I will come back sure when you are all ready to start for home."

"You will only be giving yourself trouble if you do that," said Leon, who thought his rebel friend was taking a queer way to escape. "As soon as we get your weapons we intend to turn you all loose, to go where you please."

"But I don't want to go with those rebels," said the young soldier, earnestly. "I am a Union man, and I went into the army because I had to. I will come back, sure."

"Well, go ahead, but don't let anybody see you."

When Leon led the captured horse back to his father's side he found that the escort had all been dismounted and disarmed, and were now standing there and awaiting further orders. Some were disposed to be angry and sullen, while others were laughing over what they considered a first-class surprise. Mr. Sprague was highly elated over it. He did not show it, but there was something about him that made Leon feel happy, too. The goods that were captured that day must have been worth $500,000.

"Now, Captain, you are all right, and I will bid you good-day," said Mr. Sprague. "You can go ahead, and as fast as the teamsters come up, we'll send them on after you. Silas, go back there and send up all the teamsters."

"But suppose they don't want to go?" said Silas.

"Then leave them behind. If they want to go and join the Confederate army, send them up here; but if they want to stay and join the Union forces, let them alone."

"Colonel, I suppose I can say what I please, can't I?" said the rebel captain. "You have got the dead-wood on me now, but it won't be long before I'll come back. Then I shall ask you for my sword."

In a few minutes the teamsters began to

come up, and, as they approached, Mr. Sprague told them to fall in behind the escort, which was marching down the road. Leon kept a close watch on them, but didn't count more than thirty who wanted to go back to the Confederacy. There must have been at least ten of them who wanted to stay with the Union men. The next thing was to turn the mules around and start back home. This occupied a good deal of time, for the mules were balky, and some of them would not "back;" but those five hundred men soon took the "balky" out of them, and in half an hour more the wagons were all turned around and the train was on its way to Ellisville.

CHAPTER VI.

THE MARCH HOMEWARD.

LEON remained beside his father until the wagons were turned around, and when he ordered the cavalry ahead to take its place at the advance of the column, he went with them. Forty wagons, and some of them were loaded so heavily that four mules could scarcely draw them. Everybody was pleased with the performance. If all the wagon-trains they captured were to be taken as easily as that, they had no fear but that they should have grub enough. Every driver's seat was filled with men who thought that they preferred riding to walking, and they all joined in and sang, at the top of their voices:

"John Brown's body lies a-mouldering in the grave."

How the song got down there they didn't know. Probably some of those who had been prisoners in the hands of the Federals, and there were a good many old soldiers in the lot, had heard it sung by their captors, and now that they were fighting for the Union they resolved to imitate them as far as possible. Finally, when Mr. Sprague appeared riding along beside them, somebody thought he ought to be praised for what he had done, so he called out, in tones that were heard to the farthest end of the line:

"Three cheers for Colonel Sprague. Hip, hip, hurrah!"

All the men immediately around there joined in in cheering Colonel Sprague—they had given him a new title, now—and Mr. Sprague took off his hat. As far as he went along the line everybody cheered him, and there was something in their way of talking to his father that made Leon feel very happy. He was bringing up the rear, leading his captured horse as he went, until he found himself opposite a wagon managed by his friend Tom Howe. Leon was glad to see him, for he had not spoken with him since they left Ellisville. There were three men on the driver's seat, and Tom was sitting on the knees of one and handling the reins over his four-mule team as if he had been used to it all his life.

"G'lang here!" he shouted when he saw Leon riding by. "We don't take no slack from anybody. But say, Leon, you will stand by me, won't you?"

"Of course I will stand by you," said Leon. "But I don't know what you mean."

"Do you see that leading muel there, that white one?" said Tom, pointing out the animal in question. "Well, that's mine. There ain't been anybody to lay a claim to him and I want him."

"I guess you can have him," said Leon. "But why don't you take a horse?"

"I would rather have the muel than that horse you are leading by the bits. Where did you get him?"

"I got these weapons," said Leon, showing the revolver and sword he carried about his waist and the carbine he held in his hand, "from a young fellow who gave them up to me without being asked. He has gone off in the bushes, now, to get out of sight of the other

members of the escort, but he'll be back
directly."

"Who let him go into the bushes?" inquired one of the men who was sitting on the
driver's seat with Tom.

"I did."

"Well, he has taken a rough way to escape.
Why didn't he stay here and march away with
his squad?"

"But he don't want to escape," said Leon.
"He is a Union man, and he wants to go
home with us."

"You are the most confiding man I ever
saw. You will never see him again."

"Then I shall have a horse and weapons to
give to somebody who needs them. I don't
need them myself. When you want to get that
mule, Tom, you come to me."

"I'll do it," said Tom, as he unwound his
lash and gave the leading white mule a cut
with the whip to make him pull faster; whereupon the mule's ears came back and he kicked
with both hind feet in the direction of the
wagon, barely missing the wheel-mule's head.
Leon laughed heartily. "Well, you see, he

hasn't been taught to pull in a wagon. This is his first attempt, but he is gay on horseback, and I'll bet on it. I'll teach him in two days so that he won't kick."

Leon urged his horse on ahead to catch up with the cavalry, but he had not made many steps before the bushes parted at his side and the young rebel who owned the steed he was leading came out.

"Have they gone?" said he, and he acted like one who felt overjoyed. "I told you I would come back, and here I am. May I get up and ride my horse?"

"Certainly," said Leon, and he felt so delighted to see the rebel that he could have hugged him. He didn't know what his father would say to him for allowing that man to go out in the bushes. He gave up the horse, and the young fellow swung himself into the saddle.

"I am glad you didn't give him up to some of your men who have no horses of their own," said the rebel, as he accompanied Leon toward the head of the column. "My father raised this animal, I broke him myself, and he's got just the kind of a gait that I like. Now, what are you going to do here in this county? Are you going to rebel against the Confederacy sure enough?"

"We have gone out already," said Leon. "I haven't got a copy of the resolutions with me, but you can see them when you get up to Ellisville."

"It beats anything I ever heard of," exclaimed the rebel, who burst out laughing every time he thought of it. "The idea that one county in the very heart of the Southern Confederacy should cut loose from it and say that they are Union men beats my time all holler. I told my father about it—"

"Where is your father now?" interrupted Leon.

"He is in the rebel army."

"Was he conscripted?"

"No. We didn't wait for that, but we heard enough to let us know what Jeff Davis was going to do. More than that, some of our neighbors began to talk about hanging those who did not believe as they did to the plates of their own gallery, and as we could get into

the cavalry by enlisting then, we rode down
to the county-seat one day and gave our
names in."

"Have you been in any fights?"

"Two or three; but, mind you, I always
shot high. I never drew a bullet on a Union
man in my life. I live only three or four
miles from where you stopped us, and I really
wish the authorities of Jones county would
give me permission to go back and get my
mother."

"Do you think your father would come up
here after that?"

"Of course he would. We have done nothing but think and talk about what you fellows are doing here ever since we have been
in the army. There was a distinct under-
standing between my father and myself that
whoever escaped first should bring my mother
here."

"Well, Mr.— Mr.—," began Leon.

"Dawson is my name," said the rebel.

"If you turn out to be all right I will go
with you," said Leon.

"Will you?" exclaimed the rebel, so highly

excited that he could hardly speak plainly. "I know we will succeed, for you have been in fights enough to know what it means."

"I don't understand you," said Leon. "This is as near as I have come to being in a fight."

"What! Capturing our wagon-train? You don't tell me! Well, I have seen men who had been in three or four battles that showed more nervousness than you did. You were not excited a bit."

Leon very wisely concluded that he would not say anything more on this subject just then. He never was more excited in his life than when he rode along the line and demanded the rebel's weapons. If Dawson thought he wasn't excited, so much the better for him.

"I certainly thought you had been where you had seen men knocked down by the cartload," said Dawson, looking at Leon to see what he was made of. "I have been where I have seen a whole platoon laid out at one fire, but I never go into action without feeling afraid. After this trouble is all over I would like to compare notes with you."

"To see how many times I am afraid?" asked Leon. "I don't care to compare notes with you on that, for I know I shall feel afraid all the time. I've got one chum here who won't haul in his shingle one inch to please anybody, and we'll ask him to go with us."

"Two men are all we want," said Dawson. "By the way, there was a friend of mine deserted the camp night before last, and he stole the wagon-master's horse to help him along. I don't suppose you have seen anything of him, have you?"

"We have a rebel up to Ellisville, and he says that was the way he got away. But his horse and weapons have been taken from him."

"That's all right. You wanted him to prove to you that he was true-blue before you let him have his fire-arms. But he's all hunky-dory. He told you about this wagon-train? I never saw him in a fight with Federals when he pretended to show any vim about it, but you give him rebels to shoot at and you'll hear something drop. He hasn't got the smallest sympathy for a Confederate. Why, they had him with a rope around his neck, and were going to hang him."

"He never said anything to us about that," said Leon, in surprise.

"It happened on the very morning that father and I went down to enlist," said Dawson, "and the way they acted made us believe that when they got through with him they were coming to see us. We rushed into his house and did some good talking to save the man's neck, and when they let him go he got onto his horse and went down to the county-seat with us. But didn't he give the rebels a good blessing!"

"He could say what he had a mind to in your presence, I suppose?"

"Yes, sir; and he laid down the law in good shape, I tell you. There are six men he wants to find, and they are the men who had the rope around his neck. What are you going to do with the prisoners you capture in battle?"

"I am sure I don't know," said Leon, with a laugh. "We haven't got any yet."

"You haven't been in a fight yet? How many men have you?"

"We had about three hundred fighting men, but first one Union family has come in, and then another, until we have a thousand men able to bear arms. Father said that about three hundred fighting men were all we had when this war broke out about a year ago, but they have been coming in from all sides. One man I know here has come from the mountains of Tennessee. I tell you we are going to make a good fight if the rebels get after us."

"I believe you; and these men you have now won't be a patching to what you will have by and by. But say," added Dawson, as they drew up in the rear of the cavalry, "do you really think you will be able to go with me to get my mother?"

"That depends entirely on what my father says. If he continues to let me do as I please, as he always has done, I'll go with you. There is no chance of being captured down there, I suppose?"

"Not in the least. Mobile is their nearest headquarters, and we can slip in there and get away again without any one being the wiser for it. It can be done just as easy as falling off a log."

" Well, you stay here and I will go on and ride by my father. I will tell him about you and see what he has to say."

Leon turned out and hurried on ahead to meet his father, who was riding alone in advance of the column, with his hat drawn over his eyes, as if he were thinking deeply. When he saw who the new-comer was he pushed back his hat, and beamed upon him with a smile that reminded the boy of old times.

" I tell you, father, you have done one good act in capturing this train," said Leon. " What were you thinking of?"

" Oh, there are lots of things to come after this," said Mr. Sprague. " We have got to whip the rebels in order to keep the train. Where's your horse?"

" The owner has got him ;" and taking this as his starting-point, Leon went on to give his father as much of the history of Dawson as he was acquainted with. When he told about the rebels having a rope around the neck of that man in camp his father was hardly prepared to believe it.

"But do you think the man honest?" asked Mr. Sprague.

"I know he is. No boy could talk as feelingly of his mother as he did and tell a lie about it. Now, if you will let me go down there and bring his family up here, we will make two good soldiers by the operation."

"We will see about it when the time comes," said Mr. Sprague.

That was enough for Leon, who reined his horse out of the road and halted until Dawson came up. Somehow he had taken a great fancy for the young rebel. There was something so honest about him that Leon put strong faith in everything he said. He drew up beside Dawson, and the latter's face grew more radiant than ever when Leon said that his father would "see about it."

"That is as good as saying that I may go, if something doesn't turn up in the meantime. Now, the next thing will be to get Tom to go with us. I shall feel a heap better with him alongside of me."

It was a long journey toward Ellisville, and the mules walked so slowly that it was almost midnight when they got there. Following the instructions of Mr. Sprague, the wagons were drawn up in a park in the grove, the mules were watered at the river and staked out where they had plenty of food, and the men left of their own accord and went to bed. There was no posting of sentries about the wagons to see that some backwoodsman did not slip up there to steal anything, for such a thing as theft was never heard of in that county. They knew that the things would be in the wagons in the morning in just as good shape as they were then. When Leon and Dawson, after hitching their horses and foddering them, turned to go to the opposite side of the grove, the place where that rebel was under guard, they came across Tom Howe, who had his coat off and was building a fire.

"Why, Tom, come with us," said Leon. "I am going to get something to eat before I go to bed."

"Well, sir, you can go and get it, for you

are one of these hungry fellows who always want something," replied Tom. "Do you see that muel? I ain't a-going to take my eyes off of him until your father gives him into my possession."

"You haven't had any supper, have you?"

"Nary supper. And I ain't a-going to have any, either, until I get that there muel in my hands."

"You can come back here and sleep. Tom, this is Dawson, whom I want you to be friends with. He was in that squad, but he gave up his horse and weapons to me without being asked."

The moment Leon referred to Dawson Tom put his hands behind his back as if he didn't want to say how glad he was to see him. Leon noticed the movement and went on with something which he knew would bring Tom to his senses. Tom had a mother, his father was dead, and he fairly worshipped her.

"He is going down after his mother, and I am going, too. And we want you to go with us."

"Howdy!" exclaimed Tom, and his hands

came out and he shook Dawson as if he was a friend from whom he had long been separated. "Then he's all right, of course. I'll go, but you must get my muel for me."

The boys bent their steps toward the hotel, for they knew that the landlord was a man who was determined to do what he could to help along the cause. He knew that at least a portion of the men who had gone out to capture that wagon-train had no place to get anything to eat, and he cooked up a lot of food for them, and had it spread out on his dining-room tables. He had remained up all night, and the noise the men made when they returned almost drove him wild.

"Who said those who took part with us in this useless struggle would go hungry?" said he, standing on the porch, and welcoming the men as they came up, and sending them all into the dining-room. "Ah! here's Leon and Tom Howe, I declare. Where did you get shot, boys? And a rebel, as sure as I am a foot high. Where did you take him up?"

"I am a rebel no longer," replied Dawson.

"In spite of my clothes I am as good a Union man as there is in the county."

"You are just the lads we want," said the landlord. "Haven't had anything to eat yet? No dinner, either? Then go right into the dining-room. You will find the President and the Secretary of War in there."

The boys went in and found the two officers sitting in a remote corner engaged in earnest conversation. They talked in low tones, and it was evident that they did not want anybody to hear what they were discussing, so the boys sat down and began an attack upon the food. The way the landlord's bacon, eggs and corn-bread disappeared before them would have astonished that gentleman could he have witnessed it. It made no difference to them that the food was cold, for the coffee was hot, and they finally stopped because they were ashamed to eat any more. By the time they had finished eating their supper the two high officers ceased their consultation, and Mr. Sprague hauled up a chair to the nearest table and sat down. Leon decided that this was his time. Tom Howe would certainly sleep better if he knew that the mule was his own.

" Father, there's a white mule out there in the train, and Tom Howe wants him."

" Well, he can have him, I guess," said Mr. Sprague. "Anybody else laid any claim to him ?"

" No, sir ; Tom is the only one. And he has taken a mighty queer animal to carry him through this war. He kicks."

" Tom will have to manage that to suit himself. Why don't he wait until we can capture a horse ?"

" Because he would rather have that mule than anything else."

" Tell him to take him, and welcome."

Leon found his companions in the living-room, and when he told them that the Secretary of War had given Tom the mule he wanted, Tom was delighted. He promised the others that he would get to work early in the morning to break him of kicking, and wanted them to come over and see how it was done, and then turned away to his own camp, while Leon and Dawson started out to find the camp of the rebel who was kept under guard.

"There's his lean-to right there," said Leon, after walking some distance up the road. "Do you see any comparison between that sentry and the ones you left behind? I mean, do they sit down and warm themselves by a fire when they are left on duty?"

"Not much, they don't," answered Dawson, with a laugh. "If you had our officer of the day here he would snatch that fellow bald-headed. He ought to get up, hold his arms at support and pace his beat."

"Who is it that the officer of the day is going to snatch bald-headed?" asked the sentry. He sat on a log with his rifle beside him, and he was warming his hands over the fire. He seemed to think that he could see everything that was going on, and he thought that was all that was required of him.

"The officer of the rebel army, if there was one here, would take you to task for not pacing your beat," said Leon.

"Sho! What would he do that for?" asked

the man. "That rebel hasn't moved in there
without my seeing him, and he can't get away.
Say, Johnny, are you asleep?"

"No; I am wide awake," shouted a voice
from the inside. "I wanted to see the men
that came back with that wagon-train. Well—
halloo! Dawson," exclaimed the rebel, who,
when he came out, caught sight of his old
comrade in arms. "You're here, ain't you?"

The two men shook hands as though they
had not seen each other for years. Dawson
then explained how the capture was effected,
and the rebel's eyes fairly flashed as he listened to it. When he ceased speaking the
rebel asked permission for Dawson to come
under his lean-to and share his blankets with
him, and as the sentry did not find any fault
Leon readily granted it. When he had seen
the two tuck themselves away preparatory to
a good sleep and had exchanged a few words
with their guard, Leon turned about and made
the best of his way to the hotel.

CHAPTER VII.

BREAKING THE MULE.

WHAT Mr. Sprague was talking about when Leon and his companions went in to eat their suppers was whether or not it would be a good plan to send a party of cavalrymen, say a dozen or more, down to the little creek that separated the two counties to bring them warning of a Confederate force which was coming to subdue them; for Mr. Sprague was certain that those men would be along before a great while. The rebels were not the men to stand still and allow themselves to be robbed of $500,000.

"Their scouts will be a long ways ahead of the main body, and by the time they get here we can be safe in the swamp," said Mr. Sprague. "The cavalrymen are all good shots, and by the time they get through with

9

one fire there won't be so many of them to follow up our men."

"They will shoot them down, I suppose?" said Mr. Knight.

"Of course they will have to take their chances on that. While all the rest of them are asleep one of them can be standing guard."

"I think it would be a good plan. We'll send cavalrymen down there every morning to relieve them. Perhaps you had better detail some guards for to-morrow morning. But do you say you captured that train without firing a shot?"

"It is the truth," said Mr. Sprague. "One of the soldiers said it was the prettiest surprise he every saw. The men were all prompt, and they obeyed my whistle just like clock-work."

The next morning when Leon awoke and stretched himself on the bench which served him in lieu of a bed he felt like a new man. He was not accustomed to spending so many hours in the saddle, his long ride of the day before had wearied him, and when he went to slumber he "slept for keeps," as he expressed

it.   He got up, and, after washing his hands
and face, went out on the porch and saw a
party of a dozen men gathered about a tree a
short distance away.   There was a white mule
in the party, and three or four men were
fussing around her.

"Tom has got to work to break the 'muel,'
as he calls it, from kicking," said Leon, "and
I am going down to see how it is done.   He
thinks he has got a prize there, and I hope he
has."

When Leon got up with the crowd he found
that the mule had been securely fastened to a
tree, and that there were two men engaged in
holding her head up.   You may have noticed
that when a mule wants to kick she always
puts her head down, and by holding her
head up it was impossible for her to kick
Tom, who, by bringing her tail around by
her side, was busy in tying a stone that
weighed two or three pounds, and was wrapped
up in a thick rag so that it would not bruise
her heels, fast to the end of it.   Leon saw
through the plan at once, and he laughed
heartily.

"There, now, I reckon we're all right," said Tom, as he took a finishing knot in the string with which the stone was tied. "Kick, now, and we will see how you will come out. Let go her head, boys."

When Tom said this he raised the stone and let it down against the mule's heels with a sounding whack, and the men let go their hold and backed away. In an instant you could not have told where that mule belonged. Her heels were in the air all the time; but no matter how high the stone went, it always came down, and the further it went, it came back to its place and punished her heels severely. Sometimes she seemed as if she would kick herself over her head, she stood up so straight. The men stood around and laughed heartily, until the mule, after trying in vain to rid herself of the contrivance, stopped her kicking and turned around and looked at it. She seemed to know that it was fast to her, and after looking first on one side and then on the other, and trying with more energy than before to throw off the useless appendage, which she knew did not belong

there, she drew her haunches under her,
looked at Tom and broke out into a faint
bray, as if begging him to take it off.

"There, sir, she is done with her kicking
for all time," said one of the men.

"Tom," said Leon, "don't go near her.
You know how treacherous a mule can be."

The man promptly stepped up to the mule,
undid the stone, lifted her tail, and did other
pranks which would have led even a mule
who did not know how to kick to lay back her
ears.

"I said I would break her of kicking in
less than two days, and we have broken her in
less than half an hour," said Tom, gleefully.
"Now watch me and see me ride to camp."

Tom mounted in regular Texas fashion,
placing his left hand upon the mule's shoulder and throwing his right leg over her back,
and with a "G'lang there, muel!" went down
the road at a furious pace. She loped beau-
tifully, and Tom wasn't even moved, although
he rode bare-back. Leon was satisfied that
he had got a prize, after all.

"Now all he wants is to go around that

mule forty times a day, lifting her tail and
patting her, and she won't kick him," said
the man who undid the stone. " I just know,
for I'll bet on it."

When Leon had seen the mule broken and
Tom ride away, he turned his steps toward
the camp of the rebels to see how they were
getting on. There was another sentry on
guard this time, and he was engaged in a favorite occupation, sitting on a log with his
rifle beside him, smoking a cob pipe and
warming his hands at the fire. The two rebels
were standing in the door of the lean-to, and
they greeted Leon heartily. After exchanging a few words with them Leon said :

" I am going to speak to father about you
to-day, and I think he will let you out. I am
going home this morning, and 1 want Dawson
to ride with me."

" If he lets me out I will go and be glad of
the chance," said Dawson. " But what are
you going home for ?"

" To let my mother know that I shan't be
home to-night. I reckon we are going down
after your mother."

" By George ! That's the best news I have heard since I have been a prisoner," exclaimed Dawson. " You will see father here in less than a week, and you don't want to let him get into any fight where the rebels are. He don't take any prisoners."

Leon next bent his steps toward the hotel to get his breakfast. In the living-room he met the landlord, who had three or four men around him, and was talking gleefully of the manner in which the wagon-train had been captured the day before.

" To think that our boys never fired a shot, and there were twenty-five of them rebels who were hired to defend it," said he. " Now here's Leon," he added, taking the boy's right hand in his own, throwing his left arm around his shoulder, and affectionately drawing him up to his side. " Who would think that this boy would watch over his father ? He gets close up to his side, and if anyone pops him over he is going to see about it."

" You will have to get away from this place, Mr. Faulkner," said Leon. " Your house is right on the main road, and the first party of rebels who come in here will set fire to it."

"I know all about that," said Mr. Faulkner, with a laugh. "I expect everything I have got will go up in smoke. But you see they won't burn anything but the house. Your father is going to lend me some of the wagons as soon as they are unloaded, and I am going to pile on everything I have got and take them all up to the swamp. I should like to see the rebels get them out of there."

"So would I," said Leon.

"I can't give you as good a breakfast as I could once," added Mr. Faulkner. "Bacon, eggs, corn-bread and coffee—I am almost out of coffee, now that I think of it. I shall be all out if you haven't got some in those wagons you captured yesterday. Go on and get your breakfast, the whole of you. There's many a better man than you and I dare be who is living on worse food, and he's just as good a Union man as though he stood in our ranks."

Leon went into the dining-room and found his father and Mr. Knight sitting there by themselves, and he concluded that it was a good time to talk to them about the rebels who were kept under guard.

"I have been thinking about them all the morning," said Mr. Sprague, when Leon had explained things to him, "and I don't see the need of keeping them under guard any longer; do you, Knight?"

"No, I don't. I say let them out."

"Well, I will go back with you and turn them loose," said Mr. Sprague. "That will be the way we'll work it. As fast as any rebels come in here and say they are on our side we'll take their weapons and horses away from them, if they have any, and hold them until they prove that they are just as they should be."

"Well, what do you say to my going down to Dawson's house after his mother?" said Leon.

"What do you think about it, Knight?"

"Why I say let the boy go. He has proved long ago that he knows how to handle himself in a tight place; yesterday, for instance; and he will be just as safe as he would be here in camp. By the way, Leon, we have given your father a new title. He says the Secretary of War is too long for him, and so we have promoted him to Colonel. He likes that better. Maybe if you conduct yourself all right he will make you aid-de-camp."

We are sorry to say that Mr. Knight did not pronounce this word correctly, and if there had been some boys like you, who are fresh from their books, they would have seen a good many other words whose spelling bothered him. But he knew one thing that had evidently slipped the President's mind. If his father had been promoted to colonel, Leon thought that was being promoted backwards. But then this thing would not last more than a year or two, and it did not make much difference to him what people said about it. He got no money for the position he held, none of the officers got any, and he was willing to do what he could for the sake of the county.

"I don't care if my father never promotes me to anything," said Leon. "If he will let me stay close by him, so as to be on hand if anything happens to him, I shall be satisfied."

The party having finished their breakfast arose from the table at the same time, and Mr. Sprague went out with Leon to call upon the rebels. On the way he talked more plainly to Leon than he had ever done before.

"I shan't appoint you aid-de-camp," said Mr. Sprague.

"I know why," said Leon. "If you should do a thing like that, the fellows who are not as high in authority as you are would think that you were giving me a place to keep me out of danger. I don't want anybody to think that of me."

"Well, yes; that has something to do with it. But you would be in just as much danger there as you would anywhere else. I don't want you hanging around me all the time. The men think you are doing it on purpose to shield me."

"I confess that that is what I was thinking of."

"Don't do it any more. Of course I shall be in the thickest of the fight, if we have any, but I don't want you to be there. That's the reason I am giving my consent to allow you to go down after Dawson's mother."

"Do you say I may go?" exclaimed Leon, joyfully.

"Yes; but I want you first to let your mother know we are safe and what is the reason we don't come home."

"I'll go and get Tom and Dawson to go with me. By the way, Tom has got his mule broken."

"So that he won't kick?" asked Mr. Sprague, in surprise.

"Yes, sir; and he broke him in less than half an hour."

Leon then went on to tell how Tom had operated to break the mule, and when he described her kicking he made his father laugh heartily. By this time they had reached the lean to and found the two rebels enjoying their breakfast. They arose to their feet as Mr. Sprague approached, knowing that the Secretary of War had much authority over their prisoners, but he motioned them to keep their seats. Even the sentry got up, put down his plate—for the rebels had helped him most bountifully—and held his rifle in a way that was intended to present arms. But then the Secretary didn't know whether the motion was properly executed or not. He touched his hat, however, and after bidding the rebels good-morning and lifting his hat once more out of respect to the woman who sat at the head of the table, he turned again to the sentry.

"I would like to see all the men who are on guard with you," said he. "They are around here, I suppose?"

"Oh, yes, sir; they are around here," said the sentry. Then lifting his voice he called out: "All you guards turn out. The Secretary of War wants you. Come a-lumbering!"

The men came in a hurry, three of them, some bareheaded, some swinging on their bullet-pouches as they hastened through the bushes, and all eager to see what the Secretary of War wanted. Like the good soldiers they were, they concluded that there was some business to engage in, and they were impatient to do it. But when they found out what he wanted they were just as pleased, all the same. Mr. Sprague told them in so many words that the rebels were all right, and from this time they were released from all sentry duty. The rebels were just as free in their camp as they were themselves.

"Colonel, I want to shake your hand for that," said the owner of the lean-to, and as he spoke he got up from the table and came out. "Now I want all of you boys to understand one thing. You have done nothing but call me 'Johnny' ever since I have been in camp, and now I want you to stop it. My name is Roberts, and I am as good a Union man as the best of you. If you don't believe it, wait until we get into a fight and I will show you."

All this was said in a perfectly good-natured way, and the guards, on being sent back to their lean-tos, promised that they would address him as Roberts ever afterward. They had called him "Johnny" because they did not know any other name for him.

"Now, Dawson, I am going to start for home," said Leon. "Come with me and I will get your horse and weapons for you."

When Leon and Dawson turned away the former was surprised to see standing at his side another boy, Newman by name, who was enough like Carl Swayne to have been his brother, except in one particular. Newman did not proclaim himself so much in favor of the secessionists as Carl did, but in every other way, so far as meanness was concerned, they were a good team. Leon was not the only one about there who believed that Newman was a rebel at heart, and that if he had his way he would have arrested every Union man in the county. He noticed that Newman did not go with them when they assaulted the train—he had something else that demanded his immediate attention; but he noticed, too, that when the expedition came back Newman had as much to say as anybody. There was one thing about Newman that did not look exactly right to Leon. In the early part of the year, when there was a good deal of talk about the secession of Jones county, this Newman's father had piled all his worldly goods into a one-horse wagon and started for Mobile; but in two months' time he came back. There was more fighting going on there than there was in Jones county, he said, and as he was a man of peace and did not believe in contests of any kind, he thought he and his family had better come back and stay in their own house until the trouble was over. Mind you, that was the story he told; whether or not it was the truth remains to be seen.

"Well, Leon, we got 'em, didn't we?" was the way in which Newman began the conversation.

"Got whom?" inquired Leon, and he was not very civil about it, either. He wished that Newman would keep to his own side of the walk and let him alone.

"Why, the rebels, of course," said Newman. "You have got one them with you right now."

"How many of them did you capture?" inquired Leon, poking his elbow into Dawson's ribs when he saw that he was about to reply.

"I captured one, but I let him go. You know the President said we wasn't going to take any prisoners."

"Yes, I know. But what made you let him go?"

"Oh, he told me such a funny story about his wife being sick, and all that, that I couldn't bear to keep him captive. So I just told him to clear out."

"And you let him take his weapons with him?"

"Of course," replied Newman; and then finding that Leon was getting onto rather dangerous ground he changed the subject, for he had come there to ask a favor. "Say, Leon, do you suppose that your father would give me one of them muels that we captured yesterday? I reckon I've got as much right to them as he has."

"Well, I reckon you haven't," replied Leon, indignantly.

"Just because he's a high officer, do you think he has more right to property that we capture than them that takes it?" asked Newman, getting mad in his turn. "He gave Tom Howe a muel, and Tom didn't do any more than I did."

"What's the use of telling such an outra-

geous falsehood? You was not there. Did
you see me?"

"Yes, I saw you."

"What did I do? Did you see me when I
ran from this man, and he followed after me,
swinging his sword in his hand?"

"Eh? Oh, yes, I saw you," said Newman,
looking surprised. "He came pretty near
catching you, too, and he would if that man
hadn't come up and poked a revolver in his
face. Who was that, do you know?"

"Well, Newman, I don't believe you can get
a mule to ride during this war," said Leon,
once more turning his steps towards the hotel.
"You see Tom wants to do something with this
mule, and you don't. You simply want him to
ride around, and when the fight comes you will
be miles away. That is, if you are on our side
at all," said Leon to himself. "I wouldn't be
afraid to bet that you will stay around here and
lead the rebels to our place of concealment."

Newman thrust his hands into his pockets,
pushed his hat on the back of his head, and
looked after Leon as he walked away with the
rebel by his side.

"I'll bet that boy lied to me when he spoke of that fellow being after him with a sword," said he, "and that he ever run from him a step. I am no good for a spy. I haven't got my wits about me. But his father will give me one of those mules or I'll know the reason why. It is most time for the rebels to come up here, and when they do come, mye fin lad, I'll have that horse of yours."

"Who is that fellow, anyway?" asked Dawson, after they had left Newman behind. "You don't seem to like him very well."

"Neither would you if you knew him as well as I do," replied Leon. "Ever since I got into a scrape with those logs that fellow has been down on me, and said he didn't see why I should come out all right when other men had lost their lives in attempting the same thing."

"You don't bear him any ill-will for that, I hope?" said Dawson. "He didn't dare do it, although I don't know what danger you got into."

"I ran out on the logs and started a jam, and Tom Howe fell into the water and I saved him. But that isn't what I have against him," said Leon. "You see, Newman's father has never said where he stood. When he came back to this county, and found that we were in earnest in threatening to secede, then he wanted an office, but the men were too sharp to give it to him."

"Ah! that's the trouble, is it? Let him go in and serve as a private. That's what my father and I intend to do."

"But he don't want to serve as a private. He wants the position that father holds, so that he can boss around the men and have nothing else to do. Father would give it to him in a minute if he thought he was able to fill it, but you see he don't. And mind you, I don't say this out loud, but I believe it to be so, he says if he can't be an officer he will betray us all."

"Ho-ho!" said Dawson, while a gleam of intelligence shot across his face. "He is going to turn Benedict Arnold, is he? By gracious! You fellows have something to contend with, haven't you? A spy! Well, let him come on and see how much he will make by it."

"Now, don't say that out loud," said Leon earnestly, "for I don't know that it is so. I only judge him by his actions. Now, here's the place where your weapons were left. We'll go up and see the President."

"I don't look fit to go into the President's office," said Dawson, looking down at his clothes. "I want to get home and see my wardrobe, so that I can get some clothes more befitting my station in life."

"O come on," said Leon, with a hearty laugh. "Ten to one you will find the President with a pais of jean breeches on, and a pair of cowhide boots. He is like all the rest of us, but then he will be glad to see you, for you were a rebel once."

"There's where you make a mistake," said Dawson. "I never was a rebel, although I wear the clothes. Introduce me as a Union man forced into the rebel army."

At this moment Leon opened the door that gave entrance into the office of the high dignitary of Jones county, where they found him leaning back in his chair and conversing with three or four men. He was just such a man

as Leon said he was—to the manor born. He
didn't act as though he considered himself
better than other men simply because he was
President.   Dawson took off his hat, while the
other men did not remove theirs.   He followed
Leon to a corner in which several stand of
fire-arms were stowed, and assisted him in
picking out his own weapons.   Leon gave him
the sword and revolver, and motioned him to
buckle them around him, while with the carbine in his hand he approached the President's
chair.   When he got through talking with the
men he looked up to see what Leon had to say.

"Mr. Knight, here's a good man I have
got for us," said he.   "His name is Dawson,
and although he wears the rebel uniform, he
is as much of a Union man as anyone here."

"Howdy, Dawson," said the President, nod-
ding his head.   "So you are coming over to
side with us, are you?"

"Yes, sir," said Dawson.   "I was obliged
to go into the rebel ranks to escape being
hung."

"He wants his horse and his weapons, too,"
added Leon.   "Father says he is all right."

"Let him have them," said the President.

Leon promptly handed over the carbine. "He wants to go home to-night to get his mother," said he. "There are two of us, myself and Tom Howe, going with him."

"I heard all about it from your father," said Mr. Knight. "Now, be careful of yourself, Leon. If you should get captured it would drive the first colonel I have got crazy."

The boy promised that he would look out for himself, and, with a salute from Dawson, they opened the door and went down the stairs. They saw that Mr. Sprague had already hitched the mules to the wagons and hauled them down in front of the hotel where they could be examined by all the principal men of the county. Before they had taken many steps they saw Newman walk up to the Secretary of War and accost him.

CHAPTER VIII.

REBELS IN THE REAR.

"WHAT did I tell you?" said Leon, turning to his companion. "New- man is going to strike father for one of those mules. Let us go up and see how he comes out."

"I don't think I ought to give you a mule, Newman," said Mr. Sprague, as Leon and Dawson approached within hearing distance. "You were not with us at all, yesterday."

Newman glanced at Leon and saw there was one lie nailed, but he had become so ac- customed to being caught that way that he hardly changed color. He thrust his hands into his pockets, looked up the road toward the lean-tos, and said:

"Well, you see one of our cows had strayed away and I was afraid she might not come up, so I went into the woods to find her."

"And you thought that cow was of more use to the county than stopping the train, did you?"

"It was of more use to us, 'cause, you see, we wouldn't have had any milk to put in our coffee."

"And you have milk in your coffee every day, do you? That's more than I have, and I have eight or nine cows on my place."

"Well, can I have the mule? That's what I want to know."

"No, I don't think you can."

"You have given one to Tom Howe and never asked him what he was going to do with it," said Newman, hotly.

"But I knew what Tom was going to do with his mule before I gave it to him. Whenever we get ready to go out and capture a train Tom will be on hand, and that's more than I can say in regard to you."

"Then you won't give me the mule?"

"No, I can't. You will have to go to somebody else and get one. It is Government property that comes into my hands, and I am bound to take the best of care of it."

"I'll get even with you for this some way or another," said Newman, starting to walk off.

"Newman," said Mr. Sprague, sternly, "come back here."

"Well, now, when I come back you just blow a horn to let me know it, will you?" replied Newman, still continuing on his way.

"If I ask you once more I shall put you under arrest," said Mr. Sprague. "I am not in the habit of giving orders twice."

While he was speaking there were certain other parties, who had arrived with a wagon, who happened to overhear the conversation that passed between Mr. Sprague and Newman. They dropped whatever they were about and came up to see about it, for one of the disputants had got so angry that he raised his voice a good deal above its natural key. One of them was Bud McCoy, the man who had threatened to burn Mr. Swayne's house before he got out of it. He did not like Newman any too well, for he believed that the young man was more in favor of secessionists than he was of the Union men.

"Come back here, you scoundrel!" said Bud, shaking his fists in the other's face.

"Oh, now, Bud, you haven't anything to do with it," said Newman, and he retraced his steps very slowly.

"Come faster than that," said Bud, tucking up his shirt-sleeves. "I will show you that I have something to do with it."

"I will tell my father what you are doing up here, and perhaps he will think we had better go back to Mobile," said Newman.

"Well, go back to Mobile. You belong there among the rebels more'n you do among these Union men. Your father has not got anything to do with this business. We've been talking about playing soldier for a long time, and now that we have got a constitution we are going to act. You'll see that there is a big difference between the two."

"One moment, Bud," said Mr. Sprague, when he saw that Newman had been frightened sufficiently to put a little sense into him. "You may not have been aware of the fact," he added, addressing himself to Newman, "but you were treating me in a way that I don't like when you refused to come back here. Perhaps I have more authority in this county than you think for. You talked about getting even with me. How are you going to do it?"

"I was only fooling," said Newman. "I didn't mean nothing by it."

"Well, hereafter, when you feel aggrieved by an officer, don't say that you will get even with him in some way. That looks to me as though you had something on your mind."

"I haven't; I haven't, honor bright," said Newman, wondering if Mr. Sprague knew anything further. There had been talk between his father and some of the rebel officers who had their quarters in Mobile in regard to betraying all the chief men of the Jones-County Confederacy into their hands, and this was one reason that brought him back there. But Newman didn't suppose that anybody but his own family knew anything about it.

"It looks mighty suspicious," continued Mr. Sprague. "But I can't give you that mule. It is not my business, anyway. It belongs to the quartermaster's department, and he is the man you must see."

Mr. Sprague turned on his heel and went away to inspect one of the wagons, and Leon and Dawson continued their walk toward Roberts' lean-to. To say that Leon was surprised to hear his father talk in this way would not express his feelings.

"I tell you your father can't be too strict when it comes to the pinch," said Dawson. "I didn't know he had so much in him. Well, you see he is high in authority, and it won't do to let ordinary men talk to him as that Newman did. Say, that fellow knew something he did not want to speak about."

"That's my idea exactly," said Leon. "I'll keep watch on him, and if I find anything out of the way with him I'll arrest him and take him before father."

"If you do that he'll shoot him."

"My gracious! Has it come to that?" exclaimed Leon, astonished beyond measure.

"Of course it has. I have seen three men shot to death because they tried to desert the army, and you have got to come down to that way of doing business here. You will have to be stricter, too, than they are in the army, for you have got less power to back you up. Oh, you're not going to have a picnic, I'll tell you that."

Leon was thunderstruck, for he did not believe that such things could take place in Jones county. While he was thinking about it they came up with Roberts, who had borrowed a mule to take the place of the one that had dropped dead during his rapid flight, and was engaged in packing things into his wagon. He said he was going deeper into the swamp.

"You see these houses are right on the main road, and the rebels who come in will come from Perry county," said he. "I don't propose to have what things I own burned up, and so I am going to take them where it will cost the Confederates some trouble to get at them."

"Well, say, Mr. Roberts, what do you suppose they would do to you if they should succeed in getting their hands on you?" asked Leon.

"I deserted to the enemy, didn't I?" asked Roberts.

"Yes, you did."

"And I had my rebel clothes on when I left their camp?"

Leon nodded; and Roberts, after looking at him a moment, made a turn of a rope around his neck, drew it up with his left hand and allowed his head to fall over on one side.

"That's what they would do with me," said Roberts, with a laugh. "I don't suppose they would shoot me, but they must catch me first. I'm not going to be taken prisoner. And Dawson, there, would come in for something of the kind."

Dawson smiled and said he well knew what was coming if he allowed himself to be taken prisoner, and thrust out his hand, adding:

"Well, I don't suppose I shall see you again until we get into our first fight. I am going after my mother to-night."

"So-long, old boy, and remember and don't let those Graybacks get a grip on you."

"I'll stay right there on the field until I drop," said Dawson, earnestly. "You'll never hear of my being hung."

They turned off to find their horses, after

which they drew a bee-line for Tom's camp.
Leon didn't have much to say. When men
like Dawson and Roberts could talk as they
did about falling into the hands of their old
comrades, it made him feel kind of anxious.
And if they would serve the deserters that
way, what would they do with him? He was
a traitor to the cause of Southern independence, everybody on the Pascagoula river from
the swamps down knew who he was, and if
he should unfortunately fall into the hands of
the Confederates a captive, they would without a doubt hang him without giving him
any trial at all. He had never been able to
look at it in this light before, and it made
him feel rather desperate. But here was a
fellow who would take ample revenge for his
death if such a thing should happen. It was
Tom Howe, who, when they found him, was
sitting at the foot of a tree, and he had just
been disposing of a substantial breakfast
which somebody had provided for him.

"Halloo, Leon! And you, Dawson, halloo!"
said Tom, getting upon his feet. "Well, if
you are going home now I am going with

you. I have been around that muel forty times, as that man told me to, petting her and fooling in various ways, and she never offered to kick me. But what's the matter with you, Leon? You act as though your last friends had been gobbled up by the rebels."

"Well, they haven't been gobbled up yet, but I am just thinking of what would happen to them if they were gobbled," said Leon. "Do you know what they would do with you if they caught you?"

"Hang me, I suppose. But you see, Leon, these swamps are mighty big."

"But you are going right among them to-night."

"Oh, no," said Dawson, quickly. "We'll not see a rebel from the time we leave here until we get back. I'm not going to get you in any fuss. If I thought there was a chance I wouldn't go myself."

"But we are liable to be mistaken, you know."

"I'll tell you what I'll do," said Dawson. "I'll ride on ahead, and the first glimpse I see of anything suspicious I'll warn you.

You certainly will not be captured in that way."

Tom struck up a whistle, as if to show how much he cared what the rebels might think it worth while to do, and went to work about the mule as though he had always owned her, strapped a piece of gunny-sack to serve in lieu of a saddle, felt his revolvers to make sure that they were safe, and then announced that he was ready. Their ride would have been gloomy enough, for they did not meet a single person on the way, had it not been for Dawson, who was fairly alive with stories. He was two or three years older than Leon, but, like all boys who had lived much out-of-doors, he was almost big enough to be considered a man. He was young enough in his boyish tastes and habits to be hail-fellow with Leon and Tom, and reckless enough to add a spice of danger to everything he engaged in. They did not think they had been on their way a great while before the plantation-house was in view. Leon did not see anybody about. The doors of the negro quarters were closed, and so were the rear doors of the house; and even the pickaninnies, who were usually the first to welcome him when he rode up to the bars, were nowhere in sight.

"I wonder what's been going on here?" said Leon, involuntarily sinking his voice to a whisper. "There are more people than this in the house."

"I should say there ought to be," said Tom. "We haven't seen any, yet."

"If it was a little nearer the lower end of the county I should say that some rebels had been calling here," said Dawson, in an anxious tone of voice. "I have seen many a house look that way."

Filled with forebodings, Leon hurried on until he came opposite the front bars, and on the way he saw a man lying down behind a log with a rifle in his hand, and it was pointed toward the other bank of the stream, which here ran through Mr. Sprague's property. The moment the topmost bars rattled the front door opened and his mother came out on the porch. Thank goodness she was safe.

"Why, mother, what's up?" cried Leon, throwing himself off his horse and rushing up the steps with arms spread out. "When I saw the house closed I supposed something had happened."

"Something has happened," replied his mother; and although her face was very pale, her tightly-closed lips and the way in which her hands trembled showed that she was trying to keep down some rising emotion. "The rebels are at it already."

"At what?" asked Leon, while the other boys got up close to her to hear what she had to say.

"There have been two men over on the other side of the creek, and they have got a complete map made out of all the streams and the places where they are fordable," said his mother.

"Why, how did you find it out?" asked Leon.

"One of the darkies discovered them, and I slipped out very quietly and told Mr. Giddings of it."

"Wasn't it lucky that I brought Giddings here? I knew I was proposing a good thing when I advised him to come. Well, what did Giddings do?"

"He took down his rifle and shot one of the men," said Mrs. Sprague, at the same time clinging to Leon as if she were afraid that the ghost of the slain man might come back. "This war is going to be a horrible thing. I wouldn't see the thing happen again for all the money the United States is worth. It was the first thing of the kind I ever saw done—"

"Why did you stay here and look at it?" asked Leon. "How did he know that he had a map? What made him shoot him, in the first place?"

"Well, he was acting very sly, making use of every tree and stump to cover him, so Mr. Giddings thought he would shoot them both. He went over there in our boat and got the man, and he is out there now in one of our negro cabins. And he hadn't any more than brought him over here before the other fellow shot at him."

"He didn't hit him, I suppose?"

"No; but he made the bullet sing pretty close to his head."

"I reckon that Giddings had better stay

here to-night and protect you," said Leon, after thinking a moment. " I am not coming home to-night, and neither is father. We had some work day before yesterday," he added, as if trying to draw her away from the melancholy event she had witnessed. " We captured forty wagons without firing a shot. Here's a man who was with them. Mother, let me introduce Mr. Dawson. He is going back into the country for his mother to-night, and wants Tom and me to go with him."

Mrs. Sprague smiled for the first time, shook Dawson by the hand, said she was glad to see him on the Union side if he did wear those clothes on his back, and then she turned to Tom Howe, who had just come in from hitching the horses.

" As those rebels didn't fire a shot at you the other day you don't know how it feels," said Mrs. Sprague.

" Who? Me? No, ma'am. I just covered a driver's head with my rifle and told him to hold up his hands, and he put them into his pockets and brought out his revolvers, which he handed to me. There they are," said Tom, putting his hands behind him and bringing out a pistol in each. "You see Leon had a revolver and I had none, and I just put these into my clothes and said nothing about it. If I am going to be a soldier I'll soon learn how to steal as well as anybody."

"Let's go out there and see what Giddings is doing," said Leon. "Mother, can you get us up some dinner? We have a long way to ride to-night, and we want to give our horses a little rest after we get back to Ellisville."

His mother said that dinner would be ready by the time he wanted it, and Leon walked around the house toward the place he had seen Giddings lying in ambush, followed by his companions. Giddings was on his feet now, and was standing behind a corn-crib, looking cautiously around the corner of it.

"Howdy, Leon?" he exclaimed, when he saw the boys approaching. "You had better get something between you and the woods over there, for that chap is a tolerable fair shot. I don't like the way he sent his bullet a-flying past my head."

"He didn't hit you, though," said Leon, as the boys drew up beside the mountaineer from Tennessee. They kept an eye on the woods, but all danger from that source had passed. The rebel who had been left alive had taken advantage of the bushes, crawled among them until he was out of sight, and so got himself safe off.

"And the only reason he didn't make a better shot was because he had a revolver," said Giddings. "I tell you, Leon, we are going to have trouble now. Those fellows are making a map of this whole country."

"Perhaps they are looking, too, for that wagon-train we stole from them," said Leon. "There were forty wagons in the lot, and we captured the last one of them."

"Sho!" exclaimed Giddings in disgust. "And I wasn't there to help. But let's go in and look at that man. Perhaps you know who he is."

The boys followed the man into the negro cabin with slight quakings of conscience, all except Dawson, who had seen so many dead men that he thought nothing of it. He lay

there on the floor covered with a blanket,
never to move again in this life, with bushy
black whiskers spread all down his breast,
and dressed in a uniform that had a couple of
bars on the collar. He was a fine-looking
man, and Leon was wondering how many
hearts would break when they heard of his
death.

"I hit him right in the heart," said Giddings, pointing out the mark of his bullet on
his coat with as much indifference as he
would have shown if it had been a deer instead of a man that was stretched out before
him. "Know him, any of you?"

"No, he is a stranger to me. I think the
best thing you can do, Mr. Giddings," said
Leon, reverently spreading the blanket over
the dead man's face again, "is to stay here
and keep an eye on mother. I didn't think
the rebels would ever trouble her up here."

"Did you steal much of them?" asked Giddings.

Leon replied that to the best of his knowledge it was pretty near half a million dollars'
worth.

"A half a million? Pshaw! They will be all over this county looking for them goods, and you will have to go deeper into the swamp to be rid of them. When the rebels come they won't leave a shingle of this house that you can use. They will burn them all."

"Where's the map he made out?"

"Your mother has got that, and his weapons, too. Yes, I guess the best thing I can do is to stay here. There may be some more of these Confederates where these came from."

Leon went out, spent a few moments in exchanging compliments with Giddings' wife, who was very comfortably settled in her new quarters, and went into the house to ask his mother for the map the rebel had made. While the dinner was being made ready the boys spent their time in looking it over. They were astonished to find all the streams, as far up as he had time to go, were correctly drawn, and still more amazed to see that the little creek which marked the boundary-line between their county and Perry, which was so deep at the place where the bridge extended

across it, could be forded in five different
localities.

"That man must have been a civil engi-
neer," said Dawson. "No one, without he
had some knowledge of the business, could go
over those streams in the short time he has
and make such a complete map of them."

At the end of half an hour the boys had
eaten their dinner and were well on their way
toward Ellisville, Leon having the map, for
which the man in the rebel army had given
his life, safely stowed away in one of his
pockets. He wasn't as happy now as he was
when he came that way before. Dawson's
stories of his adventures had made him a
little reckless, and he felt as though he would
like to go through some of them himself; but
unfortunately it did not come to him in quite
that way. Here was his mother liable to see
more adventures than he was, and how did he
know but a squad of rebel cavalry would
come down on her, kill her guard and carry
her off to some Southern prison-pen? Another thing, the Union men had been very
careful to hold a force on the main road which

extended into Perry county, so as to meet the Confederate troops when they came there, and now the rebels had been at work operating in their rear. It told Leon that they had got something to do before they could establish their independence.

"I know what you are thinking of, Leon," said Dawson. "I don't care how strongly a place is fortified or how closely it is watched, the enemy will get in and make a map of it. They know right where the strongest works are, and all about it."

"What do they do with a man they catch making those maps?"

"That depends. If he is in citizens' clothes they take him and shut him up; but if he is in uniform, then it's good-bye, John."

"Do they shoot him?"

"No; they hang him just as surely as they can get their hands upon him. So you see that that rebel up to your house got what he deserved. He knew what was going to happen to him in case he was caught, and he would rather be shot than hung."

Before the boys had gone a great way on

their road to Ellisville they met a party of perhaps a hundred men, some with an axe on one shoulder and a rifle on the other, accompanied by three or four wagons loaded with their household furniture. They were going up into the swamp to build boats, so that their families would not be cut off when the time came for them to retreat.

"The President sent us, but I don't look for much trouble up here," said the leader of the party, leaning on his rifle. "But then it is well to be on the safe side."

"Don't fool yourselves," said Leon. "The rebels won't come along the main road."

"Sho! How do you know?"

"Because they have got men around in your rear working at maps, and all that sort of thing," said Leon. "Here's a map that was taken off a dead rebel this morning."

As Leon produced the book the men crowded around in eagerness to see it. They looked at it in surprise, but they little thought it was a plan that would lead the attacking force miles behind them, and that when they turned they would find five hundred men in front of them, and that they could drive them pell-mell across the little stream before spoken of, and into the hands of another Confederate party who were concealed there in the bushes waiting for them. It was a scheme to clean out the Union party at one fell swoop, and nothing but Leon's going home that morning saved them from it.

"There's the little creek right there which divides our county from Perry," said Leon, pointing it out with his riding-whip, "and that map shows that it is fordable in five different places—above and below the bridge."

"Well, sir, it's amazing how he got all the little streams down there in the little time that he has had," said the leader. "Who shot this rebel?"

"Mr. Giddings. He is lying in one of father's negro cabins. I tell you this that you need not be caught napping," said Leon, putting the book where it belonged. "There may be more rebels where these came from, and you don't want to let them see what you are doing. Good-bye, and good luck to you."

Ellisville was livelier now than they had

ever seen it, except on the day of the convention. There were men scattered all over it, but the greatest number of them were around the hotel. All the chief men were there inspecting the wagons to see what there was in them, and as fast as one wagon was found to contain provisions it was pushed off on one side, to be hitched up directly and taken away into the swamp. It seemed strange that when one of them had been doing such good work, and when all the men about him were so deeply interested in what was going on before them, that there was one among them who ached for an opportunity to " throw it all into the ditch." It was Newman. He was waiting to see the quartermaster. He was going to get a mule if he could; if not, he was " going to bust up the whole thing."

CHAPTER IX.

A NIGHT EXPEDITION.

"WHO do you report to?" asked Dawson, as, following Leon's example, he pulled his horse up to a halt.

"What do I want to report to anybody for?" asked Leon. These things were entirely new to him, and he had a good many formalities to learn.

"Why, it is the rule that you must report to the men who sent you away, in order that they may know when you got back."

"Oh! Then I suppose I ought to report to father. He is busy now, but as soon as I can get his ear I'll tell him about this map. Now, Tom, you and Dawson go back to your camp, and stay there till I come. We'll make that our headquarters until we get ready to go away."

But Mr. Sprague was not so very busy that

he could not take a little time to listen to Leon. The last two wagons were loaded with clothing, and he told the person who officiated as quartermaster that it would be proper for him to call up any of the men who needed something to wear, adding:

"There are rebel uniforms in there, and I expect the men won't want to wear them, but it can't be helped. I know I shouldn't want to take off my clothes and put on a gray jacket. Well, Leon, how did you find your mother? No Confederates been near her, I suppose?"

Mr. Sprague opened his eyes in surprise when he received a warning gesture from Leon, but he followed him off on one side, out of reach of everybody. The boy then began a hurried account of what had transpired at his house, showed him the map, and told how he had left Giddings there to keep an eye on his mother. To his surprise his father never changed his countenance at all. He listened to Leon's recital with the same apparent unconcern that he would have received any ordinary piece of news.

12

"Now, father, what are you going to do about this?" said Leon, in conclusion. "It looks to me as though the rebels were getting up something, and the first thing we know they will be after us."

"I don't know what I shall do about it yet," said Mr. Sprague. "I shall want to see Knight about it first. Now, as you are going into foreign parts to-night—"

"Why, I am not going away," exclaimed Leon. "I am only going into Perry county."

"Well, that is a foreign country. That is what the rebels call the United States, and head all their news as 'foreign intelligence.' What's the reason that we can't so designate a county which they claim? You are going into Perry county to help Dawson bring his mother up here, and I must instruct you how to pass the sentries."

"Have you got some sentries out?" inquired Leon.

"We've got ten men down by that bridge, but this map you have shown me proves that they won't do much good there. Now, when you come up with them—"

Mr. Sprague took this as his starting-point, and went on to tell Leon just what he must do when he passed the sentries. It was new business to him, and he must be very careful how he acted. He must not attempt to run by them—Mr. Sprague thought that Dawson was rather careless, and was afraid he might do something to draw the sentries' fire—but must do just as he was told. When ordered to dismount and bring the countersign, " Fidelity "—could he remember it?—he must be sure not to give it until the sentry was close upon him, and then utter it in tones so low that no one but the man for whom it was intended could hear it. Leon promised compliance, repeated the countersign over to be sure he had it in his mind, then shook his father warmly by the hand and went off to Tom Howe's camp. In reply to their inquiring glances, Leon then went on to tell that his father had decided to see Mr. Knight before he determined what to do in regard to the men who had been operating in the rear, and described how he was going to work it to get by the sentries.

"That's all right," said Dawson. "We can't attempt anything wrong there, although, to tell the truth, I have run by my own sentries more than once."

"What would they do with you if they were to catch you in that business?" inquired Tom.

"Oh, if you hadn't made any effort at deserting they would put you in the guardhouse," replied Dawson, with a laugh. "They would think it was merely a little fun on your part, and they wouldn't punish you very severely. But if you were known to be a deserter, they would hang you in a minute. Now, I suppose we can wait here until it is pretty near dark, and then we must be up and doing. If you fellows don't want to go say the word, and I'll go alone."

"I shall be with you when you see your mother," said Leon.

"Here too," said Tom. "You just bet I'll stick close to Leon's coat-tails. If he gets into a row I'll be there to help."

After that there was silence in the camp, for two of the boys had something at least to think about. They were about to begin soldiering in earnest. It is true that the events of the day before had infused new confidence into them, but the attacking Union party was a great deal stronger than the Confederate escort, and a battle, if one had taken place, could have ended in but one way. Now, they were going right in among those fellows, and who knew but they might run onto a squad of rebels who were numerically their superiors, and be all taken prisoners? That was what bothered Leon. He wasn't afraid of being shot, but he was afraid of being hanged. There was something murderous about a rope and the men getting ready to haul away on it, but with a bullet the case was different.

"Well, if I am going to die I'll show myself a man," soliloquized Leon, as he rolled about under the trees watching Tom, who was getting an early supper for them. "How cool Dawson takes it."

His rebel friend lay opposite to him, on the other side of the fire, with his saddle for a pillow and his hat drawn over his face, and the regular breathing that came to Leon's ears told him he was fast asleep.

"Now, it seems to me that if I was going back among a lot of comrades who were just aching to hang me I should find something to think about to keep me awake," muttered Leon. "Maybe it is all in a lifetime. Perhaps when I have been through as many dangers as he has I can go to sleep, too."

"Supper was ready at last, Dawson aroused to eat his share of it, and the moment he was settled with a plate of bacon and corn-bread before him, he became at once full of stories. He seemed surprised because Leon told him that he was asleep.

"Well, I couldn't make the time pass quicker by staying awake, could I?" said Dawson. "You would have gone to sleep if you knew what's before you. You may see the time when you will be glad to take a wink all by yourself."

In half an hour more the boys rode out of the grove and turned their horses toward the bridge. In passing by the hotel Leon saw his father standing on the porch. He saluted him, but kept right on without stopping.

Dawson was surprised, and remarked in his quiet way that Mr. Sprague was taking the separation very coolly.

"He must have unbounded confidence in you," said he. "Most fathers would have come out to bid you good-bye."

"I did that long ago," said Leon. "My mother is the only one I am worrying about now. If the killing of that rebel will convince them that we have a body-guard out on all sides, I shall be more than pleased. They will come with a bigger force than two men to take a map next time."

The ride through the woods was a lonely one, and, finally, just as it began to grow dark, they came within sight of the bridge, and saw a sentry pacing up and down there with his piece carried at shoulder arms. One thing was evident to Leon: his father had improved his time in giving the men some instruction, or else the squad was under a corporal who understood his business. The sentry halted when he heard the sound of their horses' hoofs on the road, faced about, and brought his gun to arms port before he said a word.

"That fellow acts like an old sentinel, don't he?" said Dawson. "He has been in the service before."

"No, I reckon not," said Leon. "So far as I know, everyone of these men is as green as I am myself."

"Halt!" shouted the sentry. "Who comes there?"

"Friends with the countersign!" said Leon.

"Dismount, friends. Advance, one, with the countersign."

So far everything was all right; but the next move was something that was not down in the tactics. No sooner had Leon's voice answered the sentry than nine men came running from different parts of the woods and took up their stand directly behind the sentry. They held their guns in readiness, too, as if they meant to be on hand for anything that might happen.

"I tell you they meant to be ready for us, didn't they?" said Dawson. "You won't get the sentries in our army to answer a challenge like that."

"What would they do?"

"They would keep out of sight in the
bushes, and perhaps be ready to fire in case
anything goes wrong."

The boys had by this time dismounted, and
Leon, leaving his horse for Dawson to hold,
walked up to the sentry and whispered the
countersign, "Fidelity," in his ears.

"The countersign is correct," said the man.
"Why, Leon, where are you going? Don't
you know that you will be gobbled up if you
go beyond that bend?"

"No," said Leon, in amazement; "we are
going down after Dawson's mother."

"Well," said one of the men who stood behind the sentry," you can go, but I won't. A
little while ago two or three of us happened to
be out here, and we looked up and saw a fellow standing in the road watching us. We
called to him, but he got into the bushes before we could shoot at him."

This was something Leon had not bargained
for. The other boys had come up in obe-
dience to his signal, and they all heard what
the man had to say about the spy who was
watching them.

"Did you see more than one?" asked Dawson, who was utterly amazed to know the rebels had come between him and his mother. If that was the case he might as well go back, for all hope of bringing her into the Union camp was, as he expressed it, "up stump."

"No, I didn't see but one, and he was a Johnny, for the way he took to the bush was a caution," said the man. "That was what brought us out here in such a hurry. We didn't know but there might be others behind you, and we thought we would be ready for you."

"Well, Dawson, I am going ahead if you are," said Leon.

"Talk enough," exclaimed Dawson, placing his foot in the stirrup and swinging himself upon his horse. "All I want is a little pluck to back me up, and I will have my mother up here before you see the sun rise."

"You have got the old man's grit, I can see that easy enough," said the sentry. "Good-bye and good luck to you. We don't want to say a word to dishearten you, but if you come back here at all, you'll come a-flying. One sentry can't stop you."

The boys laughed, but anybody could see that it was forced, and in a few moments they were around the bend, out of sight. It was there that the rebel spy had been seen. They looked sharply into the woods as they passed along—every boy had his revolver drawn and hanging by his side—but the thickets were as silent as if nobody had ever been there. Leon and Tom were very pale, there was no mistake about that, but they kept as close at the heels of Dawson's horse as they could possibly get. Not a word was said until the woods had been passed and they found themselves in the midst of a long cotton-field which stretched away on both sides of them, and in the distance was a row of buildings which Dawson pointed out to them.

"If we can get there inside of that house we are all right," said he, and a person wouldn't have thought from the way he spoke that he was thinking of his mother. "There is where she lives."

"If that spy was in the bushes and saw us when we went by, what was the reason he didn't jump out and grab us?" said Tom.

"Perhaps he was alone," said Leon, who would have felt safer if that spy, whoever he was, had been among his friends. "He wants more help before he attempts to arrest us."

"Now, boys, let's keep perfectly still and ride up to the house as though we had a right there," said Dawson. "You are not afraid to shoot, are you, Tom?"

"All I ask of you is to give me a chance," returned Tom, indignantly. "Anything to keep from being made prisoner."

The boys relapsed into silence again, and presently drew up before the gate which gave entrance into the door-yard. It was an old-fashioned gate, and was held in place by a wooden pin, which was thrust into an auger-hole. The horse Dawson rode showed that he was accustomed to that way of getting in, for he moved up close to the pin, so that his rider could pull it. The gate creaked loudly on its wooden hinges, whereupon they heard a little confusion in the house, the door opened, and by the aid of the light from the fireplace the boys saw a woman and two little children fill the door.

"Oh, Bo—"

One of the children was on the point of shouting out Dawson's name, but quicker than a flash the mother's hand covered his mouth. It was no place to speak a person's name out loud.

"Sh—! Not a word out of you," said Dawson, dismounting from his horse. "You will bring the rebels on me. That's a little boy, but he is Union all over," he added, turning to Leon. "Now you stay here and hold my horse, and I will go in and get things ready. I needn't tell you to keep a good watch down the road. If you hear so much as a footstep, I want to know it."

"Now hold on a bit," said Tom, dismounting and handing his reins to Leon to hold for him. "If you are going to leave us here in silence I must take care of my muel, else she will arouse the neighborhood. You hold her head, Leon, and I will look out for her tail."

"Well, why don't you take care of it, then?" asked Leon, when he saw Tom station himself in such a position that he could readily seize her tail in moments of emergency.

"Because she isn't ready to bray yet," said Tom. "Whenever she gets ready to let the people know she is here she will bob her tail up and down. Then I will be ready to take hold of it and keep it down. Oh, there's a heap to be learned about muels the first thing you know."

Dawson laughed—he couldn't keep from laughing if he knew his mother was in danger—and went on into the house, the door of which was closed after him; so Leon didn't hear much of that greeting. And he wouldn't have learned much if he had heard it. His mother had lived in danger for the last year, and all she did was to kiss him and listen while he told of his capture.

"But I wanted to go," said he, "and father and I promised each other that whoever got away first should go to Jones county, and the one that was left in the rebel ranks should come there as soon as he could. I got away first, and now I am come after you. Pack up everything you want and be ready to load it aboard the mule-team which I will bring here as soon as possible."

"Will I be protected there?" asked his mother.

"You certainly will. There is a thousand men there, and they are growing every day. I wouldn't ask you to stir a step if I didn't think so. Your house is gone up."

"Well, I can't help that. But do you really think your father will be able to join us there?"

"He's got to take his chances; that's what I had to do. Now, mother, take everything you need and leave the rest behind for the rebels."

This was all that was said, and Dawson left the house and went out to his companions; but he knew that his mother had gone hastily to work to bundle up such things as she needed and could not possibly do without. He took his bridle from Leon's hand and with a whispered "follow me" led the way around behind a corn-crib, out of sight.

"Now I must leave you again, and you will take notice that your horses don't let anyone know they are here," said Dawson. "I am going to get a mule-team."

"Your mother is going, is she?" asked Tom.

"Of course she's going. She would look nice living in that house while she had a husband and son in the Yankee army! Of course we have seen the house for the last time. The rebels will burn it up the first time they come this way."

While Dawson was getting ready to go out and get the mule-team the boys noticed that their horses raised their heads, and pricked their ears forward and looked down the road, as if there was some object down there that attracted their attention. Dawson was the first to notice it, and he straightway grabbed his horse by the bridle and forced his head down.

"Somebody's coming," said he.

Leon speedily dismounted and took up a position by his horse's bridle. Tom gave his reins into his hand and occupied his old station by his mule's tail, and all the boys held their breath and listened. It was faint and far off, but presently they could distinctly hear the sound of a multitude of horses' hoofs upon the hard road. Nearer it came, until

Dawson, who was experienced in such matters, informed his companions in a whisper that there must be a whole platoon of cavalry approaching. It came from the south, too, and that was the direction in which the rebel headquarters were situated.

"I tell you it's lucky that we got here just in the nick of time," said Tom. "Hold on there, old muel," he continued, catching the mule's tail and pulling it down. "You mustn't let those folks know we're here. Did you see how I stopped his braying?"

Leon and Dawson were too deeply interested in what was going on in the road to pay much attention to him, and finally they could see, through the cracks in the corn-crib where the chinking had fallen out, a number of men ride past the house, or, rather, the majority of them rode by, while three drew rein and stopped there.

"By gracious! I hope mother heard them, and that she had time to put her bundles away out of sight," whispered Dawson. "Everything depends upon that."

"Where do you suppose they are going?"

asked Leon, who was so excited that he could scarcely speak.

"They are going up to Jones county to see how nearly ready for them we are," said Dawson. "I reckon they'll stop when they get to the bridge. There are some riflemen up there that act to me as if they were good shots."

"Now, here's a thing that bothers me," said Leon. "You are talking about getting a mule-team to haul your mother's things to our county, and I would like to know how we are to get it by those fellows? We'll have to wait until they go back."

Dawson did not answer at once, for he was much concerned about those three men who rode into the yard. He saw one of them dismount and go into the house, and his heart beat like a trip-hammer when he saw it. He waited for the confusion which he knew would follow when the bundles his mother had made up were exposed to view, but it did not come. In a few minutes the man came out and spoke to the two men he had left on horseback, and they went on, and the rebel turned and came directly toward the corn-crib.

"He's coming here," said Leon; and before anybody could say a word against it he had cocked his revolver, rested it in the crack, and pointed it at the man's head. He was right in front of the open doorway, and of course Leon couldn't have missed him at that distance. The rebel came on as though he knew where he was going, entered the doorway, placed his mouth close to the crack, and whispered:

"Robert!"

"For goodness' sake turn that revolver the other way!" whispered Dawson. "It is my father."

CHAPTER X.

CALE WANTS A MULE.

"I AM to go to the quartermaster, am I? It is his business to give the muels out, is it? He give one to that Tom Howe and never asked what he was going to do with him, and now he had to go and refuse to give one to me. I'll get even with you, Mr. Sprague, for that, and you just see if I don't."

It was Newman who spoke, and he leaned against the corner of the hotel and watched Mr. Sprague as he went on inspecting the wagons. He was a boy about nineteen years old, although he might have passed for thirty, judging by his looks. He didn't have a rifle; in fact he didn't have anything except the big hunk of "nigger-twist" which he took from his pocket, transferring a generous slice to his mouth. He was not a raftsman, anybody could have told that, for they generally took some pains with their personal appearance. This Newman was ragged and dirty, and looked as though he had been in the habit of sleeping wherever night overtook him. He had the appearance of being mean enough for anything, and the facts proved that he was.

"See that ole Sprague stepping around like he owned the nation," muttered Newman, shutting one eye and squirting a flow of tobacco-juice at the nearest tree. "I'll see pap, and if he thinks it can be done I am going to do it. That 'rolling officer, when he was here, told them that they couldn't have things all their own way, and I guess they will find it out. They will give me something for telling them where they can find the men, and I'll be dog-gone if I don't do it. Where's that quartermaster, I wonder? Busy, as usual, I'll bet. Well, let him work his own gait. He won't do it much longer."

Newman stayed around almost all day before he got a chance to speak to the quartermaster, and before he went away there was something that drew his attention from Mr.

Sprague to Leon. The latter and two companions came up to report what had happened at Mr. Sprague's plantation since his absence. Leon made a handsome figure, if he only knew it. He sat his horse with easy grace, was clad in a suit of blue jeans which fitted his person admirably, and he raised his hand to his father with a military salute that would have done credit to an old soldier. Newman did not hear any of his report, for it was given in tones so low that they could not reach his ears; but if he had heard any of it, it would have shown the necessity of his being up and doing.

"See how easily he touches his hat to that old civilian," said Newman, with a sneer; "while my father, who could have had that position if the folks had been a-mind to give it to him, has to go around without anybody saluting him. Such things ain't right, but I tell you I am going to make them that way. They offered my father something nice if he would betray these chief men into their hands —they didn't say what it would be, but I suppose it is some commission—and he don't seem willing to do it. I'll do it, and see what they

will give me. There's the quartermaster now,
and he don't seem to be busy."

Newman threw his tobacco out of his mouth
and walked up to the quartermaster, who stood
with his hands in his pockets and watching
some wagons that were being hitched up pre-
vious to being hauled into the swamp.

"I want to see if you will give me a muel,
please, sir," said Newman, stepping up and
trying his best to give the military salute as
he had seen Leon do.

"A mule? What do you want of a mule?"
said the officer, more than half inclined to
laugh at the boy's appearance. "You don't
want a mule to ride up to the house."

"No, sir; but I want him so as to be ready
to go with the men when they capture another
wagon-train," said Newman.

"Why, you didn't go with the men the
other day. I saw you around here the whole
time. Your father was with you, and so was
Dan."

Dan was Newman's oldest brother. All we
can say about him is that he was Cale Newman over again. Dan was the one that stole

the bacon and sweet potatoes that the family
lived on. He had courage to go where Cale
wouldn't dare show his head.

"But we would a-had to go afoot," said
Newman, in an injured tone. "I couldn't
walk so fur."

"It seems the others did it without any
trouble. You could have gone there and
showed your good-will, if you had been a-
mind to. I reckon you will find it better to
do without a mule."

"You gave Tom Howe one and said nothing about it," said Newman, growing angry
again.

"I did?" said the quartermaster.

"Old Sprague done it, and it amounts to
the same thing."

"Look here, Newman, you want to be careful how you talk about that man. He ain't
a common civilian any more."

"What is he, then, I would like to know?"

"He's got power enough to put you where
people won't hear you say that," said the officer, fastening his eyes sternly on Newman's
face. "He will put you in jail."

"Well, I'll bet he won't put me in jail, neither. My father has got friends enough to tear it up."

"Well, Cale, if you are going to hold to such doctrines as that you might as well go among the Confederates, where you belong. You don't belong here, that is certain."

"If you will give me a muel I won't hold no such docterings," said Newman. "I'll be the loyalest fellow you ever see."

The quartermaster looked at Newman in amazement.

"What kind of a fellow are you, any way?" he asked. "You are going to be loyal or not, just as you get paid for it."

"That's the way my father looks at it. You didn't give him an office, and now he's going to let you hoe your own row. Now, if I could have a muel to ride around—"

"Well, you'll not get any, I can tell you that. And, furthermore, if I hear any more such talk from you I'll have you arrested."

"My father says—"

"I've heard enough. Don't speak to me again. A man who will depend upon a mule for his loyalty don't amount to much. Now go away, and don't let me see you again."

The quartermaster was very angry as he turned away, and Newman stood and watched him while he went on inspecting the wagons. Then he took a chew of " nigger-twist," shook his head threateningly, and turned his steps toward home.

"You have heard enough, have you?" he muttered, as he followed the blind path that led through the woods toward the little shanty under which his family found shelter. " Well, I'll bet you will hear more of it before to-morrow night. If father don't give you into the hands of the rebels I will."

When Newman arrived within sight of his home he found his father sitting on the door-step smoking his pipe, while his brother Dan was stretched in a sunny spot where he could enjoy the full benefit of the warmth without going near the fire. His mother was engaged in a lazy sort of way over a blaze which had been started in the fireplace; that is to say, she was sitting down and watching a pot that had been set over the coals, while a dingy cob

pipe, like her husband's, was tightly clasped
between her teeth. The house was a tumble-
down affair, and looked as though it was about
to come to pieces, with a dirt floor, and the
door beside which Mr. Newman was sitting
was minus a hinge near the top. The family
were all of them what might have been expected by this description of their place of
abode. And the work, which might have
been accomplished by one man in three or
four days to make his house worth living in,
was not above Mr. Newman's ability, for he
showed on his face that he had seen better
times. He had been wealthy once, but now
he had lost it, and was much too lazy to go to
work and earn more. That accounted for
Cale's way of talking. He didn't say "pap"
and "mam" unless he spoke before he
thought, for he considered himself better than
those with whom he associated. The raftsmen
used to say that if Mr. Newman's work was
equal to his talk he would have a much better
house to live in.

"Well, Cale, what's the matter with you?"
inquired his father, as the new-comer ap-

proached the place where they were sitting. "You act as though you had lost your last friend."

"I want to tell you what has happened down there in town, and see if you wouldn't look so, too," said Cale, seating himself on the ground. "I asked old Sprague and the quartermaster—"

"Quartermaster nothing," exclaimed Mr. Newman. "Who gave him such an office as that? He had the handling of the mules and horses and would not give you one."

"That's just the way of it," said Cale. "Now, I want to know if such a thing is right? He gave Tom Howe one and never said nothing about it; but he wouldn't give me one for fear that I wouldn't be on hand when he was going out to capture the next wagon-train."

"No more would you," said his mother, at that moment appearing at the door to hear what Cale had to say. "You ain't on that side. The South is going to whip, and you don't want to be beholden to those fellows for anything."

"I told 'em if they would give me a muel I would be just the loyalest fellow he ever saw," said Cale.

"The more shame to you," said his mother, angrily.

"Well, I don't know about that," chimed in Mr. Newman. "If he could get a mule or one of the horses he could fly around easy, carrying dispatches and the like. He could be here to-day and see what was going on, and to-night he could get on his mule and take the news down to the Confederates. Wouldn't he give you a mule?"

"No, he wouldn't. I tried Sprague and the quartermaster, too, and they both threatened to arrest me if I talked so any more."

"Well, I do think in my soul that they are getting on a high horse," said Mr. Newman, taking the pipe from his mouth. "I'd like to see them arrest you or anybody connected with this family. Their old jail would stay up about as long as I could get to it with an axe."

"That's what I told 'em ; and he said that I mustn't talk that way any more."

"Say," said Dan, who had mustered up energy enough to straighten up during this talk and was now engaged in filling a cob pipe with some nigger-twist, "you don't suppose that the men who were captured with that wagon-train have gone on to Mobile, do you? It seems to me that they ought to be back here to-night or to-morrow. Them fellows aint't a-going to stand still and let themselves be robbed of half a million dollars' worth."

"Don't I wish I had the stuff that's in one of them wagons!" exclaimed Cale. "There's grub enough to keep our jaws wagging for one good solid year; and clothes! You just ought to see the uniforms there is in there."

"I came away before they got to inspecting the wagons," said Mr. Newman. "Somehow I couldn't manage to stay around and see the clothes and things our fellows were going to wear go to those lazy vagabonds."

That was one reason why Mr. Newman came away before the wagons were overhauled, but the principal motive that governed him was because he did not want to see others saluted. His attention was first called to it by the actions of Bud McCoy. Bud didn't care for anything, but he seemed to be carried away by his Union sentiment, and once, when he spoke to Mr. Sprague, he did it without saluting; but he thought of it at once, and came back and touched his hat to him.

"I declare, Mr. Secretary of War, I almost forgot my manners to you. I forgot that you ain't a plain raftsman any more."

Mr. Newman would have given a good deal if he could have been saluted that way, and because he was not, he didn't care to stay around where the crowd was.

"Mr. Sprague let on that he didn't want to be saluted every time a man spoke to him, but I know a story worth two of that," said Mr. Newman, getting upon his feet and pacing up and down in front of his house. "I am better able to hold that position than anybody else, because I have seen more military than they have. But no, they had to go and give it to a man who don't know a thing about it."

"That's just what I told them," said Cale.

"And what did they say?"

"They said I couldn't have the muel."

"Well, now, if those fellows come back here," said Dan, "what's the reason we can't help them get all the chief men of the county? I am in it, for one."

"Here, too," said Cale.

"You must be careful what you do," said Mr. Newman. "They have got sentries posted down there, and you can't get by them without the countersign."

"Then we'll go below the bridge and swim the creek," said Dan. "If I go into this business I shall go in all over."

"If you will do that you may be able to get me the commission of Colonel of the Confederate army," said Mr. Newman. "I never told you this before, but I shall ask that or nothing."

"A colonel!" ejaculated Cale, with intense enthusiasm. "Then you will have command. He rides a horse, doesn't he?"

"He certainly does, and he's got a commission backed by a government. He's higher than the President of the Jones-County Confederacy. That's the commission I am working for."

One would not have thought that Mr. Newman was working very hard for that commission to have seen him at that moment. In fact he did not seem to be working for anything. He was sitting there perfectly quiet and waiting for the commission to come to him

"I tell you, boys, you must work hard for that colonel's shoulder-straps," said Mrs. Newman, taking her stand in the door with her arms placed on her hips. "You won't be wearing no ragged clothes like you be now, and I'll have a silk dress to wear at all seasons. You won't catch me around cooking as I am now. I'll be a lady, and have a better pipe than this to smoke."

"And who knows but that father might get us something?" said Dan. "I'll bet if you held old Sprague's position you would give me something besides a private in your ranks."

"That's just what I am thinking of," returned Mrs. Newman. "Your father was telling me about it last night. Of course he would have a staff, and you two would come in for two of the offices mighty handy. I tell

14

you you want to work hard. Your father doesn't seem to be able to do anything."

"And what is the reason?" exclaimed Mr. Newman, taking his pipe from his mouth with one hand and extending the other toward his wife. "Do you suppose I am going to run down there among all that crowd and stand all the risk of getting my neck stretched for treachery? The boys can do what they please and nobody will say a word to them; but let me go down there and carry news of what has been going on and you will see how long you have got a husband to take care of you. It ain't safe for me to go there."

"I didn't think about your being hung," said Mrs. Newman, indifferently.

"Of course that is what they are up to, and they are thinking now how it could be done."

"Yes," exclaimed Cale, "they told me that I had best go among the rebels, where I belonged."

"Don't that prove what I said? I ain't going down there any more. But I want to see them lock you up, if they dare do it. That's what I am aching for."

But Cale didn't agree with his father's opinions in regard to locking him up, and he secretly resolved that he wouldn't say anything more in the presence of the quartermaster that would lead him to carry that resolution into effect. His father filled his pipe and sat down in his usual place in the doorway, and Cale, following the motion of Dan's head, accompanied him around behind the house. Mr. Newman didn't care where they went or what they did while they were gone. All he thought of was the carrying out of Dan's proposition to surrender the head men of the Jones-County Confederacy into the hands of the enemy. It looked like a very small piece of business for a father to put this into his sons' hands, but Mr. Newman thought he was acting just right. The boys were gone half an hour or more, and came back in time to get something to eat. They sat down to their supper in silence, and when they had got through they put on their hats and left the house. They didn't take their dogs with them, and that proved that they were not going after wild hogs.

"You just let those boys alone," said Mr. Newman, looking down the path along which they had gone with some satisfaction. "They are going to get whatever they go for."

"I think it would have been some honor to you if you had gone in their place," said his wife. "Somehow it don't seem right to leave the capturing of so many men to boys."

"Yes, and run the risk of stretching hemp," replied Mr. Newman, indignantly. "Those boys can be away from home as much as they are a-mind to and nobody will say a word; but if I go down to where the men are and find out something about them they would know in a minute if I wasn't at home, like I had oughter be. And I don't want them to ask that question. Let the boys go on. We'll have some of them men arrested the first thing you know."

"But how are they going to arrest them? Are they going to come here and take them?"

"No; it will be in a fight, likely."

"And where will you be when the fight comes off?"

"Oh, I'll be around somewhere. You look

out for yourself and let your husband look out for himself. That's the way to do it."

"I wish we had a muel to ride," said Dan, as they trudged through the woods toward the creek. "Somehow it puts me on nettles to walk. Now that Tom Howe has got a muel I don't see why we can't have one. We ought to have gone with them men that captured that train."

"But we had no guns," said Cale.

"No, but we would soon have had them. There's lots of guns in the President's head-quarters that haven't got any owners. Tom didn't have a muel, and now he's got one."

"And that's what comes of touching his hat to those civilians," said Cale, in disgust. "I bet you I wouldn't do it. Why didn't they give father a position like he ought to have had? We would have had muels by this time."

"It's my opinion that father has got his foot in it," said Dan, with a knowing shake of his head. "He has said all along that the South was going to whip, and old Sprague and the other men don't like it. "I'll bet you that if the truth was known half of them are on our side."

This was the substance of the conversation that passed between Dan and Cale on their way to the creek. Boys as they were, they had every reason to believe that one county could not stand against the whole Southern Confederacy, that the Union men in the county were going to be easily whipped out, and they wanted to be on the winning side. Perhaps there was a little hope of plunder mixed in with it, as Cale finally said:

"I'll tell you what, Dan: I don't like the way that young Sprague had of throwing on style to-day. He rode up on that colt of his and saluted the old man as if he were the owner of the State. I'd like to have him go afoot for awhile and let me ride on that horse."

"Well, he'll have to do it," returned Dan. "But he's got some other things that I'd like to have—his revolver, for instance."

Before long it began to grow dark, but the gloom that settled over the woods did not interfere with the movements of these back-

woodsmen. They kept straight ahead as
though it had been broad daylight, and finally
arrived on the banks of the creek. Without
saying a word they threw off their clothes
and prepared to plunge into the stream. If
they had known as much as Leon did they
would have looked for that ford which was but
a short distance from the place where they
swam the creek. The water was somewhat
cold, but they took it bravely, and in a few
minutes more stood on the opposite side.

"That Leon is going to have a colder place
than this," said Dan, as he shiveringly put on
his clothes. "I do wish they would turn him
and Tom over to us."

"What would you do with him?"

"I'd make him swim this creek."

"Perhaps he wouldn't do it."

"He wouldn't, eh? Wait until he sees his
revolver looking him squarely in the face. I
bet you he would go. Now, we want to be
still, for we don't know how close those sentries are to us. We must keep mum and make
as little noise as possible in going through the
woods until we find out where they are."

Cale was now perfectly willing that Dan should take the lead, for as they were getting pretty close to armed men he did not want to be the first to draw their fire; so he gradually fell behind, while Dan made his way through the bushes with an ease and celerity that was astonishing. He scarcely caused a twig to rustle. The experience which the boys had in hunting wild hogs stood them well in stead. Finally Dan pushed aside the bushes and saw the road fairly before him. There was nothing on it as far as he could see, and the bridge seemed to be empty.

"Somebody has been fooled in regard to those sentinels," said Dan.

"Go out in the road," said Cale. "You can't see anything from here."

Dan went, but had scarcely got clear of the bushes when a voice called out, in a surprised tone:

"Halt!"

"By gum, I guess you found something," whispered Cale. "You had better be geting out of there."

Dan waited to hear no more. He drew a bee-line for the bushes, and in a moment more was threading his way noisely through them. When he had gone a little ways he stopped and said to his brother:

"I didn't see anybody there."

"No, but they are there, and they saw you," said Cale, who was greatly excited. "Now, what's to be done? I wish that cavalry would come along now, and we would have those sentinels took in out of the wet. I hope they did not see you."

"Nor me. I wouldn't dare go back home again. Let's sit down here a spell."

"I—I believe I would rather go a little further away," said Cale. "Suppose some officer should come along the road?"

Dan answered this question by seating himself on the nearest log and resting his chin on his hands. He wasn't going any further, and Cale, rather than be left alone in the woods, took a place by his side. They stayed there for a quarter of an hour without saying a word, except Cale, who wished they had a gun, so that they could tumble the officer

over when he came along to see where they
went, and then they heard another challenge
to halt from the sentinel on the bridge.

"There, now, I'll bet there is somebody
else coming," said Cale, his excitement and
fear increasing tenfold.

"Well, he didn't come by here," said Dan,
who sat where he could see everybody who
passed along the road.

"No, but he came from Ellisville. Who
knows but there was someone there watching
our house, and who saw us when we came
away?"

"That's so," said Dan, but he didn't seem
to be much worried by it.

"Well, now, I say let's go a little further
back."

But Dan kept his seat with his eyes fixed
upon the road, and while his brother was trying to make up his mind whether or not he
ought to leave him they heard the clatter of
horses' hoofs on the bridge, and even Dan
began to prick his ears. It was a small party
of horsemen who were coming directly along
the road of which he kept watch. They

were walking their horses, and that made the spies eager to escape observation. Dan stretched himself out at full length in the bushes, his example being promptly followed by Cale, and in a few minutes the horsemen rode by; but they saw nothing to excite their suspicions, and in a few seconds more they passed out of hearing.

"Don't I wish I had a gun!" exclaimed Dan, raising himself on his knees and going through all the motions he would make in covering the horsemen.

"Who was it?" asked Cale.

"It was Leon, that worthless Tom Howe, and that rebel fellow that they have been running with since yesterday," said Dan. "Now I wish your squad of cavalry would come along. But you see we hain't got no guns, and each one of them has got a six-shooter."

Cale had never been more astonished in his life.

CHAPTER XI.

MR. DAWSON'S STRATEGY.

"YES, sir, I wish I had a gun in my hands," said Dan, rising to his feet and gazing down the road in the direction in which the horsemen had disappeared. "I could have tumbled that Leon Sprague off his horse just as easy as not. And I might have had if there had been any way for me to earn it."

There had been plenty of ways for him to earn a gun, or, for the matter of that, some better clothes than he wore, if it had not been for his disinclination to work. He could have gone into the woods almost any time and made a man's wages by chopping, but that was niggers' work and a little too low down for him. Mr. Newman and his boys had tried it once, but the men who had charge of them were so cross and snappish, and wanted them

to do so much more work than they did, that
they could no longer stand it. At the end of
three days they came home with their axes,
put them up in a corner, and vowed that they
would hunt wild hogs with their dogs and
stick them with their knives rather than work
under such task-masters. And if their father
wouldn't do it they might be sure that the
boys would not, for Dan and Cale looked for
better times without doing a thing to bring
them about. They preferred to be idle—they
were squatters; even the ground their house
was built upon did not belong to them—and
whenever anybody came near losing his life,
as Tom Howe had come near losing his during the last spring drive, it pleased them wonderfully. That little episode added to their
enmity against Leon Sprague. According to
their belief, Leon ought to have stood on a log
and seen him go under.

"I didn't see anybody go by," said Cale.

"I don't suppose you did," said Dan, with
something like a sneer. "You are like an
ostrich. Whenever they get frightened they
hide their heads and think their body can't

be seen. Now let's go down this way a little further, and then we'll lay in the bushes and see what's going to happen."

"What do you suppose that rebel fellow has come out here with Leon for?" said Cale. "Has he got any relatives or things down here that he is going after?"

"That's just what's a-bothering of me. I don't know, but we can watch and find out. Now we'll wait until they come back," said Dan, picking out a comfortable seat for himself against a tree where the bushes were so thick that one might have passed within five feet of him without knowing that he was there. "He's a rebel, he deserted to the enemy with a uniform on, and if we see some Confederates come along here we will tell them where he is."

"But we don't know where he is," said Cale, looking around to find an easy spot to sit down.

"Well, the rebels can easy watch here until he comes back," retorted his brother. "What's there to hinder them from jumping out on him and taking him and all that he's got into the bargain? Now, I like, when I am sitting down in this way, to talk about what I am going to do with those things we are going to take away from Leon. I speak for his revolver."

This started Cale off on a new subject, and it wasn't long before he forgot that there were armed men within less than a quarter of a mile from him. If Leon and Tom could have been dealt with as these young backwoodsmen wanted them to be it wouldn't be long before they would have changed places. They probably passed an hour in talking over their various plans, and then they were brought to an abrupt silence by the sound of horses' hoofs upon the road. The men had been advancing so cautiously that they were close upon them before they knew it. Cale, whose greatest care was to keep out of sight, at once stretched himself at full length in the bushes, while Dan, who wanted to see who the men were, raised himself to his full height and looked over the thicket. What he saw was about a dozen men, all on horseback, and noted, too, that they were all dressed in Confederate uniform; but one thing that astonished him was a revolver that was pointed straight at his head. The leader of the horsemen was an old soldier, and he could not be taken unawares.

"Halloo! By George, there's a Yank," he exclaimed. "Come out of that."

Dan was thunderstruck. He had never expected to be greeted this way by his friends, and for a moment or two he stood with his hands down by his side unable to move or speak; while Cale, uttering a smothered ejaculation, began to worm his way out of the bushes on his belly.

"Hold on! There are two of you there, and if you move another hair I will cut loose on you!" shouted the leader; and to show that he was in earnest he turned his horse and rode into the woods. His men were with him, and when Dan cleared his eyes of a mist that seemed to obstruct their vision he found that there were half a dozen revolvers looking at him. "We've got you and you might as well come out. Where do you belong?"

"Are you Confederates?" stammered Dan.

"Of course we are. What did you take us for? Come out of that."

"Well, now, if you are Confederates you want to turn those weapons the other way," said Dan, growing bolder when he heard his own voice. "I am as good a Confederate as you are."

"Oh, well, then, it is all right. Come out here on the road so that we can talk to you. Get up there, you fellow lying in those bushes. You needn't think we are going to hurt you. Now, then, what do you know? Have you seen any Confederates around here to-day?"

"No, I haven't. But say," added Dan, who had by this time taken up his stand in the road and grew bolder when he saw that none of the soldiers addressed him by name, "you want to get all the head men of Jones county in your hands, don't you?"

"Well, I should say so," exclaimed the leader, showing more enthusiasm than he had thus far exhibited. "Can you put me in the way of getting my hands onto them?"

"How much will you give?" said Dan.

15

" How much will I give?" asked the leader, as if he did not quite catch Dan's meaning.

" Yes.   My father had some talk with you fellows about it, and he says he is working for a colonel's commission.   He won't work for any less.   Now, you can afford to give me captain and my brother here lieutenant, can't you ?"

The captain, for that's who he was, was taken aback by this bold declaration on the part of Dan.   He looked hard at him to see if he was in earnest, and then looked around at his men.   There was one present, a lieutenant, who evidently measured Dan by his own estimate, for he said :

" I was there and heard all about it, Captain.   We had a long talk with the old man— what's your father's name?" he added, bending down from his saddle and trying to get a glimpse of Dan's face.

" His name is Newman," said Dan.

" And yours?"

" Dan ; and this is my brother, Cale Newman.   We are two good Confederates, dyed in the wool."

"I know you are, for I recognize the name. We had a long talk with Mr. Newman about it, and we agreed to give him a colonel's position if he would put us in the way of getting the chief men of Jones county into our hands. Now, Captain, you can afford to give two such little offices as he wants in return for his services."

"Why, yes, of course," said the captain, who fell in at once with his lieutenant's ruse. "You see, Captain—I want all of you men hereafter to address this man as captain and his brother as lieutenant—do you hear?" he added, turning to his squad; and a responsive "Yes, sir," came from all the men; although candor compels us to say that some of them wanted to laugh. Some of them looked back down the road, and others had something to to do with fixing their feet in their stirrups.

"Thank-ee, Captain; thank-ee," said Dan, who didn't know whether he was awake or dreaming. "Just give us a horse apiece and a gun, and we will lead you against those men any day."

Cale Newman scarcely believed he had heard

aright. He knew more about military matters than his brother did, and he did not know that an officer had a right to promote one to his own rank without going first through some preliminary steps. He listened in a dazed sort of way to the conference between the leader of the squad and Dan, but as no one spoke to him and addressed him as "lieutenant," he did not know whether he was an officer or not. At any rate, he decided to get home before he built any hopes upon it. His father had "seen some military" (although where he saw it, it would be hard to tell, unless he had seen some military companies march along the street), and he would know whether or not everything was just as it should be.

"You see, Captain, I was not with my officers when they talked this matter over with your father, and consequently I didn't know anything about it," said the leader of the squad. "However, I am glad to be set right on the matter. You spoke of surrendering the chief men into our hands; now, how are you going to do it?"

"I will tell you where you can get one of them right here," said Dan. "Leon Sprague has gone down the road with a rebel fellow that he has been running with since yesterday—"

"A rebel fellow?" interrupted the captain, in astonishment. "Have any of our men deserted to you?"

"Oh, yes; there's lots of them. We had 1498 men when this war broke out," replied Dan, copying what he had often heard his father say, "and now we have a thousand fighting men camped right up this road."

"Well, I declare," said the captain, turning to his lieutenant. "We came within an ace of getting right in the midst of it. They are camping right up this road, you say?"

"Yes; and they stole a big lot of provisions from you yesterday."

"We know that, dog-gone them!" said the captain. "We have come up here to see about those provisions. Do you know where they are?"

"The most of them have been hauled to the swamp."

" There !" said the lieutenant. " Then it is of no use to go any further. If those goods have been taken to the swamp they are lost to us."

" I confess it does look that way. Now, about this rebel fellow who has just gone off. What is he going after; do you know?"

" He may be out scouting, the same as you are," replied Dan.

" And he takes a couple of green boys to help him scout the same as we are ?" exclaimed the captain. " I guess not. He's got some friends down here, and he wants to get them on the other side of the line. Do you know where this boy lives or what he is ?"

" We can easy catch him as we go back," said the lieutenant. " And in the meantime I would suggest to you the propriety of going up and finding out for ourselves the number of pickets they have placed at the bridge. I believe you said there were some there ?" he continued, turning to Dan.

" There's a whole pile of them," answered Dan. " We didn't see them ourselves, because we swum the creek ; but when we got over here I went out to see if I could see anything of the sentinels, and they saw and halted me."

" But you didn't go in, did you ?"

" Not much I didn't. I took leg bail, and got into the woods. You see the men up there are acquainted with us, and if they got us they would make us stretch hemp." Another quotation from his father.

"Well, we shall have to ask you to stay here until we come back," said the captain. "We shan't be gone but a little while. Forward, and hold your sabres in so that they won't hit against your heels."

The two boys stood there in the road and saw them ride around the first bend, and they went so silent and still that one who didn't know they were there would not have suspected anything. As soon as they were out of hearing Dan showed off a little of the enthusiasm that was in him.

"Captain ! Captain Dan Newman !" said he, with a violent attempt to refrain from giving a wild hurrah. " And I never was in the army in my life ! And you are a lieutenant, Cale. But you don't seem to think much of it."

"The fact is, I don't know whether I am an officer or not," replied Cale, looking down at the ground. " I don't believe that officer had any right to promote us."

" Well, I declare, you are a dunce," said his brother, more than half inclined to get angry with him. "Didn't you hear what the officer said to his men—' I want you all to address him as captain and his brother as lieutenant' —I tell you that's enough for me."

" But this officer was a captain."

" No matter for that."

" And I don't believe that he had a right to promote you to the same rank as himself. They don't do business like that in Jones county."

" What way?"

" Why, the President has something to do with it."

"Somebody has been stuffing you. Of course they don't do business that way in Jones county; but these men are in the service, and of course they know what's right."

" Well, I am going to wait until I see

father, and if he tells me that I am an officer, why I'll have to believe it."

This was a new thing to Dan, and he did not say any more. He supposed that the next thing was to be ordered to Mobile, where his uniform, a horse and weapons would be given him, and after that he would be at liberty to take command of a body of scouts the same as this captain had done; but now he began to look at it in a different light.

"I'll tell you what is the matter with you," said Cale, after thinking the matter over. "It all comes of your wanting father to get that commission as colonel."

"Hasn't he got a right to it, I'd like to know?" retorted Dan. "He said he wouldn't work for any less."

"I know, but they didn't tell him that they would give him that commission. He told us that he was working for it; and here the rebs have gone and got on your blind side—"

"Whoop!" yelled Dan, his anger getting the start of him; and with the word he kicked out savagely at his brother, who was just a little bit too quick for him. He slipped out of the way, and Dan's momentum took him around on one foot and finally seated him rather roughly on the ground.

"That shows that you don't believe it more than I do," said Cale. "Heavens and earth! What's that?"

It was fortunate that something happened to turn Dan's mind from all thoughts of revenge, for just then there was a rapid fusillade of carbines heard up the road. Dan picked himself up, and before he could answer there came another report of rifles in reply to the first, and they were so accurately aimed that some of the bullets passed through the branches above their heads. The first alarm was given by the rebels, who wanted to see how many men there were at the bridge. They had halted a little ways from the creek, leaving two men to hold their horses, and crept up on the unconscious sentinel and brought him bleeding to the ground. A moment later they became aware that the pickets at the bridge were too strong to be carried by the small force they had at their command, for the answering volleys that came across the creek—they came thick and fast, too—showed them that the insurgents of Jones county had taken ample precautions. It demonstrated another point to their satisfaction: it showed them that they knew how to fight.

"They are shooting at us!" cried Cale, who straightway dove into the bushes.

Dan stood there in the road and didn't know what to do. While he was considering the matter the firing ceased, and then all was still. He stood there for a long time, half an hour, it seemed to him, and then he heard the sound of horses' hoofs coming from the direction of the bridge, and in a few minutes the Confederates rode up.

"Did you hit any of them?" inquired Dan.

"We hit one that we know of, and that was the sentry," said the captain. "We filled him so full of holes that he never will hold that position again. Now we will go on and report that they have got sentries at the bridge. I'll look into all the houses as I go by, and if that rebel fellow is about I'll have him, sure."

"Well, now, look here," said Dan, who

began to think now that there was some truth in what his brother told him. "What be I going to do?"

"You? Oh, yes. We shall want you to stay here, so as to be on hand, you know, the next time we come out after the Yanks. You will be right here when we want you?"

"No. I live all of twelve miles from here, and how will I know when you are coming? Couldn't you take me on to Mobile with you?"

"Why, of what use would you be there?" answered the captain, speaking before he thought. "Why—you see," he added, on receiving a nudge from his lieutenant, "your company isn't ready for you to command it."

"Couldn't you take me on your staff?"

"Well, you see, I don't have a staff," said the leader, struggling hard to keep from laughing outright. "I'll speak to the colonel about you as soon as I get back. Good-bye. Forward!"

"Of all things I ever heard of this is the beat," thought Dan, as he stood there and watched the men out of sight. "If I am a captain, I do not see what's the reason my company isn't ready for me to command it. I guess I have made a botch of this business. Well, Cale," he added, aloud, "let's catch up and go home. And Cale, I won't say anything to the old man about this."

"I reckon I wouldn't if I was in your place," said Cale.

"No; but I will depend upon you to do it for me," continued Dan, coaxingly. "You can repeat what the captain said to us without mentioning any names, can't you?"

"I suppose so."

"And all the while I will listen and be as earnest as you for disbelieving it," said Dan. "In that way we will get at the truth of the matter. But I do say that I think that that captain was up to mighty mean business. I reckon he'll find somebody else that he wants to promote in the same way, and I wish I could be there to whisper a word or two in his ear."

Cale followed along behind his brother as he bent his steps toward home, swam the creek, and just at daylight arrived within sight of his dilapidated shelter. His father was up, and a smoke lazily ascended from the chimney.

"Well, boys, what luck?" he exclaimed, when his eyes fell upon the two weary tramps coming toward him. "Did you see any rebels?"

Dan borrowed his father's plug of nigger-twist, and Cale hunted up his pipe before either of them replied. Dan cut off a generous chew, and then seated himself on the doorstep.

"You have been gone a long time," continued Mr. Newman, "and I think you must have seen something. Did you capture any of the head men of the county?"

"No," replied Dan. "We saw some Confederates, but they wouldn't go after them."

"Why, how was that?"

Dan began and told his story just as it happened, and the old man became so interested that he allowed his pipe to go out. He told about his meeting with the Confederates, described the conversation they had with them, all except the promotion, told about the firing on the pickets, and that they went back to report that they had found sentries at the bridge.

"And didn't they charge across the bridge and capture those pickets?" exclaimed Mr. Newman, in disgust.

"They didn't make nary charge that we heard of," replied Dan. "They said they would go back and report it."

"Well, if that ain't a pretty way to do business I don't want a cent. They ought to have a couple of thousand men behind them; then they could have captured the sentries, and come on up here and gobbled these men."

It was now Cale's turn to try his hand.

"Father," said he, "has a captain any right to promote a man to the same rank as himself?"

"No," said his father. "What made you ask that question?"

"Oh, I was just thinking about it."

"The captain has a right to watch his men in action, and if he sees them doing any brave act he reports it to the colonel," said Mr.

Newman. "But he has no authority to promote them himself."

The boys were satisfied. Cale stretched himself out upon his shake-down and dropped off into a dreamless slumber, while Dan threw out his tobacco, filled a pipe with nigger-twist, and sat down and thought about it. There was one thing he did not neglect to do. While he was lost in dreaming of the glory that might have been his if his promotion had been according to law, he did not forget to vow vengeance upon the captain who had presumed to play upon his credulity in that outrageous way.

"I know just how he looks," soliloquized Dan, "and if it ever comes in my way to do him a mean act he'll see how quick I'll take him up. But that promotion is what gets me. How fine that old fellow looked in his high-topped boots, slouch hat, and gloves that came up to his elbows! Never mind. I'll see the day when I will be better off than any of them."

Meanwhile there was one soldier in the captain's ranks who would have given every-

thing he possessed to have been able to have
pulled out his revolver and shot Dan down
when he talked about "that rebel fellow"
who had gone off with a couple of Yanks.
He well knew what had brought him out
there. He was Mr. Dawson, and the boy who
had escaped at the time the wagon-train was
captured was his son. The boy had lived up
to his agreement, and was now paving the
way to take his mother and younger brothers
inside the Federal lines in Jones county.

We have said that Mr. Dawson came out
and spoke to the two men who had come into
the yard with him, and they went on, while
Mr. Dawson himself came toward the corn-
crib, behind which he knew his boy was concealed. He was after a saddle, for his own,
together with his horse and weapons, had been
taken by the Jones county men when they
captured the train. He had seen his boy go
off into the bushes and drew a long breath of
relief, for he knew that his troubles were
ended. He obtained the saddle, placed it on
the old clay-bank which had been given to
him to replace the horse he had lost, and rode

16

on and overtook the line just after they had made a capture of Cale and Dan Newman. He was in something of a scrape, because if either of the boys saw or recognized him they might have mistrusted something. So he sat there on his mule, and heard what Dan had to say about that "rebel fellow," but no one thought of connecting him with it. They supposed that young Dawson was somewhere in Mobile, and that they would find him there when they got back.

The captain went into all the houses as he went along, but without finding any preparations for hurried departure. The women came to the doors as fast as they could find some clothing to put on, obediently struck a light in response to the captain's request, and then he departed with a slight apology for his intrusion. One garrulous old woman followed him to the door and inquired:

"What did you-uns think you wanted to find, anyway?"

"I just wanted to see if any of your men folks had been at home packing up goods to take them into the Yankee lines," said the captain.

"Sho! My men folks been in the Conf'drit army before you was born. They ain't seed nuthing to make 'em desert yit."

Finally they reached the house where Mr. Dawson lived, and he noticed one thing that attracted his attention at once. There was but a single dog to welcome him, and he was tied up back of the house. All the others had gone off somewhere. As the lieutenant reined his horse up close to the pin the captain turned about and said:

"Why, this is the place where one of you men live, isn't it? You came in here after a saddle, didn't you?"

"Yes, sir," replied a voice from somewhere in the line.

"Your boy is in the service, too. You don't suppose that he has deserted, do you?"

"Well, he went off into the woods, and I haven't seen him since. You can go in and see for yourself, sir."

"Seeing is believing. It will not take but a minute."

The captain dismounted from his horse and

pounded loudly upon the closed door, but met
with no response. Then he pushed open the
door and entered the house. By the flickering
light that was thrown out by the fire that was
blazing on the hearth the lieutenant found a
candle, and when he had struck a light a
scene of the greatest confusion was presented.
The bureau drawers were all thrown every
which way, and when they made their way to
the sleeping-room, not a vestige of clothing
was there on the bed.

"Gee-whizz!" shouted the captain. "Here's
where one of those fellows has been. Arrest
that man out there—the one riding the clay-
bank mule."

The men outside began riding about the
house, but no such man could be found. They
saw the place where the solitary hound had
been confined, but he was gone, and the man
on the clay-bank mule had disappeared.

"Don't you find him anywhere?" shouted
the captain, coming out of the door in great
excitement.

"No, sir. He has skipped," exclaimed one
of the men.

"He's gone off this way," shouted another.
"I hear somebody going through the field."

"Take after him, the last mother's son of
you!" commanded the captain. "And remember and don't come back without him. I tell
you I'll get fits for this, going out on a scout
and letting one of my men desert under my
very eyes!"

In an instant the captain and all his men
were in hot pursuit of the horseman whose
hoof-beats could just be heard. The chase led
through a wide cotton-field, with a high fence
at the other end, but the horseman, whoever
he was, had a long start and seemed determined
to make the most of it. Toward the fence he
held, the men scattering out so as to head him
off when he got there, and finally the captain,
who rode a splendid horse, got near enough to
the object he was pursuing to see that it was a
clay-bank mule.

"Halt!" he shouted. "We've got you, and
you might as well give up. If you don't we'll
leave you right here for the buzzards to eat.
Halt, I say."

Still there was no response, and the mule

kept on as fast as ever. The captain began to get angry, and he drew his sabre, intending to cut the man down when he got within reach of him; but just then they came within reach of the fence, and the mule turned and ran alongside of it. That brought him within reach of the captain's vision (it was so dark that they couldn't see the man on the mule's back), and the officer, after taking a look or two at the mule, drew up his horse.

"Gee-whiz!" he shouted, making use of his favorite expression; "we have been chasing that clay-bank mule, but where's the man on her? The mule was going home but the man's got off. Catch him, men, and then we'll go back and hunt for somebody else who is hidden somewhere in the bushes."

The captain was mortified in the extreme, and no doubt he was a little suspicious. At any rate, he was certain that he heard one or two of his men giggling softly to themselves. The idea of halting a clay-bank mule and telling him that if he didn't give some heed to it he would leave him there for the buzzards to eat was almost too much for them.

CHAPTER XII.

THE REBELS TAKE REVENGE.

"ROBERT," whispered a voice close to the crack where the chinking had fallen out, "is that you?"

"For goodness' sake turn that revolver the other way, Leon!" exclaimed Dawson, so full of excitement that he could scarcely speak plainly. "It is my father, and if you kill him I am gone up. What is it, pap?"

"You got away, didn't you?" continued the voice, and one would have thought there was a slight chuckle mingled with it, "and you have come here to take your mother over into Jones county."

"You're right, I have," returned Dawson, gleefully, "and you are here to help us. I've got two Yanks here with me, and they are just as good as they make them."

"I thought I heard you mention Leon's name. Is it Leon Sprague?"

"Yes, sir," returned the owner of that name. "I am here and ready to assist him in any way I can."

"I am glad to see you here," continued Mr. Dawson, "for I shall know that we are going to stand some show."

"Now, father, what shall I do first?" asked Dawson, who was impatient to get to work.

"Hitch the first two mules you can get to that wagon, and by the time you have done that your mother will be ready for you. Leave one dog behind you, so that I can readily follow your trail."

"Why, are you not going to stay, too?"

"No; I must go on with the squad, and run my risk of getting away afterward," replied Mr. Dawson. "I will be missed if I don't go with them, and I want you and your mother to get a good start. Be lively, and work as hard as you can, for I don't know when we shall be back."

"What shall I do after I get the mules hitched up?" asked Dawson. "Will it be safe for me to drive around in front of the house?"

"You can go where you please. There will be nobody to bother you. Keep up a good heart till I come."

The man went off to get his saddle, which hung in a remote corner, and Dawson kept a close watch on him as long as he remained in the crib. Leon couldn't help thinking how coolly father and son went about escaping from serving under the flag they didn't like. If they made a success of it, well and good; if they failed, it was certain death to the one of them that happened to be caught. What would Leon's own mother have said if she could have seen him at that moment? When Mr. Dawson got his saddle and turned to go out he waved his hand toward the crack as a farewell signal, and that brought the first long breath from the young fellow at Leon's side. It was plain now that all the nonsense was gone out of him.

"There goes the best father that any fellow ever had," said Dawson. "He is plucky, too, and when he next joins us he won't come so still. He'll have all that crowd after him. But now I must get to work," he added, brightening up. "You fellows can help me by staying right here and watching these animals, so that they won't arouse the whole neighborhood, while I get the team ready."

"Why don't you let one or the other of us go with you?" asked Leon.

"You'll only be in the way; and, besides, I have got plenty of negroes out there to help."

Dawson went away, and although the boys who were watching the animals caught sight of him once in a while through the cracks, it was fully half an hour before he came back. Then he had the team, which an old negro was driving, and the wagon was loaded so full that there did not seem to be room for so much as a skillet anywhere about it. Safely perched among the feather-beds was his mother, and she was having as much as she could do to keep the children quiet. On the end-board in front was Cuff, who was talking to his mules in a quiet sort of way, and it was astonishing how much speed he got out of them. Following along behind the wagon were ten or fifteen negroes, who wished her every success in her journey and promised to come to her on the following day. The dogs were there, too, all except the one that had been tied behind the house, and they seemed to think they were going off on a pleasure trip.

"Now, then," said Dawson, taking his bridle from Leon's hand and mounting his horse, "you darkies have followed us far enough. Go back now and go to bed, and remember and don't come out of your house again to-night, no matter how much noise is made here. Leave that dog tied up. Father wants him to follow our trail by. Good-bye. Now, Cuff, whip up. We don't want to stay around here any longer. Mother, take a good look at your home, for it is your last chance to see it."

"No, Robert, I will see it in my dreams, anyway," replied his mother, who was almost heart-broken at the idea of separating herself for so long a time from all her associations. "If your father only comes up with me I shall be satisfied."

"What do you think of that, Leon?" asked Dawson, as the wagon passed on out of hearing. "These rebels want killing. Father brought my mother to that house when he first married her, and we have lived there ever since. I am going to shoot every rebel that comes in my way."

Leon did not know what reply to make to this. It was probable that his own mother might be obliged to leave her home in the same way, and he didn't know how he would feel if she were turned loose in the world. It was no wonder, he thought, that Union men should talk of killing every rebel that came within reach. He knew he would feel so, too.

"There is one thing about it," said Dawson, with something that sounded like a sigh. "A woman has more pluck than a man to stand under such things. I never believed so until to-night."

The road they intended to take had evidently been explained to Cuff before they started, for he took to the lane that led through the cotton-fields, and he kept his mules on a keen trot all the way. Dawson didn't go so fast. He allowed the wagon to gradually get ahead of him, in order to cover their retreat, and of course the boys stayed behind with him. When they arrived at the cover of the woods Cuff turned into it, and in a few moments more was out of sight, while Dawson turned his horse into a fence-corner and dismounted.

"Now, we will wait here for father," said he.

"Where's your wagon?" asked Leon.

"They are going on ahead toward the bridge. Taken in connection with those pickets I saw there they will get across, too, because I believe they would turn out to help us. Now, if you see that squad coming back along the road, just hold your breath. Father is with that crowd."

Leon had never known what excitement was before. He tried to take it coolly, as Dawson did, but did not succeed very well. He threw the bridle off his horse's neck and placed it around his arm, leaned on the top rail of the fence and kept watch of the road, and all the while he kept thinking how he would have felt if his father had been with that squad of Confederates and watching for a chance to escape. Tom Howe took it philosophically, as Dawson did. He had a mother to worry over him, but all he cared for was the successful •outcome of Dawson's scheme. The baying of the lonely hound came faintly to their ears, but with the exception of that, silence reigned unbroken. They stood leaning on the fence, watching first the house and then allowing their eyes to roam as far down the road as they could reach, and finally Tom broke the stillness.

"I see some fellows away off in that direction," said he, pointing with his finger to direct the attention of his comrades, "who are coming along this way. There's a whole body of them, too."

"The time is coming," said Dawson, after he had taken a look at the advancing horsemen. "We'll know in a minute what's going to happen."

After that all was still again. The three boys stood there in the fence-corner and watched the men when they rode into the yard, and in a few minutes the baying of the hound ceased. Judging from the distance they were from the scene, there was a fearful commotion in the house. Men were seen riding rapidly about, a faint voice like a command came to their ears, and the squad suddenly vanished from view.

"Father has the start of them at last," exclaimed Dawson, so excited and nervous that he could not stand still.

"Why, how do you make that out?" asked Leon. "You must have an owl's eyes, for I can't see anything from here."

"Neither can I; but he is doing just what I would have done if I had been in his place. You don't hear the hound any longer, do you? Well, you just wait until father comes up and he will tell you that the men are chasing a riderless mule."

Leon began to understand the matter now, and he was utterly amazed at the strategy the man had used. He had dismounted from his claybank, given him a tremendous dig from some weapon or other he had in his hand, knowing that the mule would go home before he would go anywhere else, unloosed the dog, which showed him the way down the lane, and he was now coming that way with the speed of the wind. His pursuers had gone on after the mule, and were leaving him behind every moment. All this Leon went over for the benefit of Tom Howe, and Dawson simply nodded his head and then walked out in the lane to find his father. Presently he saw the hound, which sprang upon him, delighted to see him, and a long way down the lane behind him came his father.

"That's father's lope and I know it," said Dawson, addressing himself to his companions. "He'll hold that for two hours in order to beat a deer on his runway. But I am going to show him that I am a good soldier. Who comes there?" he added, in a voice pitched just loud enough to reach the fugitive's ears.

"It is I, Robert," came the joyful response; and in a few seconds Mr. Dawson came up. "By George, I have had a good race for it!" he went on, pulling his hat from his head and using his crooked finger to remove the big drops of perspiration that clung there.

"Now, let us see what those laddy-bucks are going to do with the house."

"You'll never see it again after to-night," replied Dawson. "Father, this is Leon Sprague, who has stuck to me all along."

"Leon, I am glad to meet you," said Mr. Dawson, extending his hand. "If you wait here for a few minutes you'll see what you are going to come to. The rebels are making up an organization already to go up to Jones county and clean them out."

"And, father, here's another Yank that we must not forget," said Dawson, laying his hand upon Tom Howe's shoulder. "He's little, but he don't say much. You heard about the boy that came so near losing his life during the last drive? Well, sir, he's the man, and there is the one who saved him."

"I'm no Yank," returned Tom, indignantly. "I am Tom Howe, Southern born, the same as yourself; but I hate a rebel."

"I am glad to know you, Tom, and sometime, when I get opportunity, I am going to shake hands with you. You see the reason we never knew you before is because you kept to the river

17

during your drives, and never came back into the country at all," said Mr. Dawson, turning to Leon. "Now, we will wait here a few minutes and see what those fellows are going to do with the house."

They were not obliged to wait very long, for the squad soon returned, having captured the clay-bank mule, and two of them at once proceeded to ride out the lane in which the fugitives had gone. They came on until they got within fifty yards of the woods, and there they stopped.

"I declare they are coming on in pursuit of us," whispered Leon, drawing one of his revolvers and resting it upon the top rail of the fence in readiness to shoot.

"That's the captain and the lieutenant," said Mr. Dawson. "They're not coming any further. When they see that we have gone into the woods they will go back. There isn't a man in that squad that dare trust himself within reach of these thickets."

The boys stood there and watched the two men—Leon at the bridle of his horse to hold his head down, and Tom keeping a firm hold

THE OLD HOMESTEAD INVADED.

of his mule's tail—and finally they saw one of them alight and strike a match. By the aid of the light which it threw out they examined the ground and easily saw the wagon-tracks, but they didn't care to go any nearer the woods. They held a short consultation, after which they turned their horses and rode back to the house.

"I told you they wouldn't come any further," said Mr. Dawson. "If I was in command of that squad I would think twice before I would put my men in danger of certain death by bringing them in here."

Mr. Dawson leaned upon the fence again and devoted himself to the house. He wanted to see what was going to happen to his property before he went away. He had not held this position for more than five minutes before his heart gave a violent throb, and then he became satisfied that the enemy was carrying out his plan of setting fire to the house. He saw a bright light on the inside, which grew brighter every moment, and finally the flames came out of the doors and windows. And not only the house, but the barns, the corn-crib and the negro cabins went up in smoke.

"Well, boys, I have seen enough," said Mr. Dawson, turning away to follow up the wagons. "The rebels have one enemy now that they never had before. Which way did your mother go, Robert?"

"Yes, and they have got two now," said Dawson, who was almost ready to cry when he saw the home of his boyhood going up in flames. "I'll shoot every rebel that comes across my path."

"What could you expect in war times?" said his father. "Of course, I looked for them to burn my house—indeed, I should do the same if I were on their side; but there's one thing they can't burn, and that is the ground. When these troubles are all over, if we live to see it, we have the plain land with which to start over again."

"But what have they done with our black ones?"

"Oh, they have gone."

"Gone where?"

"They are on the road towards Mobile before this time."

"Well, I'll bet you they don't keep them

there long," said Dawson, angrily. "They
will have to watch them all the time or
they'll get away. Mother went out this way,
father."

"You see, it wouldn't do for them to leave
the darkies with us," said Mr. Dawson. paus-
ing for a few moments to allow the boys time
to mount their animals, "because we are
traitors to the South. They calculate to whip
us, and when the war is ended we'll have to
get out."

"But they ain't a-going to whip us," said
Dawson.

The fugitives followed along the road—it
had been cut in better times, to enable the
planter to haul out the logs—for a mile or
more, and then they came up with the wagon,
which had halted for them to come up. They
had been within sight of the burning house
all the while, and the mother, although she had
all she could do to choke back her tears, was
endeavoring to explain the matter to her children, who could not see into it at all. When
young Robert appeared in sight, they forthwith assailed him with questions.

"Say, Bobo, what's the matter?" said the elder.

"Oh, some men wanted to burn our house, and so we had to get out and let them do it," returned Dawson.

"Go on, Cuff," said Mr. Dawson; and all he did was to reach in and give his wife a cordial grasp of the hand. "Keep right in this road until you strike the main road, and then go for the bridge the best you know how."

"But, Bobo, I don't see what them folks should want to burn our house for," said the boy. "We've always minded our own business—"

"Wait till we get to where we are going and then I will tell you all about it," said Dawson; and that settled the question of burning the house until the party reached Ellisville.

Following the directions of his master, the negro stuck to the woods-road, while Mr. Dawson and the boys stopped in a fence-corner to reconnoiter. The house was a mile away, but it threw out so much light that anything that happened around it could be plainly seen. They saw some of the men moving about, and when everything was well started they all mounted their horses and disappeared down the road in the direction of Mobile. But they had an old soldier to contend with in Mr. Dawson, who did not leave his hiding-place for an hour. He didn't know but some of the men would come back, and so get between him and the bridge and cut him off, and that was the reason he waited there in the fence-corner. While he waited there he talked, but it was not about anything connected with his recent misfortune.

"Do you boys happen to know anything about Dan Newman?" said he.

"Yes, sir, we know him," replied Leon, with a smile. "And we know Cale, too."

"Well, what sort of fellows are they?"

"It's my opinion that they are all rebels," said Leon, with emphasis. "The amount of it was that the old man expected to get some kind of a position, and when he didn't get it he turned against us."

"That's just what I supposed," said Mr.

Dawson. "Robert, I heard all about you before I ever saw you to-night."

"Who told you?" asked his son, in surprise.

"Dan Newman told me; or, rather, he told it to the captain and I overheard it."

"Was he out here?" asked Leon, and he was so surprised that he could scarcely believe he heard aright. "Was he out here among the rebels?"

"He was, and he was the one that kept the squad from running into the pickets stationed at the bridge."

Mr. Dawson then went on to tell what he knew about Dan, and before he got fairly started he had two surprised and angry boys for listeners. When he told how "that rebel fellow" had ridden on before them in company with Leon and Tom, and that he could easily capture them if they would only wait until they came back, Leon took off his hat, scratched his head and declared:

"If that fellow is at home when we get there I am going to have him arrested. I don't see why the fellow didn't wait."

"Well, I don't think he paid much attention to what Dan had to say," replied Mr. Dawson. "He preferred to go on and see how many men there were at the bridge, and when he came back he would look into all the houses and see if there had been any evidences of hasty departure. I guess he didn't find any until he got to our house, and then he found all he wanted," added Mr. Dawson, with a laugh.

"Well, now, this beats me," said Leon.

"Don't it?" replied Tom.

"There was one amusing thing that was connected with the interview," said Mr. Dawson, "and that was Dan's rapid promotion. The captain made him a captain, too, and his brother a lieutenant."

"Why, had the captain right to do that?"

"Certainly not; but the captain saw what manner of man he was, and so promoted him on the spot. I thought I had better tell you of this, so as to put you on your guard."

"Thank you; and you may be sure that we shall take advantage of it. Captain Newman! How that sounds!"

As for Tom Howe, he was almost beside himself with fury. When Leon punched him in the ribs and asked him what he thought about it, he simply shook his head and said nothing. After awhile he inquired: "Was Cale there?"

"Yes, Cale was there, but he didn't have much to say."

"No matter. He was knowing to it all, and he would have been the worst one in the lot if he had only dared."

"What would you have done, Robert?" asked Leon of his rebel friend, although the latter hadn't made any remark thus far.

"What would I have done if they had laid alongside the road and tried to capture us?" replied Dawson, and there was much more determination in his words than Leon had ever noticed before. "Well, sir, I wouldn't have been here now. Didn't you hear me say that I would drop before I would be captured? I meant every word of it. If I should be taken prisoner I would only be hanged, and I would rather be shot than that."

"Well, boys, I have seen enough to make

me believe that the rebels have gone home," said Mr. Dawson. "Now let's go and find your mother and see how much luck we will have in getting by the sentries."

"Oh, we won't have any trouble there," said Leon. "I've got the password."

"Yes; but it won't be of any use to you in broad daylight."

"Then I'll make my face pass us. Everybody about here knows Leon Sprague."

They had something more to do in coming up with the wagon, for Cuff, when he struck the main road, kept on "the best he knew how," so they had almost reached the bridge when they came within sight of his span of mules. After a short consultation it was decided that Leon and Tom should go on ahead to smooth the way for the fugitives, leaving them to follow with the team; so they galloped their horses and presently heard a voice ordering them to halt. By this time it was almost sunrise, and Leon, profiting by the experience of the old soldier, didn't say he had the countersign. He and Tom stopped and got off their horses.

"Well, I declare, it's you, ain't it?" said the one who came out to see who and what they were. "Did you see anything of the rebels last night?"

"I should say we did," returned Leon, with a laugh. "We stood right by and saw Mr. Dawson's house burn up."

"Was that before they fired into us?"

"Why, I didn't hear anything about that. Did they shoot into you?"

"Yes, sir; and they killed Bach Noble as dead as a hammer. You see he was standing guard when they crept up and had no show to defend himself; but we got the better of them."

"What did you do with Bach?"

"We laid him out there in the bushes and sent a man up to Ellisville after a wagon to take him home. He was the first man killed on our side, but I'll bet he ain't the last."

"You are sergeant of this post, are you not?"

"I reckon. That's what they call me."

"I want you to pass along this road a party of rebels who are now coming toward us. I saw their houses burned last night. They are mighty tired of fighting our fellows, and are now going over into Jones county to battle under our flag. And I will tell you another thing about them: they won't take any prisoners. Here they come now."

"Now, Leon, I reckon you'll swear by them?"

"I will, any day in the week. Ask the man any questions you want to. They have got children with them, and they wouldn't surely take them into an enemy's country."

The Dawson party approached, being beckoned to by Leon's hand, and young Robert was promptly recognized by the so-called sergeant in charge of the post. He shook him warmly by the hand, and said if the rest of the family were as strong for the Union as he was they might all come in and go on to Ellisville.

"They are as strong," said Dawson. "If you had stood where my father stood and saw your property burn up, you wouldn't have much love in you for rebels."

The party passed on over the bridge, lingered there to exchange a word with the squad on guard at the bridge and to look at the blood-stains the sentinel had left when he fell, and finally kept on the road to camp.

CHAPTER XIII.

CALE IN TROUBLE.

THE Dawson party now drew a long breath of relief. They had crossed the bridge and were now on the road to Ellisville, the pickets were between them and their pursuers, and all danger of capture was passed. Young Robert walked along beside his horse—the elder Dawson seemed determined to foot it, and his son kept him company—and, judging from the remarks exchanged between husband and wife, all peril of being made prisoners was gone. Even Cuff drew a long breath and slowed up on his mules, while Leon and Tom rode on ahead, apparently very much occupied with their own thoughts. Everybody knew what they were thinking about, and for a long time no one troubled them; but at last Dawson could stand it no longer.

"It's rather rough on you, ain't it, Leon?" said he. "To see where that sentinel shed his blood is enough to make you believe that you have not undertaken a picnic."

"I tell you, boys, you have taken something of a job on your hands," said Mr. Dawson. "I never heard of such a thing, and I am afraid before the thing is up you will find it an impossibility. The sight of a little blood don't worry me. When you belong to a company that charges a battery, and the battery opens on you and kills all but five or six of you, then it will be time for you to open your eyes."

"Well, I don't see why you took that method of finding out how many men there were at the bridge," said Leon. "Why couldn't you have made a fuss of some kind out there in the bushes and then counted the men when they came out?"

"Because it was orders," said Mr. Dawson. "If you were in the rebel army for a few short weeks you would know what that means. I fired with the balance, but I shot wild. I never fired at a Union man in my life."

"But, father, how did you come to be on this scout?" asked Dawson. "You don't belong to that company."

"Oh, no. I happened to be present when the squad was made out, and among them was an old German fellow who didn't care to go, and I borrowed his weapons and mule and went in his place. I expect he'll get tired waiting for his weapons before he sees them again. That's a pretty good carbine," added Mr. Dawson, holding his gun off at arm's length and looking at it.

"I didn't know that a man could do that," said Leon. "I thought you had to obey orders, no matter whether you wanted to or not."

"Not in a case like this. I didn't say anything to anybody about it. I got on the mule, and when the squad was called together I put in an appearance. I was afraid that something was going to happen to my family, and I couldn't bear to stay behind."

"I tell you, things turned out all right, didn't they?" said Dawson, gleefully. "You came home just in the right time to join us."

"What I want to know is, am I going

18

to get my horse?" said Mr. Dawson. "I raised him myself, and shouldn't like to part with him."

"You will get your horse all right," said Leon. "If he has been given to anybody, that man will have to give him up."

That settled the matter to the satisfaction of all the Dawson family. Leon soon began to get over the forebodings caused by that crimson stain on the floor of the bridge, and riding beside the wagon he kept up a conversation with Mrs. Dawson, who told him many things connected with the service that he hadn't dreamed of. In due time they arrived at Ellisville. Just as they were going up the main road that led past the hotel they met a squad of sentinels going down to relieve those at the bridge. It was plain that an old soldier was in command of them, for they were closed up, held their guns at a carry and marched by twos. The two officers who commanded them marched at the head. They had evidently had some time to drill their men, and the result showed that the backwoodsmen were not at all behind in military matters.

When they came up, they reined their horses out of the way and passed on without speaking.

"There's a squad that is well drilled," said Mr. Dawson. "But I do not see why you do not destroy that bridge. It seems to be a world of trouble to you."

"There's a very good reason why we don't destroy it," said Leon. "There are five other places where it can be forded."

"Why, I hadn't heard of that," exclaimed Mr. Dawson.

"Do you remember sending two men up here to make a map of the country?" asked Leon. "Well, they found it out."

"And did you let those men go back?"

"No, one of them stayed up here," said Leon, who somehow could not find it in his heart to say the man had been killed. "If we destroy the bridge, anybody like you, who is tired of serving under that old rag, won't know that they can get across, and we have nobody to send them to show where the fords are. We don't know, ourselves."

As they drew near to the porch of the hotel,

Leon saw his father standing there. He dismounted and shook him by the hand—he was certain that his father put a little more grip into the shake than usual—and presented Mr. Dawson, who, it is not necessary to say, was received with a hearty welcome.

"The first thing this man wants is his horse," said Leon.

"Was he with us when we captured that wagon-train?" asked Mr. Sprague. "If so, he can have his horse. They have not been given out yet."

"There, sir, you got your horse," added Leon, turning to Mr. Dawson. "Now the next thing is, we want to report. Is the President in his room? Then, father, I want you to come up there with Mr. Dawson. He's got some things to tell you that will astonish you."

His father replied that he didn't see how he was going to be astonished any more than he had been, but followed Leon up the stairs to the President's office. They found the gentleman there just as they had seen him before, with a pair of blue jean pants on, which were tucked in heavy cowhide boots, and no coat on. He greeted Mr. Dawson very cordially and inquired, in his hearty way:

"So you've got tired of serving under a flag that you don't like, and have come over here to cast your lot with us. Well, sir, the best we have got is yours."

"I am well aware of that, Mr. President," said Mr. Dawson. "But there is one thing that I want to post you on at once. It is about that man Dan Newman."

Mr. Knight removed the pen from behind his ear and settled back in his chair. He had been expecting to hear something from Dan Newman for a long time. Mr. Dawson began and told him the whole story of Dan's meeting with the Confederates, his sudden promotion, and all about it, and when he got done there was an expression on the President's face that few people had seen there.

"Well, Dawson, you can go down there and pick out any place you can find to draw your wagon up," said he. "You are right at home here. Sprague, what is your opinion regarding Dan Newman?"

"My opinion is that he ought to be arrested at once," replied Mr. Sprague.

"And after that are you going to try him by a court-martial?"

"That will be just as the men say. If he is not tried by court-martial he will be shipped off among his friends. They can promote him faster than we can," said Mr. Sprague, with a smile.

"Well, get to work at once. Take as many men as can surround Newman's old shanty and make prisoners of those boys. If the old man says too much, bring him along, too. Dawson, I shall send for you presently."

"Very good, sir. I will be on hand when I am wanted."

Mr. Sprague lost no time in getting his men together, and while he was hunting them up Dawson held a short interview with his father.

"Now, you take my horse," said he, "and when we get back we'll get your nag. Of course Leon is going to arrest Newman, and I am going with him. Turn into any open place you can find in the grove, and there

make your camp. You will find them all
friendly here."

Mr. Dawson mounted the horse and led the
wagon down the road, and just then Bud Mc-
Coy came up. Bud was always on hand when
he was wanted. He got so in the habit of
staying close around to Mr. Sprague that it
was not long before the men came to call him
Colonel Sprague's body-guard. But Bud
didn't mind that. He said he got more to do
by being around there than he could anywhere else, and that was what a Union volun-
teer wanted in times like these.

"What's up?" he exclaimed. "What does
the old man want with volunteers?"

"He is going out to arrest Dan Newman,"
said Leon.

"Well, there; I always thought that man
ought to be arrested," said Bud. "He has
been preaching up secession docterings till you
can't rest. What's he been doing now?"

It did not take long for Leon to make Bud
understand the matter, and as he went on to
tell what Dan had been guilty of, the scowl
on the man's face changed to one of furious

hatred. When Leon ceased he struck his fist
into his open palm with a ringing slap.

"You'll go, too, won't you?"

"Of course I'll go. I ain't a-going to stand
no fooling like that. He has said enough to
hang him higher'n Haman."

While they were talking Mr. Sprague was
seen coming at the head of five men whom
he had summoned to make the arrest. We
said he had summoned five men, but the news
of what he wanted to do had gradually worked
its way through the camp until there were
more than twenty men who were slinging on
their bullet-pouches and hurrying to catch up
with those who had been summoned. The
feeling was so great against Newman that all
hands wanted to have a finger in his arrest.
As he passed by the porch of the hotel, Leon,
Tom and Dawson joined him.

"There's one thing about it," said Leon,
looking back at the stalwart fellows behind him.
"No Newman can get away from this party."

"You're mighty right," said one of the
men. "It's a wonder to me that your father
didn't arrest him long ago."

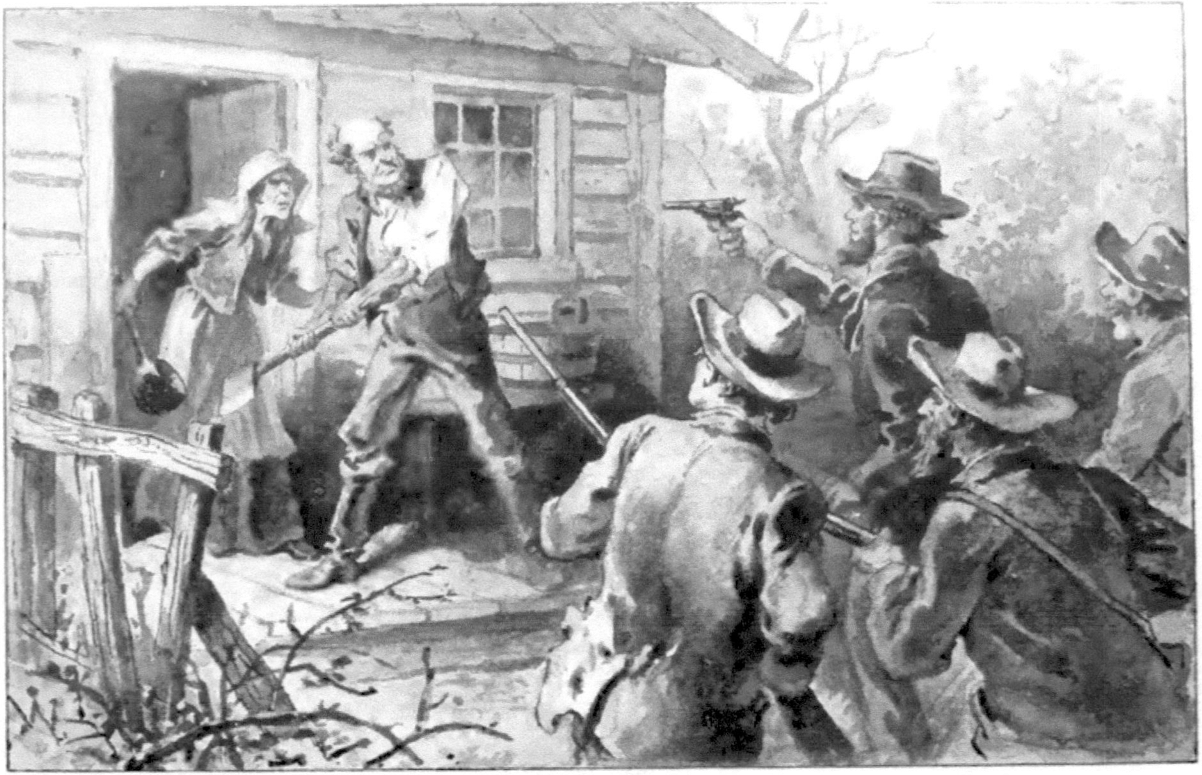

The Newmans in trouble.

"See here, boys," said Mr. Sprague, from the head of the column. "Be quiet and still. Those Newmans are like quails; they'll run and hide if they hear a twig snap. When we come up with the house I'll give the word, and then you know what to do."

Silently the men fell in behind their leader, and swiftly did they work their way toward the shanty. It was probably half a mile to where it was located, and although everybody moved so cautiously that they were certain not a twig snapped, they were not careful enough to conceal their presence from the man they were going to arrest. At length, when Mr. Sprague dashed aside the thicket and stepped out into the little space that surrounded the cabin, they saw Newman and his wife at the door. The former held in his hand an axe, and the other had a skillet, which she flourished to and fro as the men approached.

"What do you want here?" exclaimed Newman, and he lifted his axe threateningly in his hand.

"Surround the house, boys," said Mr. Sprague. "We'll talk to you in a minute."

The most of the men were prompt to act upon this suggestion, and no sooner had Bud McCoy, who was leading one squad, appeared behind the house than he caught a glimpse of Cale Newman in the act of leaving it through the window.

" Ah ! here you are, my fine lad," said Bud, seizing him by the arm. " Where's that brother of yours ?"

" Oh, now, what are you going to arrest me for ?" exclaimed Cale, who turned white and trembled in every limb. " I ain't done nothing. Father, do you see what they are doing ?"

" We hain't done you no harm yet, but just wait until we get back—"

Bud had been on the point of looking in at the window to see if he could discover anything of Dan, when, to his surprise, there came something down on his head which knocked the hat over his eyes and narrowly escaped laying him out flat. It was the skillet in the hands of the old woman ; but Bud didn't wait to see what it was. He straightened himself up by the side of the house, and when the skillet descended a second time he caught

it in his hand and came within an ace of jerking the woman through the window. He
wrested the novel weapon from her and threw
it as far as possible into the bushes.

"Say, old woman, you want to keep your
distance!" said Bud, who was so angry that
he could scarcely talk straight. "You try
that again and I'll have you through that
window!"

By this time the men from the front part
of the house had entered through the door—
the man with his axe didn't make half the battle his wife did—but no Dan was there to be
seen. You will remember that when he came
back he sat down with his pipe to smoke and
think over the perfidy of the captain in giving him promotion when he had no business
to do it, and that he had not yet gone to bed.
While smoking he was startled by a noise in
the bushes. He listened, but the noise increased and grew louder, and in an instant
it flashed upon him that his interview with
the rebel captain was known. That was
enough to start him into the bushes. Giving
his father a sign to call Cale, he was out of

sight in a moment, and all efforts to find him were useless.

"Here's one of them, colonel!" said Bud, coming around the house. " Now, where's the other?"

The man had been disarmed of his axe, and the woman didn't seem to have any more fight left in her, the powerful jerk she got from Bud satisfying her that the best thing she could do was to keep quiet; but they had plenty of talk left in them.

"Of all the mean things that I ever saw this is the beat!" said Mrs. Newman, as she gazed around at the number of men that had come there to take her boy into custody.

"It is an outrage!" chimed in Mr. Newman, stamping about over the floor as if he were almost beside himself. "They come with an army of men to take away one little fellow! I hope you feel duly ashamed of yourselves."

"Let go my coat!" exclaimed Cale to the man who held him tight by his collar to see that he did not escape. "What are you going to do with me?"

"We'll put you in jail; that's what we'll do with you," said the man. "You have preached up secession long enough."

"Say, father, are you going to let that old jail stand?" demanded Cale, trying hard to escape from the grip that held him. "You said that you would cut it down if they took any of us there."

"Where's your brother?" demanded Bud.

"He's gone where you won't find him," retorted Mrs. Newman. "Now, I want you to turn my boy loose."

"We have had enough out of you," said Mr. Sprague, who had looked all around in the hope of finding Dan hidden somewhere in the house. "If you say another word I'll take you along to keep Cale company. You two stay here and watch the cabin, one in front and one at the back," he added, pointing out two of the men he wished to obey his orders. "Don't let Newman and his wife go out of doors, and if Dan comes back here, gobble him up. I will relieve you in a couple of hours. Forward, the rest of us."

Taking Cale along the narrow path that

led through the woods was as much as two men wanted to do, he kicked and struggled so furiously. As long as he remained within reach of his father he constantly appealed to his father to "cut down the jail" so that he could not be confined there, and it was only when Mr. Sprague threatened him with the gag that he condescended to keep still. They hustled him along the half a mile that led to Ellisville, and when they arrived within sight of the grove they found all the men there to see how they had come out. Cale must have listened to some things that astonished him, for he heard one man say that hanging was too good for such as he was, and advocated that he be tied to a tree and left there. He was marched through the crowd of men, some of whom shook their fists in his face, and up the stairs that led to the President's office. Then the men let go of his collar, and in an instant every inch of standing-room was filled. There wasn't the least chance for escape.

"Well, Cale Newman," said the President, taking off his spectacles and settling back in his chair, " you tried to get those Confederates last night to go after our boys."

" I never," began Cale.

" I am not here to argue the matter with you ; I am here to tell you what you have done," said Mr. Knight. " They offered you promotion in case you would do something for them."

" Well, I'll tell you how it was," said Cale, who didn't think that he was betraying his brother by the confession he was about to make. " The captain offered to make me lieutenant, but I didn't think he had any right to do it."

" Ah !" said the President.

" Yes ; and my brother he offered to make captain. Dan was in for it, but I was a little jubius. He offered to show them where Leon and that rebel fellow was, but the captain said he would go on and see how many men they were at the bridge."

" And that was the time they killed Bach Noble," said Mr. Knight, with suppressed fury.

" Well, it was all in war times, wasn't it?"

"War times? What do you mean by that?" ejaculated the President, while a restless movement among the men told that they did not uphold anybody in thus taking the life of a sentry. Bach Noble was one of the most popular lumbermen in the county, and this method of shooting him just because it "was war times" aroused all the anger there was in them. A word from the President would have seen Cale swung up to a tree in less than no time.

"It was war times, wasn't it?" inquired Cale, who seemed to think he had said too much.

"We'll not discuss that. The Confederate captain offered you and your brother promotion. Then what?"

By a little questioning Mr. Knight got at all that had transpired during their interview with the Confederate captain, and the old soldiers that were in there were amazed when they saw how green Dan was. After thinking a moment, he said:

"I don't think that Cale has been guilty of treason. What do you men say to that?"

"No," said a voice. "But he has been giving out docterings that won't go down with this county."

"That's so," chimed in others.

"I acknowledge that," said Mr. Knight. "But I say let's shut him up and keep him until we can catch his brother. He can't be far off."

"I noticed that some of my men went into the bushes to find him," said Mr. Sprague. "Some of them haven't returned yet."

"Very well. We'll shut Cale up until we find that slippery brother, and then we'll examine them both. We'll find a room somewhere in the hotel—I see Bass Kennedy has got his corn in the jail and it would be hardly worth while to take it out for the sake of one prisoner—and, Eph, if you will keep watch of him I will relieve you in a couple of hours."

"Well, say, Knight," began Cale.

"Mister Knight, if you please. I am mister to all such fellows as you are. What were you going to say?"

"I want you to understand that you dassent hang me," said Cale, not daring to venture upon the man's surname again. Like everybody else in the county he had learned to call a man by his name without any fixture to it, and he did not care to begin now. His father had always spoken of him as "Knight," and Cale thought he was as good as the President.

"Dassent, eh?" said Mr. Knight, with a look of surprise. "You will find that we dare do anything."

"But I tell you that my father will tell the folks at Mobile about it," whined Cale, almost ready to cry.

"There you have it. Shut him up. Eph, you want to open the door every time you hear the clock strike, to see if he is there. If there is no further business before the meeting it stands adjourned."

Eph at once seized his prisoner and hurried him before the proprietor of the hotel, who at once hit upon a room that would do for his confinement.

"We'll put him high up, so that he can't get down," said he. "We'll put him up in the third story. Come on."

Taking a key from behind his desk, the proprietor led the way up the stairs until he came to a small room with only one window in it, pushed open the door and stood aside, so that Cale could enter. There was literally no furniture in the room, it all having been removed down-stairs, so that it could be ready to be moved whenever Mr. Faulkner got ready to go to the swamp.

"Now, sir, you'll stay here till you come out to be hung," said Eph, giving him a shove.

"Good mercy me!" exclaimed Mr. Faulkner, opening his eyes in surprise. "Is that what's to become of him? Well, it's a mighty hard death for a young man to die."

"Oh, no, they dassent hang me," said Cale, almost ready to cry again.

"If we do your pap will tell the folks in Mobile about it," said Eph, with a sneer. "Well, you tell your folks in Mobile to go somewhere and do something about it. Didn't you hear what our President said, that we dare do anything?"

"He ain't any more a President than I be," declared Cale, boldly.

" Let me hear you say those words again and I'll begin operations right here!" said Eph. " He's as much of a President as Jeff Davis, and I am not going to hear a word said against him. Go in there!"

" Hold on. He hasn't got a chair. I'll get one."

Mr. Faulkner was gone not more than two minutes and came back with a chair, which was pushed into the room, and then the jailer locked the door and put the key into his pocket. Cale took a look around his prison, and then walked to the window and took a good look there, too. It wasn't a great ways to the ground, and Cale was certain, if his enemies did not put a sentry there to see that he did not drop down and take himself safe off, his escape would be an assured thing. He tried the window, and was gratified to find that it yielded to his touch. Then he walked back to the chair and seated himself upon it.

" Those Union men is mighty smart," he soliloquized. " Because I am three stories up they think I am safe. I'll show them how easy it will be for me to hang by my hands

and drop down. And they talk about hanging me! I'll bet they can't do it."

The muffled tread of the sentry came to his
ears, and finally, when the clock struck, Eph
opened the door to see if he was there.

CHAPTER XIV.

LEON A PRISONER.

"AH!" said Eph, "you're there yet. You are thinking over how you can escape being hung for your treason. Well, that's a good way to put in one's time."

Cale did not answer. He sat with his elbows on his knees and his head bowed upon his hands, and he was thinking deeply—not of how he could escape being hanged, but of where he should go and what he should do in case he made the attempt at escape successful. He had heard Mr. Sprague, when he placed sentinels over his house, one in front and another behind—had heard him tell them not to let his father or mother go out of the house —and he knew it would be foolhardy to go home after that. The sentries would capture him and bring him back to his prison. Eph took an unbounded delight in bothering the boy. He knew that the most that would be done with Cale would be to ship him off among his friends, and that would be the last of him. He glanced at the window to see that it was all right, and then went out, closing the door behind him.

"That fellow keeps telling me that I am going to be hung," said Cale, raising his head and glancing at the door through which Eph had just gone out. "What would I give to be in here at night when he comes in and finds the window open and Cale Newman gone? I tell you that would be worth some money. Now, if I could only find Dan. He would know where to go and what to do."

For long hours Cale sat there and listened to the tread of the sentinel, and every time the clock struck down-stairs he lifted his head and looked at the sentinel, who opened the door and looked in. They were changed every two hours, and finally it began to grow dark. By that time Cale began to grow hungry, and while he was thinking about it the door opened and in came Mr. Faulkner, whose hands were filled with bedclothes and eatables.

" I can't bear to have any man around me who I know is hungry, even if he is going to be hung," said he. " Let me put this bread and meat on the chair. There's something for you to lie down on. It's pretty rough, I know, but I expect you get rougher at home. Good-night and pleasant dreams."

Cale examined the bedclothes as well as he could in the dark, and found that he had a pillow and, what was better than all, two quilts, which he could tear up, fasten to the chair, and thus let himself down from the window. He chuckled to himself and devoted his attention to the viands. By the time he had got through the sentry opened the door, and Cale saw a light streaming in.

"Oh, I'm here yet," said Cale.

" I know you are," said the man. " And you're going to stay there until you come out to be hung."

" All right. But you won't hang me until you catch my brother. He had the most to do with talking with that captain."

" No matter. You was knowing to it all, and that counts for a heap against you."

The sentry closed the door, and in an instant Cale was on his feet. Things had to be done in a hurry, and quietly, too, for in an hour more the man would look in to see if his prisoner was all right. It was something of a job to tear the quilts; but fortunately he had them all done at last, and when he knotted them together he was glad to see how long they were. He didn't think he would be obliged to drop more than ten feet.

The next thing was opening the window and fastening the quilts to the chair; but he accomplished it without alarming the sentinel, and drawing in a long breath, he launched himself over the side of the window and heard the chair bang loudly as he threw his weight upon the quilts. In his haste the quilts did not do much toward assisting him to the bottom, for he slid rapidly down them and landed all in a heap under the window just as the sentry opened the door to see what was going on.

"Are you there yet, Cale?" asked the man, as he looked all around the room. "By gracious, he has gone!"

With two jumps the man reached the window and leaned over and looked out. Everything was concealed by darkness, and even the crouching Cale, who was close to the wall, right under the man's gaze, escaped his notice. Then the man thought of his rifle. He rushed back into the hall and got it, fired it once out of the window, and then went down-stairs to tell the men what an extraordinary escape Cale had made. This was the time for the prisoner to make the most of his opportunity. He arose to his feet and made good time across the narrow cotton-field that lay between him and the woods, and he never ceased running until he reached the banks of a little bayou a mile back in the forest, where he stopped and sat down to rest.

"There, sir," said Cale, wiping the big drops of perspiration from his forehead. " I've done it; as sure as the world I have done it. That is the first time I ever was put in jail for something I didn't do. Let them get somebody else and talk about hanging them. Now, if I could only find Dan."

Cale did not take very long to rest himself

before he got upon his feet again and cautiously worked his way toward his father's shanty. The darkness had no effect upon Cale, for he took his course as straight as he could have done in the daytime. The sentries might have been removed by this time, but all the same he made his way stealthily through the bushes, as though the sentries were there and liable at any minute to jump out and make a prisoner of him. It would never do to be captured again, for the next time he would be put where it would be impossible for him to get away. But he walked right onto Dan, who had been up to the house for the same purpose; that is, he wanted to see if there was any chance for him to communicate with his father. As Cale was working his way cautiously through the bushes, going so still that he could not hear the thicket rattle behind him, he was startled out of a year's growth by hearing a voice close at his side mutter:

"I'll be dog-gone if there ain't Cale!"

"D—Dan, is that you?" stammered Cale, so overjoyed that he could scarely speak.

" You're right, it's me," said Dan. " Where you been ?"

"They had me shut up in jail," was the answer.

" In the calaboose?"

" No, in the hotel; and they left one window there without any sentry to guard it, and I just come out."

" Well, sir, I will say hereafter that you've got pluck. But come up here. I've got something to show you."

Cale began feeling his way toward the place where Dan was, and in a few moments he placed his hand upon his shoulder. But there was something else that he touched there. It was a revolver.

" Why, Dan, where have you been to get that?" asked Cale, in surprise.

"I have not only got that, but the man what owns it," returned Dan, with the same pride he would have exhibited had he won an enemy's colors in battle. " I've got Leon Sprague."

Cale was so astonished that he couldn't say anything just then.

"While you have been shut up in jail I have been working for the glorious cause," said Dan. "I got him just as easy as falling off a log. I've heard so much tell about Leon's courage that I was kinder afraid to tackle him; but pshaw! I handled him as easy as you would handle a baby."

Let us now go back for a moment and tell what had happened to Dan while Cale was being shut up in the hotel. When he came back from holding his interview with the Confederate captain he did not go to bed, as Cale did, but filled his pipe with negro-twist and lay down on the ground to smoke and think. He lay there for an hour—he didn't want any breakfast; besides, he was getting tired of corn-bread and bacon, anyway—building his air-castles and dreaming how proud he would be if he could only hold a position equal to the captain's.

"Boots on his feet that came up to his knees and gloves on his hands that came clear up to there," said Dan, motioning with his finger to a point on his arm that came clear up to his elbow. "And didn't he handle that horse gay? She was a frisky animal, but he managed her as easy as if he was seated in a rocking-chair. And, dog-gone him, he went and fooled me!"

By this time his father had eaten his breakfast and came out to his usual place on the threshold, pipe a-going. He took a few pulls at the tobacco, cast his eye up to the clouds to see what the weather was going to be, and was then ready to begin his topic of conversation.

"The South is going to whip," said he. "It don't stand to reason that one county in the midst of a State that's in rebellion is going to whip all the counties around her."

"But, father, do you think they are going to fight?" asked Dan.

"Fight! No, they won't. I only wish I could get my position as colonel. I would show them how to clean these men out."

"And the men here wouldn't give you the position of Secretary of War," said Dan. "What would you have done if you had got that position?"

"Eh? Well, I would have done a heap more than that old Sprague is doing, I can tell you that. I would have made you boys officers, to begin with. You would make a bully captain, Dan."

"That's just what I think, and—and—I ought to be one, too."

"Yes; and think of the money we would make. That's what makes me so down on all these officers. That must be worth six or eight thousand dollars a year."

"Whew!" whistled Dan. "And old Sprague is making that much?"

"I have no doubt of it. At any rate they might have offered it to me, and I would ask how much they was going to give. If the price didn't suit me—What's the matter?" added Mr. Newman, seeing that Dan removed his pipe from his mouth and sat up straight on the ground. "Do you hear anything?"

"Father, there is some one coming along through the bushes," said Dan, involuntarily lowering his voice to a whisper. "And they are coming fast, too."

Mr. Newman listened, and presently he heard the faint rustle of the thicket as a body of men worked its way through them. It was still very faint, but it came plainly to his ears.

"I've got to go," said Dan, hurriedly. "You call Cale."

"What have you been a-doing?" said his father, in astonishment. "You stay where you are, and if they should put one of you in the calaboose I'd cut it down as soon as I could get to it with my axe."

"I know, but I'll tell you at some future time what I have been a-doing. Call Cale."

Dan turned and made a dive for the bushes, and no sooner had he disappeared than Mr. Sprague came in sight. While Mr. Sprague was holding his colloquy with the father and mother, who stood at the door, and Bud Mc-Coy had gone around the house in time to catch Cale Newman coming out of the window, Leon noticed the pipe which Dan had thrown down, and which was not yet extinguished. He took a few pulls at it, and it went as lively as it ever did.

"Dan is out here in the bushes," said he to Tom and young Dawson, who remained close at his side. "Let's go out and capture him."

"All right," said Dawson. " Let us spread out a little, so that we will cover more ground. Be in a hurry, now."

Leon was out of sight before he had ceased speaking. He made no attempt to draw his revolver, for he did not think it would be worth while. He had always known Dan, and knew him to be a lazy, worthless fellow, but he was little prepared for what happened afterward. He was looking everywhere for Dan—he must have been half a mile or more from his friends by this time—when suddenly, as he pressed down a thicket to look into it, he felt something on his back and he was thrown violently on his face. Knowing in a minute what it was, his hand went behind him, but he felt some fingers at work with his own, and his revolver was torn from his grasp. A feeling of horror came over him when he knew that he was disarmed. The weight was lifted off his back, he was rolled over, so that he could see what he had to contend with, and his own revolver was looking him in the face. It was cocked, too, and it needed only the pressure of a finger to make all things

20

blank to him. It was Dan Newman who was bending above him. His face was very pale, but there was a glint in his eyes that spoke volumes.

"Not a word out of you," said Dan, fiercely. "Not a word out of you. Roll over, with your face downwards."

Leon had no alternative but to obey. There was shoot in Dan's eyes, and Leon saw it. He rolled over, and Dan arose to his feet and took off his coat, and then his shirt, which he proceeded to tear up into small strips. It was then a task of no difficulty to bind Leon's arms. It was done in less time than it takes to tell it, and then Leon was pulled to a sitting posture, while Dan stood and looked down at him.

"I've got you, ain't I?" said Dan, who hardly knew whether he stood on his head or his heels. "Now, what are you going to do about it?"

"I don't see that I can do anything," said Leon, wondering if he was to give up and remain a prisoner in the hands of this man. "You can do what you please with me."

"And it pleases me to take you down to Mobile and give you up to our folks," said Dan. "Mebbe they'll think that my company is in a condition for me to command it. It ain't often that a man can get the son of a Secretary of War prisoner, is it?"

Leon did not care to talk any longer. He knew what Dan was going to do with him, and he did not feel much elated over it. He sat there in silence and watched Dan, who was grinning all over and hardly knew whether or not his good fortune had stood him so well in stead or not. He wanted to be sure about it, and so began a conversation with Leon; or rather, he talked and Leon listened. He examined his revolver repeatedly, took aim at certain spots on the trees, and acted for all the world like one who was bereft of his senses. Having spent an hour in this way, and being at last satisfied that Mr. Sprague had looked around the house without being able to find him, Dan thought he would go home and hold a short consultation with his father.

"The old man will be dreadful glad I've

got you," said Dan, wondering how he was going to leave Leon so that he wouldn't arouse the whole neighborhood by his yelling, "and perhaps he'll think I had better do something else with you. I want to go home and get a shirt, too, for these nights are mighty damp."

"Does the old man believe as you do?" asked Leon. He thought it would be policy to learn all he could concerning the belief of the squatter's family, for he did not expect to remain a prisoner all his life. When he returned he would know how to go to work. The first thing he did would be to put all that family under arrest.

"Of course the old man believes as I do," said Dan. "The South is going to send men enough in here to whip you. I tell you, Leon, you fellows are crazy."

"What are you going to do with that?" asked Leon, referring to a piece of shirt which Dan was carefully folding.

"I am going to use it as a gag," said Dan. "You must think that I am a pretty smart man to go away and leave you with your mouth wide open. Now, I guess this will do."

"I assure you that I won't halloo," exclaimed Leon, who did not like to have any of Dan's clothing in his mouth. "Try me and see."

"No, I reckon I'd best be on the safe side. If you will let this go into your mouth, well and good; if not, it will have to go in anyway," said Dan, picking up his revolver.

There was but one course open to Leon, and he submitted to have a wad of shirt tucked into his mouth that almost made him sick. It was tied hard and fast, too, so that he could not get rid of it. Dan next turned his attention to his feet, which he bound with another piece of shirt, and fastened them to a tree so that he could not get up. Then he looked at the way his hands were fastened and got up, shoving the revolver into his pocket.

"I won't be gone but a little while," said Dan, straightening up the thicket in which Leon lay. "I reckon I'll bring the old man back here with me. You will be glad to see him, I know. My father might have been topnotch in this county if it hadn't been for your old man. But no, they wouldn't have him for

Secretary of War, and now they see what they made by it."

Dan took one more look at his prisoner to see that his bonds were all safe, and then went away. He was hardly out of sight before Leon began tugging and twisting at his fastenings in the hope of being able to get rid of some of them; but the harder he worked the more he exhausted himself. Dan had done his work well, and finally Leon gave it up as a bad job. Dan was gone fully an hour, and when he came back Leon noticed that he didn't have a shirt on. He noticed, too, that he was in pretty bad humor.

"They have got two sentries up there to the house, dog-gone them, and I guess they must be waiting for me," said Dan, as he began to undo the fastenings that confined Leon's mouth. "They think I'll come back after awhile, but they don't know Dan Newman."

When Leon felt the gag removed from his mouth he coughed once or twice and acted as if he was about to expel the contents of his stomach; but after awhile he was able to reply to Dan's question.

"It makes you sick, don't it?" asked Dan.

"Yes, and that shirt would make anybody sick. I suppose they have got the sentries there in order to catch you when you come back."

"But I say they don't know me," retorted Dan. "I didn't go near the house till I had looked around a bit, and then I saw those men there and I came away. They won't let me get even a shirt. I wonder if they have got Cale?"

"Where was Cale when the men came up to capture you?"

"He was in the house and fast asleep."

"Then of course they have got him. He didn't come out of the front door or I would have seen them. It rather bothers a man to be up all night, don't it?"

"Who said I was up all night?" asked Dan.

"I do. You were up all night, and held a conference with that rebel captain."

"Who's got a better right? You fellows here in this county won't give me anything, and I have a right to go where I can get to be a captain."

"Well, untie my feet, will you?" said Leon, who didn't seemed disposed to discuss this matter with Dan. "You have got them fastened to that sapling until they hurt me."

Dan was accommodating enough to untie his feet, but he didn't make any move towards untying his hands. After that he sat down and held a long talk with his prisoner, who, considering the situation in which he was placed, took the matter very coolly. He knew he couldn't get away, but there would come other times, he thought, when his hands would be at liberty, and then he would try his best at escape. They passed the afternoon in this way, and finally it began to grow dark. Leon was getting hungry, and he knew that Dan was bothered the same way, and consequently he was relieved when his captor said he would try and reach home again and get something.

"But first I must tie you up," said he.

"Now, what's the use of going to all that trouble?" said Leon, who couldn't bear the thought of having that shirt thrust into his mouth for the second time. "I didn't halloo before."

"No, of course you didn't," said Dan, with a laugh. "'Cause why, the gag wouldn't let you. I won't be gone but a little while, and then I will untie you."

Leon yielded with a very bad grace while Dan was placing the gag in his mouth; and well he might, for there was the revolver, lying within easy reach of his captor's hand. He was tied up just as he was before, and Dan, after a few parting words, disappeared in the darkness.

Oh, how I wish Tom Howe knew where I was!" panted Leon, after he had tried in vain to get rid of some of his bonds. "I'll bet you that I wouldn't be here much longer. Now, what will be done with me if I am given up to the rebels? Beyond a doubt I'll be hanged, for of course they will take revenge on my father through me. Well, if I go up there will be one less to fight them."

Dan was gone longer than he was before, and when he came back Leon was surprised to hear him talking to somebody. Of course, it was so dark that he couldn't see anything, but as his captor drew near he began to recognize Cale Newman's voice. Leon was thunderstruck. He did not know where Cale had been confined, but by some inadvertence on the part of his jailers he had got away. Leon was impatient to hear Cale's version of it.

CHAPTER XV.

A FRIEND IN NEED.

"WELL, sir, you have got him as easy as falling off a log, haven't you?" said Cale, gleefully, as he sat down on the ground beside Leon and passed his hands over him from head to foot. "It's Leon, as sure as I am alive, and you've got him tied up hard and fast," he added, as he felt of the prisoner's face.

"Hold on till I take the gag out of his mouth," said Dan. "He talks as sassy as you please."

"He does? Then I would punch him in the mouth for it," said Cale, who showed that he could be brave enough when he had the power.

"No, that won't do," said Dan, who forthwith proceeded to take the shirt out of Leon's mouth. "You are an officer—"

"Oh, get out!" sneered Cale. "I'll bet you when our officers get him into their hands they'll treat him worse than we will."

"They didn't treat them so at Mobile when we saw those prisoners brought in there," retorted Dan. "We are officers, and I'll bet you that I will get some men to command when I give this fellow up."

Leon took a few moments in which to get over the effect of the shirt being in his mouth, after which he was ready to talk to Cale; for, as we said, he was impatient to hear his version of the story of his escape.

"How did you get away, Cale?" said he.

"You thought they had me hard and fast, didn't you?" said Cale, shaking his fist at Leon. "Well, they didn't. They had me in the third story of the hotel, and once, when the sentinel wasn't looking, I tore up the quilts they had given me to sleep on and dug out."

"Didn't they have any sentry under the window?" said Leon, astonished at such a want of foresight on the part of the Union men.

"No, they didn't; and I took note of that

the first thing when I went in. I stayed up close to the building while the sentry was looking out, and when he fired his gun to let them know that I had gone I dug out across the cotton-field until I struck the woods. I wondered what I should do without Dan, and I run onto him the first thing. Now, what are you going to do with this fellow?"

"As soon as it comes daylight we'll take him down to Mobile."

"Ah! that's the place for you," said Cale, giving Leon a pinch. "You won't be riding around on that horse of yours and making us all wish we had one, too. You've got the revolver, Dan, and now I'll have the horse. I wish father could get away from the house. Mebbe he would make you stretch hemp right where you are."

"Well, Cale, as I didn't have any sleep last night I'll lie down," said Dan. "Do you reckon you can watch him while I doze a little?"

"You're right, I can," said Cale, with savage emphasis. "Give me your revolver. Now, let us see him make a move to get away.

I'll stretch him out so stiff that he won't be of any use down there at Mobile."

"That fellow has got a mighty nice shirt on that I'd like to have," said Dan, as he drew his coat about him, but couldn't confine it, for it had no buttons. "As soon as it comes daylight I'll make him shed that linen. I ain't a-going among our officers with no shirt on."

"Why don't you make him take it off now?" said Cale. "I'll watch him so that he can't run away."

"No, I guess I'd better be on the safe side. Let it go until to-morrow."

Leon was glad that he had such a reputation. He was able to sleep warm for one night at least. His clothing was comfortable, and his coat being buttoned up to the chin, and being protected from the keen wind by the thicket in which he was placed, he slept as warm as he would if he had been at home. The only thing was, his hands hurt him. He knew it would be of no use to appeal to Dan, so he gritted his teeth and said nothing. When Leon awoke it was broad daylight.

Both his captors were asleep. The revolver that Cale threatened him with was lying by his side, and all he needed was his hands at liberty to turn the tables on them in good shape.

"By gracious!" muttered Leon; and once more he began trying the effect of Dan's knots. But they were there to stay. He could not move his hands at all. "Halloo! here," he added aloud. "Do you want to go to sleep and let me run off? I am cold, and it is time I was moving."

"Well, now, I'll be shot!" said Dan, opening his eyes and rubbing them, while Cale made a clutch for the revolver. "It was good of you not to go away."

"You can thank yourself for it," said Leon. "If I could have got away I'd had my revolver in my hands, and then you would have gone to Ellisville."

"Yes; and what would we be doing all that time?" said Cale.

"You shut up!" answered Dan. "You said you could watch him, and so you did. You went fast asleep watching him."

"I only just closed my eyes, that's all," protested Cale. "If he'd a-made any move—"

"Oh, shut up, and let's be moving," interrupted Dan. "The sooner we get him where our officers are, the sooner we'll be rid of him and get something to eat."

Leon found that he was somewhat stiff when he came to get upon his feet, but before they had gone half a mile he stepped off with his accustomed free stride. Dan led the way with the revolver in his hand, and he was considerate enough to keep the bushes from striking his prisoner in the face. Leon knew how far it was to the river, but the distance seemed to lengthen out wonderfully since he last passed that way. He kept a bright lookout in the hope that he would meet some of the Union men, but in this he was disappointed.

"Now, right up that way, not more than a mile, is a company of your fellows stationed there to watch the bridge," said Dan, stopping at length. "How much would you give to holler and bring them down here?"

"Don't talk to him that way," exclaimed

Cale, disturbed by the thought. "The first thing you know he will holler."

"Then this revolver will settle his hash," said Dan, savagely. "Let him holler, if he wants to."

A little further on came the river, whereupon Dan backed off for a few feet and told Cale to undo the prisoner's hands. Cale was prompt to obey, and the first thing that Leon did when he felt his arms free was to stretch them above his head, as if he enjoyed having them at liberty once more. He did not make a motion to escape, for there was the revolver looking him in the face.

"Now take off your clothes, you two, and be ready to swim the river," said Dan.

"Am I going over there with him?" asked Cale, and he was thoroughly frightened at the prospect.

"You go first, and when you get over there you can pick up a club. I'll keep his clothes behind with me, and the revolver, too, and if he wants to run off naked let him go. I bet you he'll be glad to have his clothes again."

The two boys lost no time in taking off

21

their clothes, and there was one thing that
Leon didn't like pretty well. He would lose
his shirt by the operation; but there was no
help for it that he could see. In due time the
boys were all over, and Leon saw his shirt go
upon the back of Dan Newman.

"There, now, I feel like myself again," exclaimed Dan. "I can go among our officers
now and have a shirt on. Button your coat
up tight, Leon, and no wind can get in. Now
you must have your hands tied again."

This much being accomplished, the prisoner
and his captors went ahead at a more rapid
pace, the woods being more open, and they
held their course parallel with the main road.
Their object was to get below the bend, where
they would be out of sight of the sentries.
At the end of half an hour they emerged
from the woods, and striking the road went
on their way with increased speed.

"Don't you know some place along here
where you can go and get something to eat?"
asked Leon. "I could travel twice as fast if
I had something on my stomach."

"I was just thinking of that thing myself,"

answered Dan. "I am going to stop at the first house I meet. And remember, Leon, no trying to get away," he added, showing the revolver he still carried in his hand.

Leon didn't make any reply. He knew now that he was beyond all reach of help, and after he got something to eat—that was the first thing on the programme—he must make up his mind to face "our officers," who wouldn't be apt to treat him any too well. But first one house was passed and then another, and as neither Dan nor Cale had the courage to go in and beg something to eat, Leon finally gave it up as a bad job, and thought he would have to go on to Mobile before he could get a mouthful to stay his appetite. At last they came along to a place that Leon remembered. The first time he saw it there was a pleasant farm-house, and corn-cribs and negro quarters in abundance; but now everything had been given up to the flames, and some of the ruins were still smoking.

"Well, I declare, somebody has been burned out, here!" said Dan. " Is this the place where you came last night, Leon?"

"I was around here somewhere," replied Leon.

"Then here's where that rebel fellow lives," continued Dan. "It serves him just right. Before I take an oath to support a government and then go back on it I would deserve to be burned out myself."

Leon did not make any reply to this, for he thought that Dan might be burned out and still not lose a great deal by it; but he did not want to say so for fear of making him angry. His captors had treated him all right so far, but he knew what the consequences would be if he got them down on him. While he was thinking about it, and wondering how Tom Howe and young Dawson would look upon his absence—they certainly would know he had been captured—they came suddenly around another bend in the road, and saw before them a long line of horsemen who were travelling as though they had some place to reach before night. He took a second glance at them, and saw that they were all dressed in Confederate uniform.

"There's some of our men now!" exclaimed

Dan, so overjoyed that he took off his hat and waved it to them. "But, Cale, that ain't our captain in front, is it? He was a big man, and this is a little one. There must be a whole regiment of them, and if that is the case they are going up to whip the Union men."

Leon's heart fairly came up into his mouth. He would know soon what the rebels were going to do with him. The Confederates discovered them as soon as they came around the bend, and they kept a close watch of them until they came up. The man in front certainly was not a captain. He had a mark on his collar that no one had ever seen before.

"Well, boys, where are you going?" inquired the man; and they found out before the interview was over that his men called him colonel. Of course, Dan looked at him with a great deal of respect after he found out what his rank was.

"Yes, we've got a Yankee prisoner here," said Dan, who was expected to do all the talking. "He is the son of the Secretary of War up in Jones county."

"He is, hey?" exclaimed the colonel, beginning to show some interest in the matter. "Well, we'll send him right down to Mobile the first thing we do. Are you from Jones county?"

Dan replied that he was.

"Then you must know all about the men up there," said the colonel. "How many have they got, anyway?"

"A thousand fighting men," replied Dan. "And I tell you, you will want more men than you have got here to whip them."

"I don't know about that. We have got a thousand men here in this regiment, and they are all disciplined, and when they draw up against your crowd of bushwhackers you will see some scattering. Now, we want to get across that bridge; how far is it from here?"

"You will find it right straight up this road about twenty miles. You want to be careful, because they have got ten men hidden up there, and they are all good shots."

"We will take care of them, don't you fear. Now, after we get across the bridge we must deploy in line of battle; how far will we have to go before we can strike their main line?"

"It is ten miles from the bridge to Ellisville, and when you get there you will find all the men you want."

"Well, now, see here: suppose you go with me? You know all the crooks and turns of the road that leads—"

"But, Captain," began Dan.

"This gentleman is a colonel," interrupted the man who rode by his commanding officer's side.

"A colonel!" exclaimed Dan, somewhat surprised to find that he had found the man who held the position his father was working for. "Colonel, I am glad to meet you," he added, advancing and thrusting out a dirty, begrimed hand to the man, who merely reached down and touched the tips of it with his fingers. "My father calculates to hold the position of colonel when he has delivered up all the head men of the county into your hands. But, Colonel, I want to see this man located in Mobile. I had a heap of trouble to gobble him, and I don't want to lose him."

But that wasn't the principal reason why Dan did not want to go back. Some of the men at the bridge would be certain to recognize him, and if he escaped the bullets which they would send after him he would not dare go home.

"We'll take care of him," said the colonel. "The son of the Secretary of War is too valuable to lose."

"What do you reckon you will do with him, Colonel?"

"Hang him, probably."

Leon heard the words, and looked around at Dan and Cale. Dan smiled upon him as if he had just heard a glorious piece of news, but Cale was grinning with delight. He said to himself: "If Leon is going to be hung I'll have his horse."

"Adjutant, pick out a good, trusty man to march this fellow to Mobile," said the colonel. "A faithful fellow, mind you."

"Captain Cullom, have you such a man in your company?" said the adjutant, turning to the officer who commanded the advance of the line.

"Yes, sir. Ballard, step out here!"

The man referred to, who was one of the

leading fours of his company, urged his horse to the front and brought his hand to his hat with a military salute. Then he slung his carbine upon his shoulder and drew his revolver from his belt. Leon looked at him, and he told himself that if he had been a rebel he would have trusted that man with his life. He was young, not more than twenty-four, but he was from Texas, and had been a cowboy all his life; consequently he was a little better clad than the majority of his comrades.

"Ballard, you take this man before General Lowery and tell him that I sent him," said the colonel. "Tell him that he is the son of a high-up man of Jones county, and let him do what he pleases with him."

"Very good, sir," answered Ballard.

"I wouldn't untie his hands," continued the colonel, "but you have got your revolver in your hands and can easily stop him in case he runs for the woods."

"Very good, sir," replied Ballard. "Forward, march! Go off at one side of the road so as to be out of the way of the column."

"Now, two of the men must make room for these boys," said the colonel. "Forward!"

Dan and Cale were quickly provided with places to ride behind two of the cavalrymen, the adjutant shouted "Forward!" with all the strength of his lungs, and Leon stood at one side of the road and watched the men as they marched by. He had heard a good deal about Texas, and he finally came to the conclusion that all the soldiers were from that region. They were all long-haired, and many of them were unacquainted with combs, but there were some among them who were dressed like his cowboy, with handkerchiefs around their necks, broad tarpaulins on their heads and fine boots on their feet. A good many of them had a word to say to Ballard and his prisoner, and they were not of the kind that was calculated to encourage Leon. When Leon wasn't looking Ballard raised his pistol and took a deliberate aim at his head—a proceeding that was welcomed by shouts from all the men who saw it.

"That's the way; shoot him down!" shouted

one of the soldiers. "There will be one less Yank for us left to fight, anyway."

"Now, sonny, I guess all the men have passed," said Ballard. "Take the middle of the road and travel ahead as if you were going for the doctor. Mobile is a long ways from here."

Leon accordingly took to the road and plodded along at his best pace; but he was wearied, and his hands hurt him so that he was on the point of urging his captor to untie them for a little while, so that he could stretch his arms and get the kinks out of them. He walked along until he had got around the first bend, out of sight of the cavalrymen, and then Ballard, after looking all around and up and down the road, to make sure that there was nobody in sight, leaned forward and whispered to him:

"Say, sonny, go into the woods."

Leon turned around and faced him. He had heard that was one way the Confederates had of getting rid of their prisoners, namely, to take them into the woods and "lose" them. They would shoot them down and leave them there. Leon couldn't help himself if Ballard had decided to lose him, for his hands were tied.

"What will I go in there for?" he asked, and one wouldn't suppose that his life was in danger, to hear him talk.

"Go into the woods quick!" said Ballard. "I'm Union."

The revulsion of feeling was so great that Leon staggered and would have fallen to the ground if Ballard had not ridden up and caught him by the collar.

"Go in there quick before some one sees you!" said Ballard, looking up and down the road as he spoke. "I wouldn't hurt the hair of your head. I've wanted to get with those Jones county people ever since I have been here, and now I have got a chance at last. Go into the woods quick as you can walk. I'll untie your hands in there."

Leon waited to hear no more, but dived straight into the bushes, and he never stopped until he had gone half a mile from the road. But fast as he went, Ballard was close behind him. When he stopped his captor dismounted

and pulled a big bowie-knife from his boot.
One blow was enough, and Leon's arms were
free.

"Ballard, I never shall forget you!" said
Leon, and his voice was somewhat husky as
he spoke. "I have been wondering how I
should get away, but I never thought that
you would help me. You are a friend indeed.
But first I want to know if you have anything
to eat in your haversack? I haven't had a
bite since yesterday."

Ballard at once unslung his haversack, and
while Leon was regaling himself on the corn-
bread and bacon, which tasted wonderfully
good to him, he told Leon how he happened
to go into the service, while he knew that the
South was going to be utterly impoverished.
He owned a fine cattle-ranch in Texas, and
when the Southern men around him began to
talk of going into her service he found that
he had to go, too, or run the risk of stretching hemp.

"I didn't want to go for a long time," said
Ballard, "and when I found that my neighbors were all giving in their names, and began

to look cross-eyed at me and make remarks that people who were not for us were against us, I saw it was high time I was doing something; so I got an Englishman to take care of my place, and here I am. I tell you, there is a lot of men in the rebel army that think just the same as I do."

"Let them come over into our county and we'll treat them right," said Leon. "Father says we will have at least ten thousand men by-and-by, and it is going to take more than double that number of men to whip us. Now, Ballard, I am much obliged to you for this breakfast, and I am now able to go on. Are you going to take your horse with you?"

"Oh, I couldn't think of going anywhere without that horse," said Ballard, hastily. "I'll warrant that if the rebels went by within ten feet of us he wouldn't say a word."

Leon at once stepped out at his old pace, and Ballard kept close behind him. The woods were so thick that they couldn't stop to do much talking, and by the time it began to grow dark they were on the banks of the creek.

"Now, we are half way home," said Leon. "I would like to know just how that cavalry came out in attacking our men. I've listened every once in a while, but I didn't hear any sound of rifles or carbines."

"Probably they are too far away for us to hear them," said Ballard. "If your men will fight—"

"Oh, they will fight, and there are some of them with us who have repeatedly declared that they won't take any prisoners. If they drive our men back to the swamp they are whipped, sure. By gracious! what's that? It sounds like a couple of horses coming through the woods."

Ballard took his horse by the bridle to hold his head down in case he wanted to call to them and listened intently. Soon the measured tread of the horses could be heard coming through the woods, and in a few minutes a couple of rebels appeared on the opposite bank of the creek and but a short distance above them. One of the Confederates had no hat on, his left arm was hanging loose by his side and his companion was holding him on his horse.   They paused for a few moments, as if they didn't know what to do with the creek in front of them, and then the uninjured one urged the horses in, and in a few strokes of the hoofs they were safe across.

"I'll tell you what's the matter with our side," said Ballard, as soon as the two rebels had disappeared in the bushes. "We have been whipped!"

"Do you mean to say that our fellows have whipped the cavalry?" inquired Leon, and he was surprised and delighted to hear it.

"That is just what I mean.   If the cavalry had been successful they would have kept to the road and taken some prisoners with them; but their being scattered in this way makes me think that they have been worsted.   You saw that man who was being held on his horse?   Well, he was wounded."

"We have got to swim the creek before we can get over," said Leon.   "I am impatient to see how my father came out.   Take off your clothes and hold them above your head. I'll carry your carbine for you."

Leon worked in earnest now, for his father

had been in danger and he was not there to
share it. In hardly less time than it takes to
tell it he was on the other side of the bayou
and pulling on his clothes. Ballard was not
very far behind him, and seeing how impatient Leon was he donned his uniform with
all possible haste, after which they struck out
for Ellisville.

CHAPTER XVI.

A FIGHT AND ITS RESULTS.

LET us now return to the cavalrymen and see how they came out in their assault on the Union men who had been left to guard the bridge, and particularly to tell how Dan and Cale felt when they found themselves going back among those who would be sure to know them. Cale was frightened, and consequently he said nothing, but Dan was just scared enough to have plenty of talk in him.

"Take that man up behind you," said Captain Cullom, addressing himself to one of the leading fours of his company.

"Up you come with a jump," said the man, reaching down to catch Dan by the hand.

"Oh, now, I tell you I don't want to get up there," said Dan. "Those people at the bridge will surely know me, and I'll be tumbled off with the first volley you get."

"Get on up there," said Captain Cullom, and he reached over as if he was going to draw his sword.

"Give us your hand," said the man, getting impatient. "Now throw your leg over the back of the horse. You are Southerner enough to do that."

Dan finally made out to get on the cavalry-man's horse, but it was more the effects of the sword, which had leaped half-way out of its scabbard while the captain was talking to him. Cale was already seated behind his man, and in response to the adjutant's order, "Forward!" they moved toward the bridge. Dan was more than half-inclined to cry when he found that he must go whether he wanted to or not, and the man he was with began to torment him.

"Oh, they will give it to you if they catch you up there," said he, in a tone so low that the captain couldn't hear it. "Say, Charlie, you remember what they done to those two fellows they caught down to Mobile?"

" You 're right, I do," replied the man thus addressed. "They hung 'em up to the nearest tree."

" What did they do that for?" asked Dan.

" Because they wanted to betray their friends into our hands," said the man.

" But these ain't friends of mine," replied Dan. " I've been down on them ever since I have been here."

" No matter. You know what we will do to them if we catch them, and the others will serve you the same way. I would rather be in my boots than in yours."

" But you are going to lick them, ain't you?"

" Lick them? Of course we are. That's what we are going up here for. Have you got any friends there?"

" I've got a father and a mother."

" Then they had better get out. We're going to sweep everything clean. There won't be hide nor hair left of a Union man to-night."

" Now, if you will let me get off and go through the woods," said Dan, " I can warn my relatives."

"Can't do it," said the man, shaking his head. "Didn't you hear what the captain said? If you were in the service you would know how to obey orders."

"Silence in the ranks!" commanded Captain Cullom, and this put a stop to all conversation between them, although Dan had many things that he wanted to say.

After this they rode along in a sort of a fox trot, but Dan noticed that they didn't take as much pains to go quietly as the squad had done the night before. By the time they got to the bend Dan was certain that the pickets had heard them and taken to the bushes, and when they got around it in plain view of the bridge there was not a sentinel in sight. But before they had gone many feet along the road a voice called out:

"Halt! Who comes there?"

"Draw sabres and revolvers!" shouted the colonel, and the order was repeated by the adjutant, who galloped back along the column and yelled out the command as he went. "Forward! Charge!"

In a second Dan was flying along the road

faster than he had ever travelled on horseback before, and in another second the line was thrown into confusion by a discharge of rifles and carbines from the woods on each side of the bridge. The shots were well-aimed, too, for each man was sure of his mark. The colonel and his horse went down, and so did the two men who were carrying Dan and Cale double. The leading four were also badly cut up, and before the major could get up to command in place of his colonel a second discharge followed, which came within an ace of putting the column to a rout. Dan and Cale were on their feet as soon as they struck the ground, the former with his left arm hanging loose and the latter with a bullet-hole through both cheeks.

"I've got it now! I've got it now!" moaned Dan, and when he tried to raise his arm he saw that the lower part of it was useless.

"And I, too!" yelled Cale. "What's the matter with my face, Dan? I can't hardly talk."

But Dan wasn't staying around there to tell Cale what was the matter with his face.

In fact he didn't think anything of his brother at all, for his thoughts were wrapped up in his own wound. He gazed at the fallen men who were scattered around him, heard the major issue some rapid orders, and then he, too, fell off his horse. The pickets were evidently going for the officers, and they made short work of them. Dan saw and heard all this and then made a desperate lunge for the bushes, and Cale was close at his heels when he got there.

"Oh, my face!" groaned Cale. "I wish I knew what was the matter with it."

"Do you think there is nobody killed but yourself?" retorted Dan. "Look at this arm. It don't hurt me so much, but it feels bruised, and you have got nothing but a bullet-hole through your cheeks."

By this time the column was under command of a captain, who had little difficulty in rallying them, and Dan heard a yell such as he had never heard before, the yell of charging cavalry, and he saw the body of men sweep on toward the bridge; but when they got there they saw the Union pickets far up

the road.   But they loaded their rifles as fast
as they went, and when they turned around to
fire at their pursuers some man was certain to
go down.   At last the captain who commanded the cavalry went over also, and this
left Captain Cullom, who was the second in
rank, in charge of the regiment.

"Forward!" he shouted at the top of his
voice.   "They are going on ahead to arouse
the other men, and we must overtake them
before they get there."

Again that charging yell arose, and it was
answered by yells equally as savage from the
Union men, who turned and fired another
volley at them.   The ten miles that lay between them and Ellisville were quickly passed
over, and by the time the pickets had arrived
within sight of the camp there was not a
man to be seen.   The houses didn't look as
though there was anybody around them, but
when they came nearer they found that every
window was filled with sharpshooters.   The
church, too, was used as a barricade, and as it
stood broadside to the road we can imagine
that it must have been hot work for that col-

umn of cavalry to have stood against it. As
they came opposite the hotel the door opened
and Mr. Knight and Mr. Sprague stepped out.

"What is going on down the road?" asked
the former.

"The rebs are coming!" shouted half a
dozen voices. "They have got a whole regiment of cavalry with them. We hain't lost a
man."

"You have done nobly," said Mr. Sprague.
"Go around behind the church-house and
make your horses fast, and go in there. Be
ready to shoot when you hear us."

"This looks like a fight," said one of the
pickets, as they made their way into the
church. "Boys, I laid out one traitor the
first fire I had. It was that miserable Dan
Newman."

"And I made all haste to lay out the other
one," chimed in a second. "His brother,
Cale Newman, was there, and Bob, here, shot
the man's horse, and I took particular aim
at his head. I know I hit him, but I did not
fix him. I saw him get up and go into the
bushes."

" Here they come!" said one of the sharp-shooters, who was keeping watch at one of the windows. "There is lots of them, ain't they?"

"Yes, but it is going to take more than they have got to get away with us," said one of the pickets. "If ten men can throw a column like that into confusion, they won't stand long against the fire of five hundred."

" Now, all you men who can get there at the window fire your one shot, and then fall back and give somebody else a chance," said the quartermaster—the one who had refused to give Cale Newman a mule. "In that way we can keep up a regular fusillade on them."

The Confederates came on, yelling as they went, and there was more than one man who took note of the fact that discipline was a great thing. All those in front were coming to their death, but not one was seen to flinch. The men in the church began to wonder if Mr. Sprague had forgotten how to shoot, his signal was so long delayed, and some of the most excitable ones yelled "Fire!" as the rebels came on, but the calm voice of their leader broke in with:

"Steady there, men. Don't shoot until you have the word;" and scarcely had he got the words out of his mouth when a rifle-shot came from the hotel across the way, and an instant afterward nearly a thousand rifles and carbines cracked in unison. The slaughter was fearful. The captain, who was leading the charge, fell with a dozen bullets in his person, and when the smoke cleared away so that they could see the effect of the shot, they found that the leading company had been dismounted, and their horses were running about as if they didn't know which way to go.

"Now, you men at the window who have had a hand in this fall back," said the quartermaster; but nobody seemed to hear him. The men struggled to keep their places, and the men in the body of the church, finding that no opportunity was to be given them, opened the door and went out. Then the rebels got another volley, and it was almost as disastrous as the first. And this wasn't the worst of it. All the men came out from their hiding-places, from the hotel and from behind the trees that concealed them in the grove, and the surviving rebels, seeing nothing before them but a regiment of Union men who were backed by rifles that never missed, and more running up to join them, took to their heels and made the best of their time down the road.

"Get on your horses and follow them!" shouted Mr. Knight from the window of the hotel. "Don't let one escape!"

That was the way the rebels got scattered. The Union men pursued them on fresh horses; and some of them, seeing that their chances for escape were slim indeed, threw down their arms and surrendered, while the rest took off through the woods. That was the time that Leon and Ballard might have added some glory to their escape by capturing the two men who went across the creek, but the trouble was they didn't know how the thing had ended.

"Now, if you think they were whipped we can go up the main road," said Leon. "But I really shouldn't like to get so close to home and then have them jump onto me."

"I shouldn't like it, either," said Ballard, with a laugh. "I would be apt to fare worse

than you would. But can't we go on and reconnoitre the ground? If we find some of
your men there we'll be safe."

"Let us try it," said Leon. "Anything is
better than walking through this thick underbrush."

Leon was not more than half a mile below
the bridge, and before he had gone that distance he heard somebody talking in the road.
He raised his hand to Ballard, and the latter at
once took his horse by the head and forced it
down. Leon held on, and after carefully
feeling his way came upon several Union men
who were gathered about a rebel who had
been shot from his horse. One of the Union
men he recognized as Bud McCoy, but who the
others were he didn't know.

"Halloo! there. You licked them, didn't
you?"

"Well, I'll be dog-gone!" exclaimed the
man, as he turned about and saw Leon advancing upon him through the bushes.
"Where have you been? Your pap has been
in a heap of worry about you."

"And well he might be," said Leon. "I

have been a prisoner. Come on, Ballard; it's all right."

The men all straightend up—they were busy getting ready to remove the wounded rebel—and presently saw Ballard coming through the woods leading his horse.

"And here's the man who saved me," added Leon. "Know him, boys. His name is Ballard. He was going to take me down to Mobile, but after he got out of sight of the rebels he asked me into the woods and gave me something to eat. How many of the Confederates did you kill?"

"But first, I want to know how you came to be taken prisoner?" said Bud. "Did you run onto the rebels before you knew it? The last time I saw you, you were up to old Newman's house."

"No, I didn't run onto the rebels before I saw them," said Leon; and he knew the confession he was about to make would not meet the entire approval of Bud McCoy. "One man made a prisoner of me."

"Who was it?"

"Dan Newman."

"And you had a revolver in your pocket?"

"Yes, but he got it away from me."

"Dan Newman! Well, I'll be dog-gone! Before I would let a man like Dan Newman capture me—"

"But, Bud, he threw me down when I didn't know he was near me," protested Leon, "and when I turned over to see what had happened to me, there was my own revolver aimed straight at me."

"Well, you will never have an opportunity to get even with him now," said Bud. "He was shot right through the arm, and his brother got a bullet-hole through both cheeks."

"Why, who did that?" exclaimed Leon, who felt very much disappointed to hear it. He had always contended that no Newman could handle him, and now he would have to live with that shadow on his mind.

"I don't know; some of the pickets did it, Tom Howe was almost as worked up as your father. He's down there now, helping gather up the wounded rebels," said Bud, jerking his head down the road.

"I hope Dan will get well, for I am bound

to try my strength with him some day," said Leon. "Has anybody here got a horse that I can ride?"

"Take that gray," said one of the men, "I have got to carry this man to Ellisville, so I will have to walk."

Leon thanked him, unhitched the horse, swung himself upon his back and galloped across the bridge and down the road to the place where his two friends were at work. Tom and Dawson were surprised to see him, and while he was telling them the story he looked all around to find Dan and Cale. He want to see how badly hurt Dan was, for he believed, if they were to measure strength once more, that Dan would go under.

"There's one thing that happened about this business that you won't like," said Tom; and he spoke as though he was very much disheartened himself. "Old man Smith was badly wounded during the fight."

"Why, how did that happen?" asked Leon in surprise.

"Well, you must know that all the shooting that was done wasn't confined to our

men," said Tom. "The rebels rallied two or
three times, and every time they poured in a
volley."

"But how did Mr. Smith get hit? Wasn't
he under cover?"

"Yes; he was in the hotel with your father,
but he came out. He was just getting all ready
to fire when a bullet took him in the side and
over he went."

Leon was very sorry to hear this. He remembered that Mr. Smith had told him particularly that he had something to say to him,
and he had not been near him since. Perhaps if he went directly home he would get
there in time to hear what he had to say. He
didn't think it anything worth listening to,
but he would show his good-will. While he
was looking around at the dead and wounded
Confederates lying there—and he was really
surprised when he saw what a havoc ten guns
had made in the assaulting column—he became aware that there was a man leaning on
a rifle and keeping guard over several
prisoners. Among them were Dan and Cale.
One's arm and the other's face had been ban-

daged after a fashion, and they were waiting until the rebels were all gathered up, when they would go on to Ellisville and be placed under the care of the doctor. Leon gave his horse the rein and rode up and accosted Dan.

"Well, old fellow, I am sorry to see you in this fix," said he.

"Yes, no doubt you are glad of it," whined Dan, moving his wounded arm to a better place.

"I am, really. I was in hopes that you and I would come together again, and I wanted you to see that you couldn't take me down as easy as you did before. You handled me as easy as though I wasn't there."

"I can do it all the time," replied Dan, snappishly, for just then his arm pained him and he moved it to another position. "I can get away with you the best day you ever saw."

"Oh, it is very easy for you to talk that way now, but if you had two good arms I would try you right here."

"Say, Leon, what do you reckon those fellows will do with us after they get us to Ellisville?" said Cale, speaking with difficulty.

"I am sure I don't know. If I had my way with you I would send you among the rebels, with orders not to come back. You talk of the rebels as 'our men,' and you belong with them."

"I guess you'll stretch hemp," said the man who was acting as sentry over them.

"I hope they won't go that far, but I don't know," said Leon, as he turned his horse about and started for Ellisville.

It was getting dark by this time, but all the way Leon saw some signs of the fight. Here was a dead rebel who had been shot during the retreat, and who had fallen in the middle of the road, and he had been moved out on one side and his body covered with a blanket. A little further on he came across a wagon which was loaded with wounded Confederates, and the Union men all greeted him as though they were glad to see him. There was one thing about it, if there was any faith to be put in what the men said to him: His father had been in a constant worry ever since he failed to show up at Newman's house, and he became so satisfied that Newman was to blame for his capture—for Mr. Sprague knew that somebody had made a prisoner of him—that he sent a squad of men back to the house and placed them all in custody. Finally Leon came up to the place where the slaughter had taken effect when the Confederates got ready to make their charge, and he shuddered when he looked at it. The rebels and their horses had fallen together in a heap until they were piled on top of one another. The Union men had not got through removing them yet.

"By gracious, if those rebels could come up here from Mobile and see what I have seen to-day, I'll bet they would give up trying to conquer us," said Leon, as he once more gave his horse the rein and drew up before the hotel porch. "I didn't suppose that a battle ended in that way. I thought the dead and wounded were scattered all around, and that you had to hunt a long time before you found them, but—I never want to see another fight."

The hotel porch was empty when he got there, but a little way up toward the grove he saw a company of Confederates, all huddled together, and Union men were keeping guard over them. They were waiting there until their paroles could be made out. You see they had no printing-press in Jones county, and everything like this had to be made out by hand. He went up into the President's room, and there he found as many men as could find seats at the table engaged in writing. Some of the prisoners were there to assist them.

"The way we do this," said Mr. Knight, addressing himself to the captain who had last commanded the regiment (by the way, he was wounded, too, for a handkerchief that was wet with blood was tied around his forehead) —"the way we do this is all owing to you rebels alone. You have not hung any of our men yet; indeed, I don't know that you have had a chance, but if you had hung any of them, we should pick out as many men as had been executed and hang them to the nearest tree. We want you to understand that these paroles are matters of life and death with you. If you go into battle against us without being exchanged, and we capture you, you can expect nothing but death. I think you have found out, by the way that cavalry charged upon us, that we know how to fight. How many men had you to go back to Mobile?"

"Well, sir, I should say about two hundred."

"And how many had you in the first place?"

"We marched up here to assault you with eleven hundred men, sir."

"And only two hundred escaped! That's doing pretty good work."

Leon was astonished when he found out that so small a number of Confederates had got away, and then, seeing that the conversation between the President and the rebel captain had ceased, he began looking around for his father. He found him at last sitting at a table in a remote corner of the room, and walked up and placed his hand upon his shoulder. Mr. Sprague looked up, and finding Leon's face beaming down upon him, put his pen in his mouth and extended his hand.

"Halloo, Leon ; you have got back, haven't you ?" he exclaimed ; and for the first time in his life he saw his father's eyes filled with tears.

"Yes, sir, I have got back. Where's Mr. Smith?"

"Mr. Smith has got his death-wound, I am afraid," said his father, looking down at the paper on which he was writing with a most gloomy expression. "He wants to see you bad, and I would advise you to go down to him at once. You will find him in the parlor, lying on the sofa."

Leon waited to hear no more, but worked his way through the men toward the door, stopping to shake hands with this one, or to give a bow and a smile to another, and presently found himself in the parlor. The doctor was there and bending over the wounded man, and so was a distant relative of his, who seemed determined that the doctor should not exchange any words with Mr. Smith without he could hear them. Leon had never liked that man, Leonard Smith. It is true that he had never worked for his father, nor for Mr. Smith, either, for there was something about him that neither of the gentlemen approved of. He was constantly telling around that he was going to have a lot of money one of these days, and nobody knew where he was going to get it. Mr. Smith had a little, just how much no one knew, and it was very clear to everyone that Leonard Smith wouldn't get any of it when he got done with it. Mr. Smith had often been heard to declare:

"I'll never help a man who is too lazy to help himself. What does that Leonard Smith do to earn his living? He works at the logs about half the time, and the balance he spends in visiting me. I have often told him to go to work, but he won't do it. He is a sort of second cousin to me, but all the same he has no claim on me."

When Leon came into the parlor Mr. Smith turned his head and saw him. With more strength than a person of his injuries would be likely to show he thrust out his hand and welcomed him in his cheery way.

"Why, Leon, where have you been?" exclaimed the wounded man. "Come here and tell me all about it. Now, doctor, I can get along without any more help until I get

through with Leon. Take everybody out of
the room."

The only person in the room besides the
doctor and Leon was this Leonard Smith, and
he didn't seem inclined to move. He walked
back toward the foot of the sofa and leaned
upon it, and there he seemed determined to
stay.

"I want you to go, too," said Mr. Smith,
in angry tones. "Take him out with you,
doctor."

"I guess I had better stay here," said Leonard. "You might want me to hand you
your water or something."

"I reckon this man I have got here is
enough to hand me my water or anything
else," retorted Mr. Smith. "Doctor, I want
to see Leon about something particular, and I
would thank you to take that fellow out of
the room. I haven't got but a short time to
live—"

"Come, now, Leonard, go out of the room,"
said the doctor.

Leonard waited a moment, just long enough
to cast a glance of mingled hate and rage

upon Mr. Smith and Leon, and then went out, banging the door after him.

"That's all right," said Mr. Smith. "Now, lock the door. It will take not more than a minute, but what little I do say I want to reach your ears, and your ears alone. Pull up a chair and sit down."

Leon complied. He fastened the door, and then drew a chair close to the wounded man's side and leaned over him.

CHAPTER XVII.

THE EVENTS OF A WEEK.

"THAT'S all right," repeated Mr. Smith, as Leon seated himself close by his side. "I didn't want that Leonard Smith to hear a word I had to say to you, for he is a slippery fellow, and I don't deny that I have detected him in efforts to steal money from me. The funds I have got— Put your hand inside my vest and pull out my pocket-book."

Leon arose to his feet and was about to comply with the man's request when the door of the parlor was tried with a careful hand, but the lock prevented intrusion.

"That's Leonard," said Mr. Smith. "Let him work. He has got rid of the doctor and was coming in to hear what I had to say to you. That's it," he continued, as Leon drew out a pocket-book which was made so large that it would contain bills at full length.

"Now, put it in your pocket and button it up and give it to your father the first thing you do. My will is in there, and my money is all bequeathed to you."

Leon gasped, but he had never thought of anything like this, and he didn't know what to say to it. Finally he stammered:

"Do you think it right, Mr. Smith, to take all this money away from Leonard and give it to me, who—"

"I have a right to do what I please with my own," interrupted Mr. Smith. "I have worked hard for every cent of it, and I have made it all. The money is all in gold, and the will tells where to find it; but don't you let Leonard get hold of the pocket-book, for if you do he will cheat you out of it. Keep watch of him the first thing you do, and don't let him catch you off your guard. Now, Leon, that's all. Hand me a drink of water. This fever, or something else in me, is burning me up."

Leon made all haste to bring the wounded man a tumbler of water from the table, and when he had drained it he thought it wise to

provide for the use of the money in case Mr.
Smith's injuries should not be as severe as
they thought.

"Of course, if you get well," he began.

"Why, then, of course, I'll get the money
back. I understand that; but, Leon, you
don't want to talk about such things. I know
when I am done for as well as anybody. Now
you may unlock the door and let Leonard in.
After that, take the money up and give it to
your father. It is all willed to you, mind you,
but of course your father will have full charge
of it until you are twenty-one. Now unlock
the door."

Leon lingered a moment. Something told
him that he would not see Mr. Smith alive
again, and he wanted to bid him good-bye,
but he didn't know how to go about it. The
wounded man was getting impatient, so he
stepped up and shook him by the hand; after
that he unlocked the door, and he unlocked it
so suddenly that it came open with a jerk,
and Leonard Smith, who was leaning over
with his ear close to the key-hole in the hope
of hearing something that would be of use to

him, came into the parlor on all-fours. He
didn't apologize for his abrupt entrance, and
neither did Leon for letting him into the
room so suddenly, while Mr. Smith looked
the disgust he could not express in words.

"If I were in that man's place I should
feel so ashamed of myself that I couldn't look
Mr. Smith in the face," said Leon, as he
bounded up the stairs that led to the President's room. "But I suppose he has been
caught in so many tricks that he isn't
ashamed of anything. Father," he added, in
a whisper, "this is what Mr. Smith wanted to
see me about. This pocket-book has got his
will in it, and tells us where to find his
money. How much of it there is I don't
know; but he wanted me to give it into your
hands, with instructions to look out for Leonard Smith."

"Ah!" said Mr. Sprague, taking the pocket-
book and slipping it inside his vest. "So
Leonard has got onto it in some way or another, has he?"

"Yes; and it was all Mr. Smith could do
to get him out of the parlor when he wanted

to talk to me. He says don't you let Leonard catch you off your guard one instant, for if you do he will cheat you out of it."

"Why, if the money is made over to you I don't see what Leonard can have to do with it."

"But he will find out where the money is hidden, and go there and dig it up."

"Well, I reckon Mr. Leonard won't get it now," said Mr. Sprague, buttoning his vest.

"No, I don't think he will. Now, hadn't you better go down and see Mr. Smith? He thinks he isn't going to last much longer."

"I will go down and see him now. I hope he will get well, so that he can have this money back again."

Mr. Sprague laid down his pen and got upon his feet, and just then there was a rumble of wagons in front of the house, which told them that some of the wounded had arrived. Leon went down to assist them and to look for Ballard, whom he wanted to introduce to the President, while his father went on to the parlor. Leon found that there were four wagon-loads of wounded rebels there, and while he was looking around watching for a chance to lend a hand his father came to the door and beckoned to him.

"He has gone," said he, when Leon approached within speaking distance.

"Is he dead?"

"Yes; and all his pockets are turned inside out."

Leon followed his father into the parlor, and they found no one there except the doctor and Leonard Smith. The doctor shook his head and turned and went out, while Leonard stood in his accustomed place at the foot of the sofa, and did nothing but glare at the father and son. The pockets had evidently been searched, and Leonard did not have time to put them back again before the doctor came in. Leon drew a long breath of relief when he saw how mad Leonard was. He had arrived home just in the nick of time. If he had delayed his coming half an hour the pocket-book would now be in the possession of one whom Mr. Smith did not want to have it. But it was plain Leonard did not intend to give it up in this way. As Leon took hold of

the sheet to spread it reverently over the dead
man's face, Leonard suddenly aroused himself
and seemed determined to find out where the
pocket-book was.

"I would thank you to give up what you
got from him when I went out," said he, and
he was so angry that he could scarcely form
the words into a sentence.

"What did I get?" inquired Leon, while
his father straightened up and looked at him
without speaking.

"You got a pocket-book, or something else,
in which he kept his will," said Leonard.
"That pocket-book is mine, and I am bound to
have it."

"It's safe," replied Mr. Sprague. "I'll tell
you what I will do in order to find out
whether it is in the possession of the one who
ought to have it. As soon as these troubles
are all over I will take out the will and read
it in the presence of the men—"

"But I don't intend to remain out of my
money so long," interrupted Leonard. "Some
of these rebels might come here and dig down
and find it. If I have it now it will be safe."

24

"How do you know it is in the ground?"

"Well, I just suppose it is. I don't know any other place he could put it where it would equally safe."

"I told you that I would read the will in the presence of the men and let them decide who owns the money. More than that I cannot promise."

"Now, I will just tell you what's the gospel truth," said Leonard, leaving his place at the foot of the sofa and striding up and shaking both his clinched hands in Mr. Sprague's face.

"Put down your hands or I will have you arrested in a minute!" said Mr. Sprague, not in the least alarmed by the other's threatening manner.

"I will shake my fists in your face or in anybody else's face who intends to rob me of my birthright!" exclaimed Leonard, at the same time allowing his hands to fall by his side. "I tell you that I will camp on that place every night, and woe be to the man or boy who comes there after that money. He will not get away with it."

"I hope you have said enough in the presence of this dead man—"

"He was my cousin; that is what he was," shouted Leonard.

"— of this dead man to make you ashamed of yourself," said Mr. Sprague. "Now, we will go out."

"But I want you to understand what I said about camping on that place," said Leonard. "The man or boy who gets that money don't get away with it."

Mr. Sprague and Leon went out without making any reply, the former going back to the President's room to resume his work upon the paroles, and his son to wander aimlessly about, with no disposition to do any work, although he saw plenty of it before him. After awhile he found Tom Howe, and both his friends with him. They were tired of removing wounded rebels and were now going up to Tom's camp for a good nap. Ballard was evidently much impressed with the sharp-shooting the Union men had done, and declared that he had never seen the beat.

"I don't see how any of our fellows came

out alive," said he, and his astonishment was
so great that he threw his arms about his
head. "You Union men are dead shots!"

"Well, there are plenty of deer and bear
loose in the swamps, and squirrels in abundance," said Leon, "and you can't expect that
men who sometimes have to depend on them
for a living will miss them every time."

"Come on, Leon," said Dawson. "You'll
have to go up to Tom's camp, too. We
haven't heard your story yet."

Leon began his story as they walked along,
and as he did not have very much to tell, anyway, his companions knew all about it by the
time they got to the place where Tom had left
his mule. Tom was disgusted when Leon
told him about his being captured by one
man, and more than all by such a man as
Dan Newman, but he was elated just as much
when Leon told how Ballard had taken him
into the woods and given him something to
eat.

"Howdy, Mr. Ballard," said Tom, walking
up and shaking the Texas rebel by the hand.
"I didn't get a chance to shake hands with

you before, but now I am glad to see you. That boy is a friend of mine, and if you do anything for him it is as though you did it for me. Now, we will take some supper and then go to bed."

While Tom was kindling the fire Leon related to him the particulars of Mr. Smith's death, and to say that Tom felt quite as badly as Leon did would be telling nothing but the truth. He did not say anything about the will which he had given into his father's care, or about the trouble that Leonard Smith had threatened to make on account of it, for something told him that he had better keep that to himself. Thus far, he and Mr. Sprague were the only ones that knew anything about it. Of course, he would have been perfectly willing to have trusted Tom with his secret, but there were other men there, Ballard and Dawson, of whom he knew nothing. How did he know that they would not hunt for the money and make off with it? It was hidden in the ground somewhere. Leonard seemed to think that that was the place he would go to find it, and if he told everybody of it

they would dig Mr. Smith's farm full of holes
but that they would find it.

"I don't think I had better say anything
about that," said Leon to himself, after he
had thought the matter over. "I will talk
about it to father the first chance I get. These
men will all be poor when this war is settled,
and they may fight about the money as readily
as they fired into that regiment of cavalry."

During the week following there was nothing happened that would be of interest to you,
although it was full of interest to the Union
men of Jones county. In the first place, as
soon as they had eaten breakfast, the prisoners
who had been captured the day before were summoned to the hotel, and there signed their paroles. They did it, too, knowing full well what
was to be expected if they didn't keep them, for
Mr. Knight was there, and he went over the
same speech he had delivered to the captain
in his room. There were a number of wagons,
and the wounded were placed carefully in
them, and they were to be taken away and
delivered to their friends. There were also
two hundred Union men with them who were

to guard them as far as the bridge, and then they were to bid them good-bye and come back.

"I hope," said Mr. Knight, after he had got through with his speech, "that you all have been treated right since you have been here."

"Oh, yes, sir," responded a dozen voices. "You have treated us like we were your own."

"Then I hope that if you get any of my boys in the Confederate lines you will treat them in the same way. That's all. Go on."

Mr. Knight did not raise any objections when the men took off their hats and gave him a cheer. He simply bowed and went up the stairs that led to his room.

The next thing was taking Mr. Smith and Bach Noble, and several other men who had been killed and wounded during the fight with the cavalry, to their homes. It was done with rather more of solemnity than had yet been displayed, and a long line followed after each man who had given up his life in defence of the flag. Mr. Sprague and Leon went with the man who had bequeathed them all he had

in this world to give, and saw a grave dug
where he had always said he would wish to be
laid, and when the ceremony was over they
came back to the hotel very much depressed
in spirits. And it was a long time before
they got over thinking about Mr. Smith. He
was so lively and full of fun that he was
sadly missed, but it was not long before something else demanded their attention. There
was one thing that Leon was glad to see.
Leonard Smith was not present at the funeral.
It was not the man he cared for—it was the
money he thought he had laid away, and
which he believed he was in duty bound to
get, seeing that Mr. Smith had no one else to
bestow it upon. But he saw that he was not
likely to get it by fair means, and so he kept
out of the way.

There was another thing that happened
during the week that made the Union men
draw a long breath of relief. The boats
which that squad had been sent up to build
were all done, and now it needed nothing
but a strong force of Confederates, much too
large to be handled by them, to send the last

man of them over to the island, where they would be comparatively safe. They were now ready to fight, and they didn't care how soon it was forced upon them. During that week, too, a large number of men, probably two hundred of them in all, came in to give themselves up. Some of them were on foot, and others had their wagons along loaded with their families and household furniture. They had heard the particulars of the capture of that wagon-train, and believing that the men in Jones county were in earnest, and that they did not intend to be forced into the rebel army, they watched their opportunity and came in by night. And this wasn't the worst of it. There were more came in every day, until Leon wondered where they should get food for them all.

"I don't think the rebels knew how many fighting men there were about here," said he. "We must have as many as twenty-five hundred men here."

"Yes, and I guess if you had said double that you wouldn't have been far out of the way," said Ballard, who stuck close to the boys wherever they went. "It will take ten thousand men to whip us."

"Do you suppose that Jeff Davis can send that number of men up here? We are only one little part of the Confederacy, and I should think he would want to save his men for something else."

"He may now, but he won't after a while. When Mobile becomes surrounded by Union troops, as she certainly will, he will need all the men he can get."

And there was one other thing that happened during this week that caused Leon and Tom to look at each other in perfect astonishment. It proved that the chief men of the county, although they might act so very innocent, were not to be taken unawares. They had spies out. Some of them went to Mobile to see what they could find there that was worth looking at, especially to keep track of that strong force which they knew would be sent against them sooner or later, and the others went up into the interior of the State to keep a lookout for some more wagon-trains. These men took their lives in their hands, for every one of them that went into the Confederate lines was dressed in a rebel uniform. If they were caught and could not make a good excuse in regard to the regiment and company they belonged to, they would be hanged. Leon had been so very busy ever since he came into camp that he had not had time to learn all these things; but there was one other thing that he did learn which afforded him infinite gratification. It was what happened to Mr. Newman and family. They had been arrested as soon as Mr. Sprague found out, or rather mistrusted, that one of their number could tell more about Leon's absence than any one else, and Bass Kennedy's corn being thrown out of the calaboose, they were chucked in there, and guards placed over them to be sure that they stayed, too. Of course, Mr. Sprague was very much astonished when he learned that Dan had made a prisoner of Leon and had been wounded and captured by the pickets, and when he was brought to Ellisville he had him put into the jail with his father and mother. On the morning that the prisoners were sent away they were given a

wagon to themselves and forwarded to the
rebels in Mobile, and Leon never heard of
them afterward. We may tell you, however,
that Dan's arm was amputated when he got
among the doctors, and Cale never recovered
his good looks. He looked as if his jaws were
sunk in, and all the negro-twist he could get in
them would not make them look any different.

By this time everything had been got ready
for the visit of that force which was to crush
out the rebellion of the Jones-County Confederacy. We don't say that Mr. Sprague
and the other chief men looked upon it as
boys' play, because they knew well enough
what it meant. The actions of the regiment
of cavalry which came in there, as well as the
threats they had made that they were "going
to sweep everything clean," and that before
night there wouldn't be a Union man left,
showed them that they couldn't hope for any
mercy. The head men of the Confederacy
would be hanged, and the others would be
forced into the rebel army. Mr. Sprague
talked this all over with Leon, but the latter
did not exhibit any signs of wavering.

"Well, I suppose if that is what we have got to contend with we can't meet it any too soon," said Leon, compressing his mouth firmly, as he always did whenever his courage was tested to the utmost. "I never thought that this thing was coming through all right. Such an exploit was never thought of before."

"I know it; and that is what makes us think we shall come through with flying colors. There's one thing about it: We won't fight against our old flag."

In spite of all the constant work there was for him to do at headquarters, Mr. Sprague found opportunity to go home and assist his wife in packing up for the island, which was the place the backwoodsmen had decided upon to make their last stand. It was a piece of ground in the midst of the swamp, entirely surrounded by water, and now that the inside of it had been cleared of all underbrush, which had been piled around the outside of it to answer for a breastwork, the island seemed to be a larger camp than the force of men at their disposal needed. Leon went up and saw it.

He took his mother over in one of the boats, making their stock swim behind, and through a long, winding pathway, made of corduroy logs, and obstructed at every turn by numerous barricades, and when he came at last into the cleared space he was astonished.

"Why, father, we haven't got men enough to fill up that space," said he. "There's room enough for ten thousand men."

"Don't worry yourself," said his father, with a smile. "This war is not half over yet. By the time we have our first fight here we'll have more men than we want."

We must not forget to say that Tom Howe's mother and Mr. Giddings and his family went with them. They all settled right down close together, and seemed as happy and contented there as they would have been under their own roofs. Mr. Giddings especially was the source of constant merriment to the boys. It didn't make any difference to him that he was so far from his mountain home, but he pitched right in and had a good time. Of course, he was careful of his rifle. Whenever he could get his hands upon that he seemed to throw care to the winds. It was on this very day that Mr. Sprague thought it best to speak to Leon about that will. The boy didn't know anything about it, and if anything happened to him during the fights that followed he wanted Leon to know where to get the money. Mr. Sprague, in the presence of his wife, had examined the will a few days before, and the result almost took his breath away. There were a few gold-pieces in the pocket-book, perhaps a hundred dollars or two, and a few bills payable; but they were all marked off, as if to show Mr. Sprague that Mr. Smith did not want to press the men for the money. Among these bills was the will, and when Mr. Sprague came to examine it his hand shook and he passed it over to his wife, saying:

"My goodness! Mary, who would have supposed that Mr. Smith was worth so much money? We dare not say anything about this, for if we do our lives will not be worth a moment's purchase. These men around us will fight as hard to keep the money here as they will to keep the rebels away. Now, what had we better do?"

CHAPTER XVIII.

COLEMAN PROVES HIS HONESTY.

MRS. SPRAGUE fastened her eyes on the document, and as she read the color all left her face. She looked around. There was plenty of opportunity for her to be overheard now, for they were living in a brush lean-to, and there were people constantly passing back and forth almost within reach of them. There were plenty of folks there that could be trusted with their secret, but there were lots more from whom it must be kept at all hazards.

"And do you think that some of these people will fight for this money?" she said in an earnest whisper.

"There are lots of them that will do it," returned her husband. "You see we will be as poor as they make them when this thing is ended, and where they are going to get money to start on, I don't know. I tell you, we

mustn't let anybody know it. Put that away
and I will go out and call Leon."

The heir of all this wealth was found assisting Mr. Giddings, who was just putting
the finishing touches on his brush shanty preparatory to getting his family under it. He
looked up when he saw his father approaching, and he had never seen him look so white
before; but he was warned by the signal his
father made him, and so he didn't say a word.
His mother handed him the will when he entered their brush lean-to, and in less time
than it takes to tell it Leon was master of its
contents.

"A hundred thousand dollars!" he gasped.

"Sh! Not so loud," cautioned his mother.
"You don't want everybody to know it, do
you? Sit down here and tell us what you
think of it."

"To think that old Mr. Smith, who went
about with his knees and elbows out, should
be worth so much money!" said Leon. "It is
no wonder that that fellow wanted to fight
for it."

"Yes, and you must be careful what you
25

say around where he can hear it," said his father, who had taken up a position in the door of the lean-to so that he could partially screen Leon while reading the will. "If he finds out where that money is hid, it's all up with you."

"But he won't find it," said Leon, who quickly copied after his father and spoke in an almost inaudible whisper. "He has got it hidden in the pig-pen. I was there while he was laying that floor along in the early part of the war, and he said then that I might some day dig up something under it. I couldn't think then what he meant, although I know it now."

"Well, you had better let your mother take care of the will," said Mr. Sprague, "and then if anything happens to us she will know right where to go and get the money. I tell you that is a good deal more than we thought we were going to have."

Leon was almost overwhelmed by the result of the last few minutes, and if he could have had his own way he would have been glad to get off somewhere by himself and think the matter over. But now it was impossible. Everywhere he went there was somebody around, and it seemed to Leon, now that he thought about it, that those who knew about Mr. Smith's will had a way of looking at him as though they knew the secrets of what was hidden under the pig-pen. Of course, it was all imagination on his part, but still he wanted to get away and talk the matter over with Tom Howe.

"Mustn't I take anybody into my confidence at all, not even Tom?" said he.

"Take nobody into your confidence," said his father, earnestly. "You don't know what sort of a fellow Tom is. He may be all right to have around where there's a jam of logs in the river, but you don't want to say anything to him about this money business."

"Well, when are you going to get it? We'll have to go away from here in order to use it."

"We'll go to it after this war is settled, and not before. Of course, we shall have to go away from here, for we can't use it around where Leonard Smith is. And here's another

thing I want to tell you. Remember and keep
close within reach of me, and don't let Smith
or anybody else get you off on one side. If
you do, you will suffer for it."

Leon smiled and wondered what sort of a
story Smith could make up to draw him off in
the woods, and it wasn't so very long before
he found out. Ever since the night that Mr.
Smith died, Leonard had been half-crazy. He
had no idea how much the will in the pocket-
book contained, but he was certain that it was
enough to keep him all his days without work.
This was what this lazy vagabond was building his hopes upon. Anyway, he didn't want
the Spragues to have it, and what was more
he was determined that they shouldn't. If
there was any way by which could get the will,
or any means to learn the hiding-place of the
money, why then it would be clear sailing
with him. Leon undoubtedly had time to
read the will and find out where the money
was concealed, and if he could get him off by
himself somewhere he would find out where
that money was concealed, or he would leave
Leon hanging to a tree in the woods. It took

him two days to come to this decision, and all
the while he roamed about over Mr. Smith's
place, poking into every place that he could
think of where there was the least chance of
hiding money. When the funeral procession
came there he slunk into the woods, but when
they went away again he came out and re-
newed his endeavors to find the fortune.

"There is money hidden somewhere about
here, and I am as certain of it as that I am
alive," said Leonard Smith, when the men
who had composed the funeral procession had
gone away. "If it were not that Leon has
the secret stowed away in his head I would
up-end him the moment I saw him; but if I
can get him in the woods and make preparations to hang him, I'll find out where the
money is. I can't do anything by myself,
and I must have somebody to help me. Now,
who shall I get?"

Fortunately it was an easy thing for Leonard Smith to decide upon this question. He
thought over all the worthless fellows who
occurred to his mind just then, and finally
hit upon one who was just about of as much

use in the world as he was. Caleb Coleman
was on the island beyond a doubt—he was
always around where he was certain there was
no danger—and if he could only get over
there and see him he was sure that he could
induce him to lend a hand in finding the
money. But the trouble was he did not care
to go around where Leon was.

"I don't know whether that boy is certain
that I am looking for the money or not, but
he acts as if he did," said Smith, as he took a
look around to make sure that he had not
missed any place where he thought there was
a chance of hiding the money.

He had removed every pile of boards there
was about the farm-house and had dug under
them until he saw that the earth had not recently been disturbed, and then threw the piles
of boards back again. He had even been in
the cow-stable and plied his search there; but
with all his looking he could not find any
place which bore the appearance of having
been dug over, and he was almost inclined to
give up his search in despair. But he had
one more trump card to play, and the more

he thought of it the more confident he became
that it would surely work.

"Here's one thing that I have got to blame
old Sprague for," said Smith, as he picked up
his rifle—nobody ever thought of going
abroad without a rifle in war times—and
turned his steps toward the island. "He's
gone and sent off that Newman family, and
if they were here I would know right where
to go to find three good men to assist me; but
seeing that he couldn't mind his own business,
I suppose Coleman is the best one I can get.
I'll bet I will make his eyes open if I promise
him one thousand dollars in gold."

Smith had not yet been over to the island,
but it was no trouble at all for him to get
there, for the boats were constantly employed
in carrying over the household furniture of
the refugees. He did not know that there
were so many men in the county before, and
when he came to look closely at them he found
that the most of them were strangers. A great
many of them, too, were dressed in rebel uniform, and they worked like honest men who
were anxious to take their families to a

place of safety; but he did not see Coleman there.

"I'll bet I'll find him on the island, laid down alongside the fire," said Smith, as his boat touched the shore and he jumped off. "You may be sure that he wouldn't do any work while there is anybody to do it for him."

Smith was surprised to find that no one on the island had missed him, for nobody spoke to him. The majority of the men were busy building their houses and getting their household goods under cover, and well they might be. After they got through here they were to march in a body down to the hotel and meet the assault of that force which was coming to crush out the last vestige of the Jones-County Confederacy. The men all acted with a feverish eagerness, as if they were impatient to get at it. Smith thought, too, that if that invading force succeeded in following the Union men to their island they were bound to be whipped. The passage through the cane was long and winding, and at every turn there were barricades erected, behind which three or four hundred men could have resisted a thousand. These breastworks of logs had been thrown up by the party who came out to build the boats and without any orders from headquarters, and Mr. Sprague showed what he thought of them by praising the men without stint.

"You will make good soldiers some day," said he. "The rebels can't get in here any way they can fix it. They are bound to come in column when they assault these breastworks, because the cane is so thick that they can't come in any other way, and before they can get in here they won't have a man left."

"There's one of them now," muttered Smith, as he caught sight of Mr. Sprague standing in the door of his lean-to. If Smith had only known it, Leon was in the act of reading the will. "If I can get a-hold of that boy of yours I'll soon know as much as he does. He knows where the money is, and he will tell it all sooner than be hung."

Mr. Sprague bowed to Smith as he passed by, but the latter didn't pay any attention to him. The man wanted to know where he could find Coleman, but he was much too sharp to speak to Mr. Sprague about it. He kept on a little further, and found somebody of whom he could make inquiries. Another thing that attracted Smith's attention right here was the air of neatness and order with which all the lean-tos were arranged. They were laid off in streets, so that one could go the whole length of them on the darkest of nights without stumbling over a brush shanty which contained some sleeping occupants.

"You will find Caleb up there on the out-skirts of the camp," said the man of whom he made inquiries. "He's got sick of poleing the boats over, and so has gone up to camp to lie down."

"Then he isn't doing any work at all?" asked Smith.

"Work? Naw. He says he hain't got but a little time to stay with his folks, and so he intends to see them all he can. When we go down there to meet the rebels, he is going to stay in camp."

"Then he is just the man I want," said Smith to himself, as he pursued his way toward Coleman's lean-to. "I aint a-going to meet the rebels myself, and consequently I don't blame him."

Smith followed along up the street until he came to the end of it, and there he found Coleman. The lean-to that he had over him was not very secure, but Coleman didn't seem to mind that. He lay stretched out on the bedding with his pipe in his mouth, and three or four dogs and as many children kept him company.

"Why don't you put a roof on your lean-to?" asked Smith. "When it rains you'll wish you had paid more attention to it."

"Well, when it rains I can't fix it; and now it don't need it," replied Coleman with a laugh. "It will do."

"Why don't you get out and pole the boats over?"

"Oh, there'll be plenty of men besides me to do that little thing," replied Coleman. "Besides, I've poled some of them over until I am all tired out."

"Well, get up, if you can. I want to see you."

"Anything particular?"

"You will think so when you hear it," replied Smith, impatiently. "Kick some of those dogs out of the way and come along with me."

Coleman arose with an effort, laid the children carefully aside and followed after Smith, who led the way around on the outside of the lean-to, being particular to keep out of sight of Mr. Sprague at the other end of the street. There he threw himself down upon the leaves and waited for Coleman to join him.

"Sit up closer—not so far off," he said, when the man halted at least five feet away. "I have got something in particular that I want to say to you, and I don't want anybody to overhear it."

"It seems to me that you are mighty friendly, now that the old man is dead and you have come into his fortune," said Coleman, moving up closer. "How much did you make out of that? I think I have heard you say that you wanted as much as twenty-five or thirty thousand dollars."

"That's what I said," answered Smith,

frowning fiercely. "But the trouble is I have not got it."

"Who has got it, then?" demanded Coleman, looking surprised.

"That little snipe, Leon Sprague. Smith had no business to give it to him, but he did, and I am left out in the cold."

"I say! That's a pretty how-de-do, ain't it?"

"I should say so. Now, I will give you a thousand dollars if you will help me to get it."

"That's a power of money, ain't it? But how can I help you?"

"By going to Leon and telling him that I want to see him in the woods," said Smith, sinking his voice almost to a whisper. "If I once get him out there, away from everybody, I will tell him that if he wants to see daylight again he can tell me where that money is."

"Good gracious! What are you going to do with him? Kill him?"

Smith nodded.

"Then you can get somebody else to help you get that money," said Coleman, drawing a long breath. "You won't get any help out of me."

"But think of the thousand dollars," said Smith, who began to see that he had made a mistake.

"I don't care if it's twice a thousand dollars. I wouldn't dare show my face in Jones county again."

"You needn't come back to Jones county," said Smith, who began to fear that he had run against a snag when he least expected it. "I am not coming back. I am going over to the rebels."

"Well, there! That's just what I expected you to do. Here you promise to support this government, and then go back on it the first chance you get!"

"You say you won't meet the rebels," retorted Smith.

"I know it; but I didn't say I was going over to them. Good land! You can get somebody else to help you," said Coleman, rising to his feet. "That's a little too dangerous a piece of business for me. If that's all you wanted to say I'll go back."

"Well, here, hold on a minute," exclaimed Smith, who saw that it would not do to permit Coleman to go back among his friends feeling as he did now. "There is all of twenty-five or thirty thousand dollars in that will, and Leon knows where it is."

"Let him keep it. That's what I say."

"Now, suppose, instead of hanging him," continued Smith, paying no heed to the interruption, "we will just make believe to hang him—pull him up until he sees stars and then pull him down again. We could do that."

"No, we couldn't. Leon's eyes would be unbandaged, and he could easy see who pulled him up. I tell you you had better get somebody else."

"Well, I supposed you were willing to work hard for a thousand dollars," said Smith, in disgust. "But you are willing to live along just as you are now, without any thought for the morrow. Thank goodness, there are plenty of men in this party who will help me."

"Then you had better get one of them."

"You won't say anything about what I have told you?"

"Never a word; only, don't mention it to me again. I would rather be poor all my life than make a living in that dishonest way."

"Say, Coleman, sit down here a minute. I want to whisper something to you."

The man was a long time in sitting down. He seemed to think that Smith had some other terms to disclose which would lead him into his scheme, whether he wanted to or not.

"I will give you five thousand dollars," said Smith, in an earnest undertone. "Just think of that! Here you will be as poor as Job's turkey, and that amount of money will easily set you on your feet."

"I don't care if it's ten thousand. I won't do it."

"Well, Coleman, I was only just fooling you," said Smith, and in order to give color to his words he leaned back and laughed heartily. "You will do to tie to."

"Yes?" said Coleman, and he laughed, too, but it was a different sort of laugh. "You have an awful funny way of fooling a fellow, I must say. If you were not in earnest when you sat down here I shall miss my guess."

Coleman got upon his feet again, and Smith was so angry that he let him go without compelling him to promise over again that he would not tell anybody of the scheme that had been proposed to him. He laid down on his bed and filled his pipe, but he rolled over to see where Smith went.

"That fellow is a-going to get himself in a power of disturbance the first thing he knows," said he to his wife, as he saw Smith moving down toward Mr. Sprague's end of the street. "He is fixing himself to get hung."

"Good land! How is that?" exclaimed the woman.

In spite of the fact that he had promised Smith that he would not say a word about it, it did not take Coleman long to go over his interview with him, and when he told of the amount of money that had been offered him his wife fairly gasped for breath.

"I know that is a big sum," continued Coleman, "but just think of the danger there will be. If Leon gets off in the woods and don't come back they will hunt high and low for him, and it won't take them long to deter-

mine who it was that had a hand in his taking off.   If they make-believe they were going to hang him, why, of course. he will know
who it was and he'll tell of it when he comes
back.   I think I was pretty smart in keeping
out of it.   There goes Smith off toward the
boats.   Now I believe I'll go and see Leon."

Smith had evidently missed his guess by a
long ways when he selected Coleman to assist
him.   He had never known anything against
this man's honesty.   He supposed, of course,
that a fellow who hated to work as bad as he
did, and who was content to lay around home
all the time in company with the dogs and
the children in preference to handling an axe,
ought to be willing to engage in anything
that he thought would bring him money; but
as it happened, there were some honest men
in that party, although they did wear ragged
jackets.   Without further thought Coleman
arose and sauntered off toward Mr. Sprague's
end of the street, and when he came opposite
their lean-to he found the boy he wanted to
see, talking with his mother.

   "Well, Caleb, what can I do for you to-day?" asked Mr. Sprague, who still occupied his old position in the door of the lean-to.

"Not a thing," replied Coleman. "But I want to see Leon for about five minutes."

"Do you want him to go out in the woods with you?" said Mr. Sprague, with a wink that spoke volumes.

"Eh? No; but I want to tell him to keep away from the woods," replied Coleman, who wondered if Mr. Sprague knew all about it.

"Well, you might just as well come in here and tell it," said Mr. Sprague, taking Coleman by the arm. "There are no secrets between us."

Coleman went, and in a few minutes was seated on a trunk revealing the scheme that had been proposed to him. Leon and his father exchanged significant glances, and the boy thought how wise Mr. Sprague had been when he advised him to stick closely by his side and to let nothing draw him away.

"I did say that I wouldn't tell this to anybody," said Coleman, in conclusion. "And I won't tell it to any one except you-uns, who are so deeply interested in it. You won't tell on me?"

"Did he say how much he was going to get?" asked Leon, after his father had made the required promise.

Coleman replied that he thought he was going to get twenty-five or thirty thousand dollars, and this proved that Mr. Smith did not know anything of the value of the deceased man's legacy.

"That's a heap of money," said Leon. "And now, Coleman, I'll tell you what we will do with you. If you will stay around with Smith and learn all you can in regard to his plans you shall not lose anything by it. I want to find out if he gets somebody else to assist him."

Coleman promised, and having had his talk out went away.

"I can easily give him a thousand dollars to pay him for the trouble he has taken," said Leon.

"But you must remember that you haven't got the money yet," said his father.

"Oh, I know I shall have some trouble in getting it," said Leon, while that firm expression settled about his mouth. "When this trouble is over that fellow is going to camp on the place, and just as likely as not he will shoot down everybody who goes anywhere near the money."

"Leon, I am afraid to have you go there," said Mrs. Sprague.

"But think of the money! I tell you that will set us up. Then I can get an education. That's one thing I will never have if I stay down here."

The matter was settled for the time being by Mrs. Sprague's putting the will into her bosom and pinning it fast; then Leon went out and mingled with his fellow-refugees. But his feelings were very different from those which he had experienced when he followed his father into the lean-to. When he came to think of what the will bequeathed him it fairly took his breath away. It would get them a little home somewhere, his mother would be obliged to do no more work, and, better than all, he would have money enough left to send him to school.

"Well, Leon, you seem to be particularly happy, and so am I," said Mr. Giddings, as he took his seat near the door of his lean-to, pulled off his hat and wiped the big drops of perspiration from his forehead. "Or rather, I should be happy if my brothers were out of prison. I expect they have been executed by this time."

"If I thought that, it would make me shoot to kill," said Leon.

"Oh, won't I, when I get the chance!" replied Mr. Giddings, with so much excitement that Leon was glad he was not a rebel. "I am waiting for the colonel to say the word and get me down there where I will have full swing at them, and then every one that I pull on goes up. I tell you, you don't know anything about rebellion down here."

This started Mr. Giddings on his favorite subject of conversation, and Leon sat there and listened to him until they were called to supper.

CHAPTER XIX.

CONCLUSION.

BUT two adventures remain to be told regarding Leon Sprague's life as a Jones county Confederate soldier. One was the first real fight in which he bore a part, though to tell the truth he didn't remember much about it, and the other the exploit he went through in getting the money that had been bequeathed to him.

It took one hundred men to guard the island, and although there was no necessity for having this number of men out, the colonel thought it best to be on the safe side. He selected the men, posted them himself, and sat up nearly all night to make sure that they were doing their duty. At the first peep of day the men were all aroused, and, having had breakfast, were getting ready to march down to the hotel. How Leon's eyes opened

when he saw the men all in line after they
had got across the stream! His father said
that there were at least three thousand of
them—enough to whip four times their number of rebels, if they were brought against
them. They were going back to the hotel
because it was the first point that the rebels
would strike in Jones county; and, more than
that, they had things very neatly fixed there
for the reception of any body of men who
might be brought against them. A long line
of breastworks extended across the edge of
the woods, one side being flanked by a deep
swamp and the other by the river, so it was
impossible to get behind them. They calculated to whip the men right there. If they
didn't, the island would be their next halting
place. The women had congregated on the
edge of the island to see them off, and after
giving them a hearty cheer to ease their hearts
when they were away, the cavalcade set out
on its journey.

"Now bring on your rebs!" said Dawson.

Nearly two-thirds of the men were on
horseback. They had attempted to form col-

umn of fours as nearly as they could, and aided by some old soldiers, of whom there were a goodly number in the ranks, they managed to hit the right number at last, and before the brigade had marched a mile it was going along as orderly as any old body of cavalrymen could have exhibited. Leon was riding in the first four in company with Mr. Giddings, Dawson and Tom Howe, and he was as lively and jolly as could be. He looked all around, but he couldn't see either Smith or Coleman. But, in spite of the fact that there were men enough to protect him, he wished that Smith was out of the way.

"I declare, it is always so," soliloquized Leon. "When you get everything going just as you want it to, there is always somebody to step in and knock the thing into a cocked hat. Smith won't get the money, and he might as well give up trying."

"Bring on your rebs, I say," repeated Dawson, raising his carbine and looking all around. "We're ready for a fight!"

"You may sing a different tune from that," said Mr. Giddings.

"I know I may, but I hope not," said Dawson. "I want to keep up long enough to pay the rebels for burning our house."

It was three o'clock when they arrived within sight of Ellisville, and then Mr. Dawson, who had been riding all the way with Mr. Sprague, took command. Under his supervision the Union men were all posted behind the breastworks, and each one knew where he belonged. His camp was right where he halted, and all the men had to do was to throw off their arms, picket their horses and wait for dinner and supper, which were to be served together. If there was anything to which Leon objected it was to being held down with a firm hand. He wanted to go with his father, for by doing that he knew that he would be in a fair way to learn all the news that happened within the borders of the Jones-County Confederacy, as well as some things that occurred outside of it; so he climbed the breastworks and went down to the porch of the hotel, where he found all the chief men of the county gathered and holding a consultation with his father.

"I thought it best to burn the bridge, and move our pickets up nearer headquarters, for it would put the rebels to some trouble to swim their horses over the creek," Mr. Knight was saying to his father when he came up. "If we only had our breastworks built nearer the creek we could whip them before they ever got across."

"I think that is the best way, and I wondered long ago that you didn't think of it before," said Mr. Sprague. "Halloo! there is something coming, down there. And what's that waving over them? It is a white flag, as sure as I live! Knight, you are getting to be a big man when the enemy comes to consult you in that way."

"I declare, I believe that's what it is!" said Mr. Knight, after he and the other chief men of the party had taken a good view of it. "Now, we don't want them to see how many men we have got, and I want you to order them all into the breastworks out of sight. Tell them that we will describe the whole thing to them after the rebels go away."

The chief men went off at once to obey the

order, and by time the two Confederates got up to the hotel porch there wasn't more than a half-dozen of them in sight—just enough to act as body-guard for the President. There were two rebels in the party, and with them were four pickets whom they had picked up after they had swam their horses across the creek.

"Here's a couple of gentlemen who want to see the President," said one of the pickets. "They have come to us with General Lowery's compliments and want us to surrender."

"Well, I guess they can take General Lowery's compliments back to him and say we didn't come out here to surrender" said Mr. Knight.

"I want to see—are you the President?" asked one of the rebels, opening his eyes in surprise.

"I have that honor," replied Mr. Knight.

The rebels looked at him in profound astonishment. If any of the other men standing around had said that he was the President of the Jones-County Confederacy, they

might have believed it; but for this man, who
stood there with his coat off, his hands in his
pockets and his hat perched on the back of
his head—for him to say that he was the head
and front of that rebellion, was almost too
much. The rebels looked at him, and then
they looked at the men standing around.
There didn't seem to be but a few of them,
and perhaps it was not going to be much to
whip them, after all.

"General Lowery wants you to surrender
at once," said the rebel, who had grown bolder
since he looked around.

"You have my answer, sir," said Mr.
Knight.

"If you surrender, we will let the privates
off if they will enlist in the army," said the
colonel, for Leon made out that that was his
rank. "But the chief men of the party will
have to go under arrest and be tried for treason."

"That's very kind of General Lowery, but
somehow we are not ready to be tried yet. We
won't surrender."

"Why, my goodness, my friend, there won't

be a living man of you left by this time to-morrow. How many men have you got here, anyway?"

"About five thousand."

"Why, I don't see anybody."

"Of course you don't; but if you bring your four thousand four hundred men up here—"

"Have you had spies out?" asked the rebel, more surprised than ever.

"We know how many men you have, and we know that we outnumber them," said Mr. Knight.

"Then, of course, you won't surrender if you have that number of men. Then we may as well go back."

"I think it would be as well. We are bound to kill and capture some of the men you bring against us, and to-morrow we'll send them inside of your lines with their paroles."

"Yes? Well, their paroles won't amount to a row of pins."

"I think they will. If we capture any of the men without being exchanged we'll hang them to the nearest tree. Good-morning, sir."

It was right on the rebel's tongue to tell Mr. Knight to look out or he would get hung himself, but he didn't say it. After looking all around to make sure that there were no Union men in sight he wheeled his horse and rode off, accompanied by the pickets. No sooner were they out of sight around the first bend than the men began to pour out of their breastworks, and in five minutes more the hotel grounds in front of the porch were just black with an eager, excited crowd, all anxious to hear what the rebels had to say. Mr. Sprague took the part of spokesman, and when he told them what the Confederates had said about there not being one Union man left alive by this time to-morrow, the announcement was received with whoops and yells.

"Let them bring their men on!" shouted Bud McCoy. "We are all ready for them."

"You must remember that the demand for a surrender comes before a fight," said Mr. Sprague. "They may be up here in an hour,

and I think I had better send some men down
there to reinforce those pickets."

"I'll go for one," and "I'll go for another,"
were the exclamations that arose from the
crowd, and in less time than it takes to tell it
five hundred men were all mounted and armed,
and rode up to the porch to listen to their
final instructions from Mr. Knight. Leon
wanted to go, too, but a positive shake of the
head from his father told him that that thing
wouldn't do at all.

"You will get fighting enough if you stay
right here," said Mr. Sprague. "You do your
duty here under my eye and that is all I shall
ask of you."

"Make as good a fight as you can, boys,"
said Mr. Knight. "Only, don't let them get
behind you. Be sure and retreat while you
have the chance.'

The reinforcements rode on down the road
with Mr. Dawson in command, and as soon as
they were out of sight a silence fell upon the
men they had left behind. All were listening
for the first report of a carbine or rifle that
should announce the opening of the battle.

One hour passed, and then two, and just as darkness came down to conceal the movements of the rebels the long-wished-for report came. It was followed by a moment's silence, and then it seemed as if a hurricane was going through the woods. The Confederates had deployed their line until it reached the woods, where it was lost to view, and in that manner charged across the stream and through the timber. But where were the Union men who were to oppose them? For three miles they went through the woods, and then all of a sudden the opposition came when they least expected it. It was the report of a carbine in the hands of young Dawson, and the nearest colonel threw up his arms and fell from his horse. A moment afterward the woods were fairly aflame in advance of them. Scarcely a yell was heard, for the Union men fought as though they had life and liberty at stake.

"Fire low, boys," said Mr. Dawson, as he loaded up for another shot. "If you strike a man in the legs it will take two to carry him off."

27

The Union men fired three times before they thought of retreat, and the middle of the line was not only thrown into confusion, but it was annihilated, so that their officers could not get anybody to charge upon their concealed enemy; but the wings were all right—they were stretched out so far in the woods that they could easily wrap around the Union men and capture them all—and they hastily got on their horses and beat a quick retreat. The company that came along the road was badly cut up. They were marching in column of fours, and it was their intention, after they got the Union men in full flight, to follow them in, and they would go with such rapidity that they would take the breastworks at once. But after the smoke had cleared away there wasn't more than a dozen men left. The riders had been shot down, and the horses, having no one to control them, were running frantically about, trampling the dead and dying under their feet.

"That's pretty well done for the first time," said Mr. Dawson, when he had made up his mind that all of his battalion were in the road. The rest were in the woods, and could easily fight their way to Ellisville. "Now, boys, give them as good as they send."

The retreat to Ellisville was accomplished in short order, and when the rebels broke from the woods and uttered their charging yell they couldn't see a single man. They were all behind their breastworks.

"I tell you we gave it to them down there in the woods," said Dawson, as he rode along behind the breastworks until he found Leon and Tom. "You ought to have been along. I reckon I have paid the rebels for burning our house. I lifted one officer out of his saddle as clean as a whistle."

"Did you kill him?" asked Leon.

"Well, I reckon so. He threw his arms above his head, and that is a pretty good sign that he was done for."

"Did you hear any bullets come near you?" inquired Leon, who shuddered when he thought how coolly Dawson could talk of shooting another in cold blood.

"Yes, sir, I heard them; but the rebels fired too high. I saw one man clap his hand to his mouth and say 'Oh!' but I didn't see who it was. There they come!" said Dawson, grasping his carbine with a firmer hold and creeping up to an opening in the breastworks. "Now, Leon, show what you are made of."

"It is certain death to send those fellows up here!" said Leon. "I wish I could warn them away."

"Haw! haw!" laughed Dawson. "They know what is behind here better than we can tell them. If they don't, they will soon find it out."

Mr. Sprague stood a little ways from Leon with his rifle in his hand. He had charge of the brigade now, and it was his duty to give the order to fire. Nearer and nearer came the rebels, yelling like so many mad men, but the report of Mr. Sprague's gun couldn't be heard. As soon as the men saw him raise his piece to his shoulder they all fired, and the way the rebels went down before it was certain proof that their bullets had not all been thrown away. But these men were not to be defeated by one volley. They kept on until they reached the breastworks, and then they found that they were too high to be scaled by their horses. The Union men on the other side reached over and fired their guns in their faces, until the Confederates could stand it no longer. They turned their horses and fled, and did not stop until they were safe in the woods, from which they had just emerged.

"Long live the Jones-County Confederacy!" shouted some one in the ranks; and the shout was taken up by all the men in the line.

"Let's go after them!" said another. "We can easy whip them."

"No, stay where you are," said Mr. Sprague, who got his instructions from Mr. Knight. "We can whip them here, but if we should get out of line of the breastworks they might prove too much for us."

It was the occasion of no little difficulty for the Confederate officers to rally their men, and the trouble was that those who belonged to the right and left wings reported that it was impossible to flank the Union position. Those on the right said that there was a swamp in which many men had been killed in their efforts to get around it, and the men

who belonged on the left reported that there
was the river there, and that any attempt to
get by it would be useless. General Lowery
began to see that the Union men were not to be
easily whipped, but he used all his eloquence
and authority to induce them to make an effort to carry the centre of the line. He dismounted some of his men with instructions to
go and throw down the breastworks, and the
rebel cavalry was to be close behind them and
go in at the openings they had made. This
was the plan that General Lee decided on
when he made the attempt to split Grant's
lines by his assault on Fort Steadman. He
had half his army in that exploit, but his effort ended just as General Lowery's did to
split the Union lines here. The second attempt was grandly made, and the fight lasted
a little longer than it did at first; but the dismounted men were quickly picked off, the
cavalry began dropping here and there, and
finally, without a word from anybody, they all
took to their heels. This time there was
nothing said about pursuit, for the Union
men had their blood up, and nobody could

have controlled them. By the time the rebels
were in the woods the Union men had
mounted their horses and started after them.
Leon was in this exploit, and his father did
not tell him to stay behind. He didn't find
any Confederates on the way, but he assisted
in making some noise, so he did just as much
as anybody.

This was the last attempt that was made to
break up the Jones-county Confederacy. The
rebels saw that the Union men were in earnest and they gave it up as a bad job. A week
afterward a big wagon-train was captured and
taken to their place of refuge on the island,
and after that the Union men breathed a good
deal easier. They were going to have grub
enough to support them, no matter what happened. About this time, too, some more men
began to come in, and Leon saw the army
grow from one thousand men to more than
twenty thousand. Of course with such an
army as that the Confederates wouldn't try to
whip them. They minded their own business,
going out whenever they thought that their
provisions were getting low, and picking up

wagon-trains and taking them where they would do the most good. Of course, too, these parties when they went out always captured some papers, which were read until they almost crumbled to pieces. When the rebels were defeated at Vicksburg and Gettysburg the Union men drew a long breath of relief, for they thought that the war was almost ended and that they could go home; but there were some severe battles to be fought before their flag could wave over the entire country. One day, long months after this, when Leon had got so tired of being a soldier that he wished that the Confederacy would sink or do something else that would wipe it out of existence, he was out with a party of skirmishers, when they ran plump onto a rebel soldier who had a gun on his shoulder, and acted as though he was going somewhere. In an instant Bud McCoy's pistol was aimed at his breast.

"Put up your revolver, young man!" said the rebel, who did not seem at all abashed by finding himself in the company of Union men. "You belong down in Jones county, don't you? Well, I want to say that you are behind the times. General Lee has surrendered!"

Bud and the rest were so astonished that they could not say a word.

"It's a fact," continued the rebel. "I wasn't there, because I was in our Western army, but I heard of it, and more than five thousand of us escaped that night. The Confederacy has gone up!"

"I tell you I am glad of it," replied Leon. "Why didn't you surrender when you got whipped at Gettysburg?"

"A good many men said it ought to have been done," answered the rebel, "but I wasn't at the head of affairs. You had better let me go, for I want to reach home and see my wife. I haven't seen her since I went into the service."

The foragers were only too glad to let him go. They would have passed anybody who brought such news as that; and, furthermore, they wheeled their horses and went back to Ellisville with much more speed than they had shown in coming out. There was joy on

the island when they told what the rebel had
said to them, and some of the men fired off
their guns in ecstacy; but Mr. Knight said
that the rebels had so long been accustomed
to lying that they didn't know when they
spoke the truth, and suggested that it would
be better for them if they sent a couple of
men down to Mobile to see what was going
on there. Any number of men offered themselves, but two were promptly sent, and while
they were gone the refugees hardly knew what
to do with themselves. In due time the men
came back, and, better than all, they swung a
paper over their heads.

"It's a Yankee paper, and now we'll get at
the truth of the matter," said one of the mes-
sengers. "Yes, sir, Lee has surrendered;
that whole army has surrendered, and the
fortifications down at Mobile are just black
with Yankees!"

Cheers long and loud rent the air at this
announcement, so that it was a long time before Mr. Sprague could read what the paper
said in regard to Lee's surrender. When he
read it, the cheers once more broke out afresh.

"They said that we couldn't take this county out of the Confederacy," said Mr. Knight. "I reckon we've done something that nobody else could do."

A day or two after this, companies of Union cavalry began scouting about Mobile to see if they could find any rebels, and some of them presented themselves before Mr. Knight. The officer listened in amazement while he was told the story, and when Mr. Knight had got through he laughed until he could hardly sit on his horse. The Union men all laughed, too; and, taken all together, it was a jolly party—very different from what they felt while they were resisting the cavalry that tried so hard to overpower them. The officer told them that they could go home, that the war was ended, and that they would never be called upon to fight for the flag again.

After that there was a good deal of excitement in and around Ellisville, for the refugees were making efforts to go home. The bridge over the bayou that had been burned to keep the rebels from getting across so easily was rebuilt, and after that Leon and his father

had their hands full in saying good-bye to
the Union men, who wished them every success in life. Then they went home and went
to work, getting their ground ready to plant
a supply of cotton, glad indeed to handle
a plow once more instead of a rifle. Their
object was to throw Smith off the scent. They
had seen him a few times during the last few
months, but he had nothing to say to them ;
but the sequel proved that he knew what he
was talking about when he threatened to
camp on his cousin's place and shoot the man
or boy who came there for the money. He
lived in Mr. Smith's house, for the rebels had
not had time to set the buildings on fire; but
it was close to the pig-pen, so it would be next
to impossible for them to go there and dig for
what was hidden in it, and every day he rode
over the plantation, to make sure that the
Spragues had not dug in some other place.
Mr. Sprague kept close watch of his movements, and one day announced to Leon his
plan of action.

"We will go there and hunt for that money
to-night," said he. "But, mind you, we won't

dig where it is. We will go down into the
lower part of the plantation and dig there,
and when we come away we'll leave a shovel
there. How will that do? He will be sure
to see the shovel, and at night he will watch
that place and leave the pig-pen free for
us."

Leon didn't see that anything else could be
done, so he readily fell in with his father's
proposal. When night came they set out,
and selecting a place where some brush had
been thrown to get it out of the way, they
threw it aside, and in a few minutes had a
hole dug there that was six feet deep. Then
they placed a shovel in a conspicuous position
and went home, wondering what was to be the
result of Mr. Sprague's new scheme. They
were not long in finding out. The next day
about ten o'clock Leonard Smith rode by on
his horse, and, seeing the father and son employed in plowing the field, stopped and had a
word to say to them.

"You didn't get the money last night, did
you?" he asked, while his face was white with
fury. "I know where it is now, and I will

give you fair warning that if either of you go there again I will shoot you."

Mr. Sprague made no reply, and Smith rode off. When night came they set out again—only, this time they went on horseback, and told Mrs. Sprague that if she heard them going by some time during the night—she must pack up the next day and go to Mobile. Mr. Sprague and Leon were armed, of course. They went up the road until they came to Mr. Smith's gate, and there Mr. Sprague left Leon while he went ahead to reconnoitre. He was gone half an hour, and when he came back his words were full of news.

"There's nobody about the house," said he, and one wouldn't think that he had a hundred thousand dollars at stake. "Now, we must go quickly. Stay by the horses' heads, so that they won't call out. I will do the digging."

With a heart that beat like a trip-hammer Leon dismounted, passed the shovel over to his father, and followed along after him when he led the way toward the pig-pen. The house was all dark, and it didn't look as

though anybody lived there, but Leon couldn't
help drawing a long breath when he thought
of the unerring rifle that was hidden somewhere about.   His father got into the pen and
pried up the boards, and he did it without
causing anything to creak.   Then by putting
down his shovel in various positions he found
where the earth had been disturbed, and then
he went to work.   Never had he worked so
hard before, but it seemed an age to Leon, as
he stood there holding fast to the horses.   At
length, to his great relief, his father seized
something and held it over the side of the
pen.

"Leon, he exclaimed, "here's one of them !"

How heavy it was !   But just as Leon was
going to take it he heard the sound of horses'
hoofs up Mr. Smith's lane.   His horses heard
it, too, and raised their heads to see what was
coming.

"Father, father, they are coming back !"
he faltered.   "Can't you find the other one?"

"Yes, here it is.   "Now, you get on your
horse and ride for dear life and I will stay behind. I will keep them from overtaking you."

Leon was on his horse in a moment, the other valise was passed up to him, and in another second he was flying down the road. Mr. Sprague was close behind him, but before they had gone far they heard some muttered ejaculations from the horsemen, followed by the command :

"I declare, there is that Sprague, Halt! I say halt!"

But Leon and his father were not given to halting. Their horses went faster than ever, and by the time Smith—for he was one of the party—had lingered to look at the pig-pen, they were far out of sight. Then followed a volley from their carbines—not one or two of them—but from a dozen which proved that Smith had found more than one man to assist him. But all the balls went high or wild, and Mr. Sprague and Leon got safely off. They crossed the bridge, travelled rapidly along the road that led to Mobile, and by ten o'clock the next day had the money safely in the bank. On the next day but one Mrs. Sprague came along. She told a pretty thrilling story about what had happened to her

THE HIDDEN FORTUNE SAFE AT LAST.

since Mr. Sprague left. Smith was so mad to think they had got away with the money that he burned her house over her head, and did not even leave her a negro cabin to go in to.

Here we will leave Leon Sprague, only stating that he came on to Clayton, where Mr. Sprague had some friends, who gave him a cordial welcome. They purchased a neat little house which had been deserted by its owner during the war, and as they now lived there six years it began to look very home-like. He made the acquaintance of Bob Nellis almost as soon as he got into town, through him learned of the academy at which the latter was preparing for college, and went with him and entered his name on the books when he went there next term. Of course he was in the lowest class, but he studied his books night and day, and the result was very soon apparent. In two years he was up with boys of his own age.

We said that Joe Lutkin had not forgotten the raid he was going to make on that watering place the time he talked of stealing all the jewels. He made it, and perhaps we shall

see what came of it.   His son Hank got a
boat about this time; and what he did with it,
and how it took Joe Lufkin almost two hundred miles to sea, shall be told in " The Cruise
of the Ten-Ton Cutter."